Also by the author

Gringa

Beyond Deserving

Walking Dunes

More Than Allies

Opal on Dry Ground

OPAL
ON
DRY
GROUND

a novel

Sandra Scofield

Villard Books New York 1994

Copyright © 1994 by Sandra Scofield

All rights reserved under International and Pan-American Copyright
Conventions. Published in the United States by Villard Books, a
division of Random House, Inc., New York, and simultaneously in
Canada by Random House of Canada Limited, Toronto.

Grateful acknowledgment is made to Sheep Meadow Press for permission
to reprint four lines from "The Magnificat" by Chana Bloch. Published
in *The Secrets of the Tribe*. Copyright © 1980 by Sheep Meadow Press.
Reprinted by permission of Sheep Meadow Press.

Villard Books is a registered trademark of Random House, Inc.

Library of Congress Cataloging-in-Publication Data
Scofield, Sandra Jean
Opal on dry ground: a novel/Sandra Scofield.
p.   cm.
ISBN 0-679-42397-4
1. Mothers and daughters—Texas—Fiction.   2. Middle aged women—
Texas—Fiction.   3. Marriage—Texas—Fiction.   I. Title.
PS3569.C58406   1994
813'.54—dc20   93-45787

Manufactured in the United States of America on acid-free paper
2 4 6 8 9 7 5 3
First Edition

For the mothers and daughters,

the sisters and cousins

in my family—

and especially for Mae

Now the fingers and toes are formed

the doctor says.

Nothing to worry about. Nothing

to worry about.

—*Chana Bloch, "The Magnificat"*

Acknowledgments

My heartfelt gratitude to my publisher, Diane Reverand, for opening this door; to Rosemary Ahern for her support and friendship; and to my agent, Emma Sweeney, for being all she is.

Contents

The Queen's
Bread
Pudding

In a Texas town along the Gulf of Mexico, where a bug in your bed might be two inches long, and there is often the taste of salt on your skin, Clancy Thatcher, who has reclaimed her maiden name, swings her legs around to get out of bed, and falls over. The bed is dismantled, the mattress on the carpet, and it is an abrupt if minor surprise to lose her balance so close to the ground. She reminds herself that the coming days will be jam-packed with demands for adaptation, but that soon enough she will find some new cranny where she can settle into routine.

Routine soothes her.

She dresses and then comes back to the mattress and lies down across it sideways, thinking dreamily of her dog, Halo, whom she misses fiercely, with more emotion than she has felt for anything else ever, except her parents' divorce when she was not quite twelve. Halo liked to lick Clancy's long, thin arms, which Clancy liked to extend for the licking, sometimes for most of the news with Tom Brokaw, whom her ex-husband thinks he resembles, when he surely does not. Clancy never spoke during the news, pretending absorption, although she often closed her eyes against the sight of mouths talking, talking.

Halo lives with Clancy's ex-husband Jeeter, who has now assumed his real name, Jeremy, and acts as if he has always dressed like a Dallas stockbroker and not in tooled boots and plaid cowboy shirts the way he did when she married him a couple of years ago. Clancy found Halo at the pound. She had been crying a lot, and both Jeeter and Clancy's mother said that what she better do was go to a counselor. They thought she ought to find a new job, or have a baby. She figured out on her own that it was easier to get a dog.

Halo is a big wonderful mutt with golden Lab in her. She was still a puppy when Clancy brought her home. Jeeter was full of advice about raising and training her. He did help Clancy turn the back porch—which is enclosed, Southern style—into an oversized playpen for the pup. Halo has a big soft corduroy bed stuffed with cedar chips, and rawhide bones and balls. Clancy used to come home at lunch from the bank and eat a carton of yogurt while she sat on the step from the house onto the porch and talked to Halo. "Work is shit today," she'd say, with no one's ears but Halo's to hear it. She would say whatever was on her mind. "Jeeter's going to make chimichangas tonight. I swear, I don't know why anybody who lives in Texas would ever want to cook Mexican food, do you?" If they had Mexican food, though, she could drink a beer, and beer made her sleepy, and this was good. "If Jeeter cooks," she told Halo, "that more or less takes care of the evening."

Clancy used to watch the clock, wanting so much to go to bed. It is easier since she went to a doctor who put her on Elavil, which, like beer, makes her sleepy. She could go to bed right after supper, if she had a mind to. She always went to bed before Jeeter; he said trying to wake her up later was like making love to a dead woman. He liked to watch the sports channel, then come to bed in his red Jockeys. Wrestling matches and stock car races made him horny.

When Jeeter came home one day and said he wanted to

divorce Clancy, he said he would pay all her moving expenses and the deposit on a new place if he could keep the house. All they had invested in the house was money Jeeter had borrowed from his daddy, and Jeeter had done all the work to make the yard look good, so she said yes.

She didn't care about the house. The best thing that ever happened in it was when Halo pooped on the rug in front of the TV one night while Jeeter was doing sit-ups. Clancy laughed so hard her eyes filled up and she was looking at Jeeter through water, like rain. She picked the poop up with a napkin and carried it outside to the garbage, and then took Halo out on her leash, although it was nine o'clock and she usually would be going to bed.

The trouble was, Clancy couldn't find a place that would let her take her dog. She had to move fast—the sight of Jeeter turned her stomach, once he told her he didn't love her—so she took an apartment. She told Jeeter she was going to look for a little house, one of those dumpy frame houses that sometimes have a lot of stuff in the yard, and shades but no curtains, no carpet, and nobody who minds dogs, cats, kids, dope, or what.

All around her, Clancy's belongings are piled. She bought a special carton at the U-Haul so she could hang her clothes, but now she wonders if they will stay that way, on hangers riding in the back of her mother's husband's truck. Besides the box of clothes, there is just her little TV. She is leaving her lamps, and the persimmon-red rug and toilet seat cover in the bathroom. The manager says she will try to sell Clancy's couch to a new renter, and if she can't, she will buy it herself, although for less than Clancy thinks she should get—it does let down. Clancy ran a small ad in the newspaper for a week, and she sold a few things that way, but she felt discomfited by strangers poking around in her belongings, and she hated the idea that someone would try to bargain with her about their worth, so she gave away a lot of household goods, like dish towels and skillets and those racks you hang on the door for shoes. She saw someone eyeing the Bundt pan she used exactly once, and she said, "Oh, go on, take it, why don't you?" The woman's eyes creased and she said, "Think *not*," suspiciously, but someone else said, "Why, thank you!" and "Are you *sure*?" and took it and bought a pie plate, to be fair. If, to get out alive, Clancy had to list everything she owned a week ago, she probably couldn't; already she has forgotten, and it makes her feel stupid, and a little cheated, to have thought she needed so many things she obviously didn't.

The manager offered to take Clancy's cache of paperback novels, too, but Clancy has lined them up in two brown bags; sometimes it is soothing to read the same book twice. She has a wide range of interests: She likes true-story accounts of scandalous crimes, glitzy contemporary novels about seduction and betrayal and ultimate love, and all kinds of historical romances, except Regency ones, which are too silly to believe. She likes books with endings that tie life up neatly, leaving you with the idea that now you know *how it will be*. It is her own life's lack of resolution—what's to become of her—that is so depressing.

It is, in fact, incredibly depressing to be going to her mother's, but Clancy has been depressed for a long, long time and there is nothing new in that. She does all right at work by being attentive. She whispers to herself as she works. She does everything exactly right, and now her boss is crushed that she is leaving. There will be more work for him because the next secretary will probably be just a secretary instead of a skilled loan officer on a secretary's salary.

Her boss takes her to lunch, despite her earnest protestations—she has never been able to eat around anyone other than family—and says that she has been a "perfect jewel" and "a darlin' " and "one in a million." He has not given her a raise in seventeen months. He orders peanut butter mousse pie for them both. He says he has decided not to give her a letter of recommendation—today is her last day, and she has reminded him for the third time—because he wants her to tell anybody who is seriously interested to call him, collect. That way, he says, they will know how serious he is when he says she is the best. Although grateful, Clancy hates to think of her boss on the phone with a stranger, talking about her.

"This is good," she says of the pie, which is neither pie nor pudding, and both salty and sweet. She wishes she could tell him to write down what he knows about her and be done with it. She is neat and punctual. She never makes personal phone calls. She can spell, use an adding machine, type, use a desktop computer. She can run the department whether he is there or not. When she is at work there is nothing else on her mind.

He won't know to say any of that. He can't understand a person who has nothing going on in her life anymore, since she moved out of her second marriage and left her dog behind.

"They put out a little recipe book," her boss says when they are standing up. "Let me get you one, a going-away present." She waits by the door while he pays for things. Later, at home, she sits on her mattress and opens the book at random. There is a recipe for Harvey Wallbanger Souf-flé. There are Rio Grande Corn Muffins and The Queen's Bread Pudding. She doesn't know anyone who would make any of the dishes in the book. She puts it in the bathroom, above the toilet, as a housewarming present for the next tenant.

2

Opal and Russell Duffy are in a McDonald's just before closing. The kids who are left this time of night are sweeping or wiping up or standing around.

"There's no reason to stop," Russell argues. "I'm one *hunnerd* percent awake. I like to drive at night."

Opal is holding her left thumb in her right hand. If she couldn't see it, she would swear the thumb was black and blue and twice its size, it throbs so much. She considers the state of her legs, where the twisted veins, warm to the touch and bluish, pool with blood. She wants to lie down. She thinks of herself lying in the bed of the pickup, staring into the cold December sky.

"They want to close, Russell. They want to go home. It's eleven already."

A boy with his hair shaved close to his skull, so that the indentations show like the landscape of a tiny planet, leans over the trash can and stares at them. He wears several earrings, some of them high on the ear, where it must have hurt to pierce. Opal thinks he is watching Russell's jaws work as a way to will him to hurry. It gives her a spooky feeling; you can't tell these days who is a witch or voodoo artist or just plain nuts. People have been shot to death for things no worse than being too long with your french fries. "I want to go," she insists.

Russell, with his back to the boy, is rubbing a bit of

bread in the last smear of catsup on the yellow wrapper of his special-order double cheeseburger. "Inna minute," he says. Sometimes he talks like a much dumber man than he is, to provoke her. She never says how little she cares. What she hates is when he speaks with authority about VCRs and UFOs and telephone systems, about the way Mexicans are taking over Texas, about the price of anything.

They drive all night. Russell's maroon Ford runs steady as a ship on a calm sea, cutting through the long stretch of dark winter quiet. The pickup is all that is left of Russell's entrepreneurial days; when she married him, he owned a filling station. Now he is in college, free-floating in math and science, promising Opal early retirement. He is forty-nine years old. His pickup says SERVICE IS OUR BEST PRODUCT on both doors.

"I told him he'd be dead if we drove all night," Opal tells Clancy. They are in a pancake house drinking coffee while Russell sleeps on Clancy's couch back in the apartment. When they left him he was snoring, one hand backside down on the floor, his fingers out like worms.

"Jeeter always did that, too. Acted like motels were rip-offs specially out to get him. I could always sleep. You know me."

"There isn't any reason we couldn't have stopped tonight." Yesterday was the last day of classes before Christmas break, so Russell can quit pretending to go, Opal thinks. He couldn't leave before two o'clock yesterday because of chem lab. "Chem lab," my foot, she thinks. She suspects he spends chemistry lab in doughnut shops, with cops on break.

She lifts her thumb to her mouth and sucks at the

knuckle. The thumb is sending out roots like a fertilized plant. It hurts all the way to her elbow. At fifty-eight, she is worse off than her poor mother was at the same age. Her bones are brittle, her joints inflamed, her colon spastic. Her arteries are jamming and her heart is swollen. She tends toward phlebitis, and she is fat. Five years ago she was still a size ten, and her lover was a bushy-browed Jewish psychiatrist. He used to come over on Sunday morning with *The New York Times*. She was working two jobs to get ahead. The sting was going out of her divorce. She had hopes. Out of all the hard times, she had salvaged a bit of cheer. She thought of herself as a person with a sense of humor. She and the children's father used to love a pun. They would tell one another jokes in the middle of anything, even *that*. She has worked around doctors for forty years; she knows nothing is sacred.

The psychiatrist announced one day that he was going to Israel, for good. He bought her a Honda, which she gave to Clancy. He warned her she was getting too old to go for cheap. "You're a great dancer, you keep your eyes open in bed," he cited, implying value rapidly diminishing. He was the first man to teach her that there are sharp edges on a shard of pleasure. He was so full of last-minute admonitions, he had to talk fast to get them all in. He was still talking at the airport gate. "Drink milk; better, take calcium. Watch your varicose veins. Cut the kids' cords, Opal, and tell your mother to mind her own business." All this for free.

She had been taking her car to an Exxon station where the owner seemed honest, even kind. Russell Duffy. He wasn't one of those smart-ass mechanics who make a woman feel stupid. He did extra things for her without charge. The same week her lover landed in Tel Aviv, she broke down while Russell was giving her change. "Hey, hold on," he said. "Don't you go nowheres." He still had her keys in his hand. In two minutes he had locked up the station. She followed him home and waited while he changed. They had dinner at a steakhouse where it was so dark she couldn't see what she was eating. He told her his wife had left him a while ago, for no special reason. He had an obese son, dumb as a post, married to a perfect match, and a daughter Clancy's age, married to a Mexican—the kind of disappointments that go on and on, especially since there were grandkids. He had a paid-for four-bedroom house and the station. He didn't drink. He watched too much TV. He was lonely. Worse bargains could be made.

Opal took a long time making up her mind. She would have liked to do better. She couldn't tell how smart he was, a man who knew his children were ignorant.

While Clancy is in the ladies' room, Opal thinks of how Jeeter had paced around the kitchen at her house, hot to get on the road home. Both of Clancy's husbands had a lot of nervous energy. Funny that Clancy would pick them. When she was ten or so, she started coming home from school and lying down right away. She wouldn't even kick off her shoes. It worried Opal no end to come in and find her daughter's long skinny body on her bed like a board. She made her get up. She gave her something to do—sort laundry, peel carrots. Of course by then she would have been on the bed for hours, not asleep, not doing anything.

Opal thinks she remembers telling Jeeter all that. She remembers saying, "She was so calm, just when her daddy and I were getting bad with one another. She didn't want to know about it. It's like she went away inside her head, back then, and never got all the way back." She did say it.

She remembers now how her face flushed when she realized it was the same as saying Clancy was crazy, when
Clancy is probably the sanest one in the family. Opal hopes
what she said didn't have anything to do with Jeeter wanting a divorce.

Clancy comes back and says she has paid. This both
exasperates and touches Opal, who always pays.

"I want to go over to Jeeter's and tell my dog good-bye,"
Clancy says. If you did not speak English, you would never
be able to guess what she is saying, because she never
shows any expression. "He'll be at work now."

Opal checks her watch. It is ten o'clock.

Clancy laughs shortly. "Jeeter, I mean."

On the way, Clancy tells her mother that Jeeter has married again. The woman is a financial planner in the American Express office with Jeeter.

"Good God," Opal says. "Your divorce was just final
last month."

"Well, Mother, what do you think this was all about?"
Clancy smiles, as though she has fooled Opal in some small
way.

"I don't know how you could let him sell your piano,"
Opal says, because she cannot help herself.

"I quit playing weeks after I married him. He used to
line his beer bottles up on the lid." Clancy glances at her
mother, who paid for the piano a long time ago. "Sorry,
though."

"I thought he was a sweet boy," Opal says sadly. "I
remember he used to pet you. You'd sit beside him at our
table and he would stroke your arm and pat your hand."
Opal often mourns the past.

"I guess it was boring for him. It was boring for me, too,
but I didn't mind, you see." Clancy seems so calm. Yet on

the phone she told her mother that during lunch she was going to her car and sitting there and crying. She said she was hearing things at night, living alone.

"How could you walk away like that, with nothing?" Opal's heart sinks when she sees the house. It is in a little development of nine houses tucked close together, but each so charming. She thinks Jeeter called this "Cape Cod." The house has gray clapboard siding, and a trim of creamy white and burgundy. It has bay windows and, in the back, French doors opening onto a wide screened porch. Nobody in the family has had a house with what you would call style before.

"Do you have a key?" Opal asks softly.

"No need to whisper, Mother." Clancy leads the way to the backyard. "Halo will be in the yard or on the porch. I wish I could hug her before I leave for good."

They go through the gate of a cedar fence. Inside is the cold wall of a cyclone fence that takes up about a third of the yard. Inside, the lush grass is trampled in an egg-shaped path worn by the dog's pacing.

"God," Clancy says.

"See, he made a place for Halo," Opal says brightly, trying to cheer Clancy up. She liked both of Clancy's husbands right up until the end, not like Joy's at all.

"He doesn't want Halo in his garden," Clancy says. "Jeeter's little prison." Between the house and the pen is a pretty bed of lavender and purple delphiniums, bordered by creeping candytuft. Clancy tries to put her hand in the fence to open the gate, but she can't work the latch.

"Oh, my." Opal sees Halo first. "Oh, my," she says again. The dog is growling low in the throat, its ears are back. Its pretty cream color is marred by random liver-colored markings.

"Here, Halo, here, peachy, it's me, it's your mama," Clancy croons. The dog barks once, loudly. Clancy goes down on her knees, her face against the fence. "Here, girl, here, Halo."

The sight of her daughter on her knees begging a dog to come just about does Opal in. She stands back four feet or so from the fence, holding her sore thumb. Tears are trickling out of the outside corners of her eyes. She has a feeling they will run into snow, once they get away from the Gulf.

"Here, girl; here, girl," Clancy says over and over. The dog comes closer, taking a long arced route. "I used to kiss her good night. I let her lick my face." Clancy stands up and wipes her hands on her jeans. "Well, shit."

The dog begins to whine, and lies down with its front paws out. Clancy has already started toward the gate.

"I think she remembers now," Opal pleads. She can't believe Clancy has turned her back on Halo.

"Jeeter told me he was going to train her to be a killer. He made a big joke of it. A sweetheart like that."

"Jeeter was sure funny," Opal says, exactly as though he has died. She thought Jeeter understood Clancy, understood that she has special needs. When she was four she had polio, after polio had all but disappeared. A light case, but months in bed, nevertheless. She never complained. It affected her heart.

The dog yelps a few times, but Clancy and Opal are on the other side of the fence, headed for the car. The dog sounds far away and lonely.

"Maybe we could get a dog," Opal offers.

"You already have a cat."

"Russell's."

Clancy shrugs. "I'm not into spare parts, Mother. No husbands, no dogs."

When they get back they see that Russell has woken up, found a neighbor to help with the couch, and loaded the pickup.

"I wasn't going to take the couch," Clancy says when she sees what he has done.

"There's that little front room by the door?" Russell says. "Your mother's got her sewing machine in there?" He sticks his head way forward to see if she understands. "You can put your couch in that room."

"It does make down into a good bed," Clancy says. She hopes she will have a bedroom at Russell's house.

"That's good to know," Russell says, "in case somebody else comes to stay." By the time he has the whole sentence out, he is chuckling, really enjoying himself. He winks at Opal. Opal wants to slap him. "You never know who'll drop by," he says to her.

Opal climbs back in Clancy's car to wait while Clancy turns her keys in to the apartment manager. Russell leans on the car and sticks his head in the window. "You first and I follow, or the other way around?"

"We'll drive behind you," Opal says. It is insane to turn around and make a drive like this. It's nearly as bad as driving to Chicago and back. "Men are so much better at directions." Her sarcasm is lost on Russell. He bangs the car once with the flat of his hand. Clancy gets in the driver's seat.

"On the road again—" Russell sings. He loves to drive, not a bad trait in a Texan.

"Just relax, Mother," Clancy says as she starts the car. "Lay back, why don't you?"

They run into snow north of Sweetwater. It blows lightly across the road like shreds of cottonwood tuft. Opal dozes.

She feels light, too, almost light enough to float, except for the blood heavy in her feet. The blood cannot push hard enough against gravity to make its way back to her heart. In her dream her feet are gouty. Nobody can see the blood inside, seeping backward, pushing the walls of her veins. People think she swells because she eats too much. So much is wrong. Her children are sad. Her mother is dead. She has to be responsible for some of it.

3

Late Monday morning, Clancy takes the garbage out to the alley. "Watcha doing?" her sister's daughter, Heather, asks as Clancy goes by. Joy's daughter is a surly girl, pretty, but always mad at something. Opal says it is Joy's fault that Heather is spoiled and sour.

"It's not even your garbage," Heather says, rolling her eyes. Her bare feet are propped up on the table. She is painting her toenails. Beside the polish sits a quart of Coke with the cap off. Russell's old cat, Chocolate, lies stretched out on the end of the table by the window, where sun falls on her like yellow gauze.

The day is cold and bright. Opal predicted wind and snow, but the sky is clear and blue. Clancy never paid much attention to the sky until she lived on the coast, but Jeeter told her you better pay attention or you will get caught in the wrong kind of weather. You could be blown off an underpass or swept out to sea. Clancy prefers the Panhandle sky, for its color, vastness, and familiarity.

She hears a neighbor calling, "Ginger, here, Ginger. Good girl. Sit." Clancy puts the garbage lid on and looks over the top of the fence. A woman in tight twill pants and a loopy knitted sweater has her finger in the air, talking to her German shepherd. The backyard is laid out with white hurdles.

"She's sure pretty," Clancy calls. The woman glances up,

smiles, and goes on with her instructions to the dog. The dog is off her leash. The neighbor says, "Hup," and the dog clears two hurdles with easy grace. "Sit," says the neighbor. She waves at Clancy. "She's not much more than a pup," she tells her. "We're just getting started." The dog comes over and puts her beautiful nose in the woman's crotch. "Oh, Ginger, naughty dog," the woman says, falling to her knees. She bends over and puts her face down in the dog's ruff. Clancy goes back inside.

She has been waiting for some time for a turn in the bathroom. Joy was up and off to work before eight, but Heather, out of school for Christmas vacation, took nearly an hour to wash her hair. Now Russell's daughter, Tanya, is in the bathroom with her baby, Rosa, who is walking but not yet talking. Every once in a while Rosa shrieks and Tanya laughs.

Opal is at the table, cutting coupons from the Sunday paper. She looks tired and mad. She spent an hour cleaning up dishes from the two days she was gone. Clancy doesn't want to try to talk to her while they are both still worn out, but she doesn't want to go back to her couch, now made up in the little room by the front door, either. Sure enough, when they got home, there was Tanya in the spare bedroom. "What do you know?" Russell said. "It won't last two days. She only brought the baby. Georgie's with his dad." Tanya, however, says she is never going back, because Hector has a girlfriend, a waitress at the club he manages.

Russell is finally up out of bed. He is in the kitchen on the phone, talking heartily about good deals on phone systems. When he isn't talking, he keeps his mouth open and his head stuck out, taking in whatever the other person is saying on the phone, staying ready to talk back. When he hangs up, Opal says, "We are not putting money into any schemes, Russell Duffy. Call your union and get on a pipeline if you want to make money." Russell brags about his experiences all over Texas, and keeps a special rack in the laundry closet hung with hats from jobs he's worked, but he hasn't gone near an oil well in the two years since he married Opal. He says it wouldn't be fair to go off and leave her in Lubbock in his big old house. Of course Joy and Heather moved in two months after he married Opal, but he hasn't felt he had to offer a different reason, all that time.

"Is it okay if I shower in your bathroom?" Clancy asks him when she feels sure Opal hasn't just launched an argument. The last thing she wants is to be in the middle of, or even witness to, an argument. Jeeter told her once, "Clancy, your ass is so tight you're going to start belching shit." She was the only person he was crude with; around everyone else, he was pure honey.

Russell says, "Be my guest, hon." As she walks by, she sees him pull a chair up to the table next to Opal. He is going to try to sweet-talk her into something. Clancy wonders what happened to the gas station he used to own. She wonders what happened to college, which is what she thought he was doing these days. She wonders if *she* will ever go to college, if it would be worth the trouble.

She wonders how they will ever get through Christmas.

She comes back through in her pink terry-cloth robe, rubbing her hair with a towel, and Opal says tensely, "Why don't we go down to the bank and take care of opening your account, sugar? And get some groceries." She looks around the gloomy kitchen. "Since nobody ever does." Russell is now in the living room listening to *Headline*

News. "Hell, I never," he yells. "Them sons of bitches." Opal says, "If they listened to Russell he could get the hostages home, save the nation's cities, and turn Russia on its ear. There isn't any problem he can't solve by talking." She twists her mouth and looks at Clancy woefully. "I've got to quit working one of these days," she says. "Wouldn't you think he could get a job? Shouldn't Joy give me a little rent?"

"God, Mother, I am *sorry*," Clancy says sharply. "I promise you," she adds testily, "*I* won't be around long." She is tired or she wouldn't give in to temper like that. Usually she is unprovokable, another fault that drove Jeeter crazy. She used to stretch out on the couch, and he would sit on the end with her feet in his lap, tickling the bottoms for an hour at a stretch. He thought her not being ticklish was something she controlled. He thought she was a bad sport.

At least he can't say she didn't try, when it came to sex, which is what she thought really mattered to him. Her mother told her both times when she got married: Do it whenever he wants to, it will keep other things from getting out of hand. Time did tell, though, and it doesn't seem to have worked for any of them, Joy included, although Joy has a boyfriend fifteen years younger than she is, a pre-med student who sleeps over a couple nights a week and eats with them more often than that. Opal says Joy is easier to live with if Mick spends the night, but she says she wonders what Heather thinks of her mother and her boy-toy, what she tells her daddy when she visits him in Amarillo. Clancy wonders why it's anybody's business, although of course it is Opal and Russell's house. She doesn't think Russell minds who sleeps there. She doesn't think Opal minds, either; Opal likes a full house.

"You know I didn't mean you, Clancy darling," Opal says. She slumps forward on her arms on the table. "And I don't know what Joy can manage on what she makes, with her damned house payments still hanging over her head. Everybody's doing what they can, I guess. A body can't do more than that."

"I'll get dressed," Clancy says. She doesn't want to hear about Russell. It seems to her he's what her mother's got, and she's not at all sure where her mother would be if she wasn't in Russell's paid-for house.

Opal and Clancy eat cups of raspberry frozen yogurt at the mall. After two bites Clancy is full, and looks around for a garbage can while Opal stands in front of a window display of velveteen bomber jackets. What Clancy would really like to do is sit someplace alone and listen to the buzz in her head. She thinks the sound might be something like the music some people say they hear, or maybe radio channels. She knows it doesn't mean you are crazy, because she read in "Dear Abby" that it is a true sound and not the invention of the person who hears it. She made the big mistake once of telling Jeeter about it, and he threw it back at her when he was angry, and said if the noise started to be people talking, to let him know so he could carry her off to the nuthouse. Clancy thinks she hears the noise because she has a sensitive inner ear, which might be what is called the seat of the soul; the noise is there for anyone to hear, but most people are too keyed up to listen. There's so much rock music and TV and people arguing, you miss the subtle transmissions coming from God and the universe. She tries to pay attention; someday she'll figure out what she's supposed to know; she's sure it's a message bigger than "Spend" or "Dance" or "Feel good." She thinks it will cure her depression, if anything will.

"You'd look good in a jacket like that," Opal is saying. "You can wear that blousy style because you're so thin." Her voice is wistful. She has given Clancy and Joy all her clothes from when she was a much smaller size.

"I have plenty of clothes for work," Clancy says. It doesn't matter what she wears, otherwise. Right now she has on jeans and a pink striped polo shirt that used to be Jeeter's and a corduroy blazer. Opal is wearing a raincoat over a plaid skirt and blouse; with the coat buttoned, she looks pregnant, except for her age.

They go into B. Dalton's. Opal buys a Weight Watchers cookbook. Clancy buys a book on obedience training for dogs. Opal wants to pay for Clancy's book, but Clancy won't let her. She feels she is on a long slide down into dependence, and she would like to hold on to the sides of the tunnel as long as she can. It's probably silly, but she thinks that the longer she takes care of herself in small ways, the faster she will be in charge again in ways that really matter. She knows this visit is going to last a while, but a stopover isn't your life. She does plan to move on.

4

The woman who helps Clancy open an account at the bank remembers her from her last year of high school, when she had a couple of dates with her son Chuck Martin. "Whenever I see your mother, I always ask, 'How's that Clancy?' Don't I?" She looks at Opal, who smiles back. Opal wears a polite and respectful look. Clancy thinks it is funny that Opal, who is always saying outrageous things about doctors, acts in a bank as if she is in church. As if Mrs.-Chuck's-mother-Martin knows anything special. Opal doesn't have any idea how tedious and dumb it is in a bank, moving pieces of paper from one desk to another while most of the money moves around as numbers on a computer screen.

Clancy says she is fine. She says she has moved back to Lubbock, and that is why she needs to move her money from her old bank, where she used to work.

Mrs. Martin is excited to hear this. "I tried to get Chuckie interested in banking, but you remember how he hates to dress up." All Clancy remembers about Chuck is the disagreeable smell he put off sitting beside her in his souped-up Chevy. She always assumed he didn't bathe, or wore the same socks day after day, or had a glandular problem.

She nods agreeably to Chuck's mother.

Mrs. Martin adds, "Chuckie works in a Radio Shack out by Texas Tech." Clancy smiles and fills out the signature cards. She should tell Mrs. Martin to tell Chuckie hello for her, but he is probably married by now, and if he isn't, she would rather die than have him call her.

Opal speaks perkily. "Clancy had this real good job in Corpus, so we're hoping she'll do as well here. She was secretary to a bank vice president. There wouldn't be any jobs here, would there?"

Mrs. Martin has the look of someone whose Dexedrine just kicked in. "Oh, oh," she says. She holds one finger up: *Wait*. She leaves them to talk with a young man at a desk across the room, and comes back elated. It seems there *is* a job. Suddenly she looks concerned. "It's a special job, and I don't know what your experience is. It's being the administrative assistant to the president!"

Clancy would like to put the woman's mind at ease. Look, she could say, I could do anybody's job in this place, give me a couple days. Maybe even the president's, once I got to know it.

She knows that some people resent being under the supervision of other people whose work they could do themselves (like her mother and every doctor she ever worked for), but this arrangement gives Clancy secret pleasure and confidence. She is young and patient, and eventually other people older than she will retire or die or move to better jobs, and something will open up for her. She doesn't mind waiting, because she doesn't have anything else to do.

"My boss in Corpus said they were grooming me to be a loan officer," she says. "They paid for me to take two college courses."

This is good news to Mrs. Martin. She gives Clancy her temporary checks and receipt, beaming. "Can you wait a sec?"

"Come on, let's move over to the couch," Opal says. She

and Clancy go to a loveseat by a table with a carafe of coffee and plastic cups neatly arranged. Opal groans as she sits down, and then looks amazed at the sound she has made. "What do you think, honey?" she whispers to Clancy.

"God, Mother, I haven't been here one whole day yet. Are you scared I'll live with you forever?" Immediately Clancy is sorry for her remark—she only meant to tease— because her mother's face crumples. "I didn't *mean* anything," she tells her. Opal, her head tilted at a regal angle, begins turning the pages of a money magazine and acts as if Clancy is speaking Chinese.

When Mrs. Martin appears beside them, it is with a certain Mr. Riddler's name and the address of the proper branch, written on the back of a withdrawal slip. Mr. Riddler, it seems, can see her right away, if she can get over.

"Oh, my," Opal cries. "She's not dressed up at all."

Mrs. Martin's brow furrows as she sees Opal's worry, but she says, "I did tell him it was all unexpected, a stroke of luck."

Outside, Opal says, unconvincingly, "If he likes you it probably won't matter what you've got on."

"Don't you think if he's smart enough to run a bank, he can figure out I wouldn't wear jeans to work?" Clancy says. She is losing patience with the whole enterprise, and would like to give Mr. Riddle Fiddle, who has nothing to do this afternoon, her old boss's number so he can call him up, and the two men can figure out her life on the phone.

Which, give or take a few details, is exactly what happens.

* * *

Mr. Riddler wants to hear what she did in her old job, and wants to know if she liked it. She considers her opinion completely irrelevant, but she says she loved it. He wants to hear about the courses she took, too. He is a nice, bland man in his fifties who has obviously never been in the sun except to come and go from his car. He doesn't have the deep creases at the corners of his eyes and across his forehead that you see on ranchers and cotton farmers and all the other good ole boys who make up the backbone of his bank's business.

She tells him about Introduction to Accounting and Principles of Financial Planning, and doesn't say that Jeeter dismissed them as elementary. When he asks why she has moved back to Lubbock—something else that isn't any of his business—she says she only left in the first place because her husband got a job in Corpus. (This is true. It was her first husband, a driller, though.) She says she stayed after her divorce because she liked her job, but then she decided she could find a fine job in Lubbock, too, and be closer to her mother, who seems to need her. "Also, I hated the humidity," she says. Mr. Riddler smiles.

When she goes home at six, she has the job. Her old boss told Mr. Riddler on the phone that Clancy had practically done his job for him, and Clancy laughed and said he was awful nice. She didn't say it was true, and that her old boss was a dreamy man who had recently fallen in love with a kindergarten teacher and was always making sketches of the house he hoped to build when they had the downpayment and a lot they could afford.

When Clancy tells Opal her salary, Opal's hand flies to her mouth. "Don't tell Joy! That's more than she makes." Clancy doesn't add that her salary will go up after the

training period is over, nor that she resents having a training period in the first place, which she sees as a way to save
money on her for six weeks. She doesn't say that it still
isn't very much money if you are trying to make it on your
own for the rest of your life. You could not pay her enough
to do what Joy does, working in a doctor's office. You'd
think Joy would know better, after all the years of Opal's
complaints. It is Clancy's observation that hardly anyone
ever learns from past mistakes, their own or anyone else's.
Why else do they say that history repeats itself? Joy married three men in a row who all turned out to be mean as
rattlers poked with a stick. And she, Clancy, sure can't
throw stones, since both her husbands left her for other
women who, they said, had more in common with them.

The way Clancy sees it, Joy makes men mad, whereas
she bores them to death.

"Hot damn!" Russell says when he hears the news. "We
oughta celebrate. Let's go to the Big Steer and have steak."

Opal has already put a tuna casserole in the oven. "What
do you think I've been standing here doing?"

Heather prances in and rummages through the cupboard
while they all watch her. She turns around and says, "What
are y'all looking at!" She has found a box of caramel corn.
She takes a quart bottle of Coke out of the refrigerator and
heads back to her room, where she has her own little TV.
"I am making supper!" Opal calls as Heather disappears.
Clancy can't tell who Opal thinks she is telling.

Like a character on a set, Heather has crossed Tanya on
her way into the kitchen. It all reminds Clancy of one of
those comedies on TV where there is a family, and neighbors from across the hall and upstairs, except on the show
she's thinking of, everybody's black.

"Can you take me to the store?" Tanya asks her daddy. "I don't have nothing left to feed Rosa."

"Good Lord," says Opal. "That baby can eat *food,* can't she? I have a casserole in the oven and that will do fine. She doesn't need to eat out of jars. Her digestive tract won't ever develop, Tanya Ann."

Russell gives Opal a dirty look and says, "Okay, Tanny, but bring Rosaritoo with us." He never calls his kids by their names. He calls the baby "Rosaritoo" or "Rosakid," and he calls his son, Buddy, "Bones," which is a big joke because Buddy is so fat. He's never pulled any of that on Opal's family.

Clancy cuts in. "Do you have any chow mein noodles? For on top of the casserole? I love tuna and noodles that way."

Russell says, "So much for going out, huh? Maybe some other night?"

"Sure," Clancy says.

"Oh, sure," Opal says. "We'll go out and celebrate when *you* get a job."

5

Clancy hasn't been taking her Elavil. She wonders if that is all right. Now, for example, it is past midnight and she is nowhere near ready to go to sleep. She feels like throwing up, too. Before she started taking the antidepressant, she used to cry a lot at night and feel so heavy, she didn't want to get out of bed in the morning. She felt all the time like someone trying to swim in molasses. Now when she gets to feeling bad, she tries to do something to distract herself. Usually she reads, or sits and listens to the noise in her head. She sometimes wonders if she might think of a good plot for her own life, if she could sort out words or images in all that buzzing between her ears. She wonders if her nighttime dreams, which she never remembers, are scratching to get into her daytime consciousness, and, when they do, if she will have some big insight, the way characters in books do. Of course, in books, circumstances are arranged tidily so that insight comes on the heels of a suitable crisis, whereas in Clancy's life the crises go on and on, dragged out so that they aren't even interesting enough to think about telling somebody else, let alone writing them down. And nobody in a book is ever thirty; thirty is too old to be pretty and too young to matter.

She is sitting on her pulled-out couch in the dark, wishing Tanya would go home so that she can get moved in and put her clothes in the closet. She has been re-reading a novel about a Texas girl who goes to New York and ends up running a modeling agency, something Clancy would never be interested in doing, but she finds all the details about metropolitan life absorbing enough that she doesn't think about how she can't fall asleep. She tells herself that a little insomnia might balance out over the long run, when you think of all the nights she went to bed at seven o'clock. Being in a house with other people helps. She can hear Heather's TV from down the hall, and Joy and Mick giggling in Joy's room. She doesn't mind the sounds, or the idea of her sister with this long-legged boy, maybe their legs all wrapped around one another. She isn't interested in sex anymore; sex makes demands on you, on the spur of the moment, when there's no time to think what you want to do or say.

She hears cars on the boulevard at the end of the block, and sirens. She can hear her own pulse if she leans back and puts her ear against the couch.

She has dozed a moment. She opens her eyes and there is her mother on the arm of the couch, staring down at her.

"I'm okay," she says right away.

Opal brushes Clancy's hair back off her forehead. "You look awful."

"Oh, thanks a lot."

"Are you taking your medication?" Her mother thinks everything would be solved if Clancy got the right dosage. As if her depression isn't *about* anything, as if it is a flipped switch in her body, or something in the drinking water.

She shrugs.

"How much have you been taking?"

Clancy knows she sounds like her teenage self, speaking only because she has to. "A hundred milligrams a day, two doses, split, or sometimes twenty-five in the morning and the rest at night." She gives her mother the information resentfully, like she used to recite where she'd been when she got home late, or her plans for cleaning house or doing dishes, like she was supposed to. Now, she's *supposed* to take pills and get better.

"You stopped when you left Corpus?"

Clancy's face burns. She is actually glad to discuss this with her mother; she doesn't really know the right thing to do. But shouldn't some things be private? Next will Opal ask her what kind of birth control she uses?

Not that it matters. She hasn't had sex since last winter, when the big news broke. The night before Jeeter said he wanted a divorce, they Did It. He got one more time in.

She tells her mother about not being sleepy, and about feeling nauseated.

"That drowsiness?" her mother answers. "That's just an immediate side effect. It's not what the medication is about. The real effect—on your mood—that's delayed, ten days, two weeks. Who told you to stop?"

"I just stopped, okay? Starting that night we left. I was feeling fine. I am fine."

"And next week you could crash. You shouldn't stop all at once."

Her mother's voice drones on. Her mother loves to give advice about medication, and enemas, and vitamins and exercise and having things cut off or out. Now she says Clancy is playing games with the balance of her body chemistry. She asks her, "Have you got any left?"

So Clancy agrees to take fifty milligrams at night for a while. Opal says it is a trifling dosage, but better than nothing. She says Clancy is going to have to see a doctor here soon. Clancy knows very well that if Opal wants, she can get a prescription for anything she asks for from her boss, who is an orthopedic surgeon. Opal has a kitchen drawer absolutely stuffed with drug samples and old prescriptions; you could be a junkie for six months right here in Opal's house. This is notice that she won't cough up Elavil for Clancy. She wants Clancy to *see somebody*. She thinks Clancy needs help.

Clancy looks at her mother carefully. "You do know I'm okay, don't you? I'm not going to crash on you? I'm past that. It never was that bad, really. I don't think I ever really loved Jeeter, I just liked the company."

"Well, there's plenty of that here!" You can tell a block away that Opal doesn't like Tanya.

"I do like it," Clancy says. It has only now occurred to her. "It's better here than with Jeeter." She starts to cry. "I was always lonesome, Mama. I never didn't miss you."

Opal says, "I'll get you some water, sweetheart."

"Right," Clancy says. She takes the Elavil out of her purse and holds it while she waits for the water. She shakes it gently, near her ear, like a baby's rattle.

The book she bought says the first trick to teach a dog is shaking hands. The book says it is essential for shy dogs. You put your dog in a corner so she can't get away. Once you teach her to shake hands with strangers, she'll be friendly and let them pet her. Clancy wants a dog people will like, a dog that takes up a lot of time in a nice way. After the dog learns to shake hands, you can teach her to roll over. You can teach her any number of tricks. There isn't any reason Clancy can't have a dog like that for company, once she has her own place.

Christmas morning, Heather dresses in jeans and a discarded blue sweater of her father's. In the kitchen she finds Opal has made a big pan of cinnamon rolls, and cornbread for dressing. She has stuffed a turkey and put it in the oven. She has made three pies. And still she is making something else.

"What's that?" Heather asks her.

Opal squints at her new cookbook. "Asparagus Swiss Roll Appetizers, for people to eat while you wait for the turkey."

"Ick." Heather pulls a big fat roll out of the pan. The icing has flecks of orange peel in it.

"Merry Christmas, Heather," Opal says crisply.

"Yeah." Heather puts her roll on a saucer and carries it in to the couch.

"Don't drip," Opal admonishes.

Heather switches on the television and roams the channels. There are only boring parades, news, reruns of cartoons. She leaves cartoons on with the sound down low.

Her mother appears. She is still wearing her nightclothes—a Texas Tech T-shirt of Mick's and black tap pants. "Has it begun?" she asks.

Heather holds up a strip of roll. "Opal's cooking. Nobody's here."

Joy gets a cup of coffee and returns to sit by Heather. On

TV a Christmas tree is being demolished by a dog chasing a cat. Heather and her mother watch it until the dog has been leashed and the cat is purring over a bowl of cream.

"Wonder where the mice went," Joy says.

"Oh, Mommy," Heather says.

They hear Rosa screaming. She bursts into the room, followed by her mother. Tanya shrieks, "Come here so I can brush your hair!" Rosa heads straight for the Christmas tree, which is so tall it brushes the ceiling, and throws presents into the room, behind her.

"Now, wait a minute!" Opal cries from the kitchen. "Tanya, you do something."

Tanya grabs Rosa by the arm and jerks her away from the presents. "Those aren't *yours*," she says.

"Russell!" Opal shouts.

He comes in from the backyard, as if on cue.

"It's Christmas, Russell!" Opal says. "Give that child a present."

"Why, sure," Russell says. Rosa, still held by her mother, has gone silent. In her outgrown pink pajama suit, she looks a little smashed together. Russell sits in his lounge chair and beckons her with his finger. "Come here, come here, Rosaritere," he chants. Rosa takes a timid step in his direction. Tanya lets go. Rosa takes another step, and another.

Russell reaches behind the chair and pulls out a large silver package with a multicolored bow. He makes a big show of reading the card. "This is for the littlest girl in the Duffy house," he says. Rosa watches. "It is for the *best* little girl."

Opal rushes over. "What about Buddy's boy?"

"They're not coming until tomorrow. They went to Crane, to Leeanne's grandparents." He looks up at Opal. "You *know*."

"And Heather?"

Rosa has now reached Russell, her arms still at her sides. She gazes at the present. She has walked through a field of overturned gifts.

"I'm not a *baby*!" Heather says, although she hopes she will get something to surprise her, not just jeans. "I can wait."

Rosa reaches for the present; Russell holds it above his head. Rosa wails.

"Daddy!" says Tanya.

"Oh, for God's sake, give her the damned doll!" Joy snaps.

"Joy!" Opal scolds.

Heather jumps up and snatches the gift from Russell. Before he can say a word, Heather is on the floor with Rosa, helping her take off the paper. It is a lot of fun to rip into the expensive foil wrapping. Heather remembers the Christmas she was four, when she opened a present a few days before Christmas, a package this size, a doll. It had a hard face and a soft body, dressed in a ruffly dress and bonnet. This one is a Cabbage Patch doll, fat and stupid-looking, and Rosa regards it with a suspicious air.

"Look, Rosie," Heather says, "it's so soft." She clasps it against her, then holds it out to the little girl. "Tell it, '*Te amo.*' "

Rosa looks around at the adults, then back to the doll. She has a funny expression, a look of concentration.

"Rosa!" Tanya shouts.

"Ohh!" Opal cries.

Rosa's pink pajamas have darkened at the crotch. Rosa is peeing as she stands there.

"Shit," Tanya grumbles, snatching the child away. The Cabbage Patch doll drops to the floor. Heather picks it up and carries it back to the couch, by her mother. Opal, a spoon in her hand, busies herself rearranging the presents by the tree.

"Remember my doll?" Heather says.

Joy squeezes her eyes, then opens them again. She pulls her legs up and hugs her knees. "Your daddy made you give it to the Goodwill, one of his lessons to be learned."

"I guess I learned. I never opened anything early again."

"Honestly, Joy," Opal says from across the room. "We can see everything you've got."

Clancy wanders through on her way to coffee.

"I know you'll want to shop the after-Christmas sales," Joy tells Heather. "So I'm just giving you money for Christmas."

Clancy sits down on the other side of Heather, cradling a mug. "Me, too," she says. "I couldn't fight the crowds."

"Oh, that's all right," Heather says, disappointed. She wonders how much money.

They hear Rosa screaming from the bathroom.

Russell finds a parade on TV.

Opal says, "You might as well open yours, Heather." She says this as if Heather has been making the fuss.

"I can wait on everybody else," Heather says. She isn't especially curious.

"We're all here, why don't we just do it!" Opal says. She lays her spoon down on the kitchen table with a *whack*. "Russell, turn that damned TV off."

Russell turns the sound on mute.

Joy says sourly, "I haven't even had my second cup of coffee."

Clancy says, "I haven't finished this one."

They all stare at one another.

Opal more or less marches to the other couch and plops herself down. "Heather, yours is that big green package from Mervyn's."

Heather is agitated, like someone called to the front of the room to be bawled out, and at the same time, she feels a gush of such ample sadness that she longs to curl up on her mother's lap and shut her eyes.

"Heather!" her mother says.

Heather picks up the assigned gift without enthusiasm. She knows it's clothing, something her grandmother thinks she should wear, and she knows she will end up exchanging it—this part she actually likes—and Opal's feelings will be hurt and she will swear she is never going to choose anything for anyone ever again. She takes the present back to the couch and undoes it.

The gift is an electric-blue jacket, a lightweight fake material like she sees rich kids wearing at school. When you crush it between your fingers, it snaps back, but it is soft, and light, and a tiny bit fuzzy.

"Ooh, like," Clancy says.

"It's pretty," Heather says, almost in a whisper.

"It's bright enough," her mother says.

"Don't act so surprised!" Opal says.

"I didn't know what it was," Heather answers.

"That it's pretty."

"Mother," Joy says.

"Now you," her mother says.

Joy sighs. "What would I want for Christmas!"

"The package with the candy canes on the bow," Opal says.

Joy drags herself off the couch, picks up the package, holds it for an instant, then drops it to the floor and rushes out of the room. They hear her door slam hard.

"I'll be dipped in shit," Russell says.

"It's Mick," Opal says bitterly.

"It's not Mick, it's *Christmas*," Heather says. "Why do they even *have* it!" She runs into her mother's room.

Joy lies facedown on her bed, her crying muffled by the pillow.

"You're really pretty, Mommy," Heather says.

Joy groans.

"I hate men," Heather says. "I hate Christmas."

Joy turns over. "Me, too, pumpkin," she says. She holds out her arms.

Heather, changed now into a nice sweater of her mother's, enters the household again. Clancy is curled up on the couch reading one of her paperbacks. Russell's parents, Imogene and Papa Duffy, have arrived. Mr. Duffy is at the table, staring at a scrapbook of photographs. Imogene sits on one side of him, Russell on the other.

"See, Papa, that's old Dog Man Slater, over in Farmington," Imogene shouts. "We put your pipeline pictures in a book."

Mr. Duffy mumbles something nobody can understand.

Opal is laying out pickles and olives on cut-glass dishes. The television, tuned to a parade, is blaring at no one.

"Look here, Papa," Imogene says. Heather wonders why Imogene calls her husband "Papa." "This was in Appalochicola, right before you went to Miami, when it was still *American*."

Heather moves to the edge of the kitchen group. Opal says, "Would you like to frost the cookies?" She holds up a bottle of red dye.

"Sure." Heather is glad for something to do.

"Wash," Opal says.

"Well, *sure*," Heather says, although she doesn't see the point.

Russell says something about a pig and laughs loudly. Mr. Duffy says, "Ha, ha, ha," like he's pretending something is funny. Heather doesn't think Mr. Duffy is following along.

The phone rings and Heather grabs it. It is Mick Jasonbee. "I'm in Plains," he says. "Merry Christmas."

"Just a minute," she says. She lays the phone down. "It's Mick," she whispers to Opal.

Mr. Duffy slumps in his chair, his head rolling to the side.

"Go get Joy," Opal says. She gives the phone a dirty look.

Joy walks to the phone so slowly that Heather wants to get behind her and give her a shove. Joy picks up the phone, says, *"What?"* and then, a few seconds later, slams it down and returns to her room.

Opal rolls her eyes.

"What?" Heather demands.

"Here," Opal says. She pushes a small jar of colored candy beads toward Heather. "Make them fancy."

"What'd he want?" Heather asks. She misses Mick, misses how her mother acts when he's around. Sometimes they all play Crazy Eights when Mick is there.

Imogene says, "We'll put him on your bed," and scrapes her chair back as she stands up.

"Nothing, I'd say," Opal says.

Wayne Ronnander comes in the garage door without knocking. Russell and his mother are dragging his father out of the room. Opal says, "You're early," and Heather feels tears bubbling up. Her father comes to her and gives her a hug that lasts exactly two seconds. He backs away and looks her over.

"I think you're gaining weight," he says.

"She's wearing a *sweater,* Wayne," Opal says.

Heather blinks. "So *what!*"

"I came to take you to my mother's for dinner," Wayne says. He is wearing a suit, with a red tie.

"I didn't hear anything about that!" Opal says.

Wayne gives her his look. It is a familiar one. It says: You don't know because I didn't tell you. Heather has seen it a thousand times.

"We're eating right away, so I won't be late driving back to Amarillo," he says.

"Daddy—" Heather says. She's not sure what she wants to say, only that she's suddenly more unhappy than she was before he arrived.

"Are you ready? Packed?"

"Daddy—"

"Where's your mother?"

"She's not here," Opal says quickly.

"On Christmas Day?"

"Free country," Opal says.

"Daddy—"

"Wayne, we're having dinner in an hour. We weren't expecting you to take Heather away." Opal holds her eyebrows arched up high. Probably she thinks she looks more important that way. She looks surprised, though, when there's nothing to be surprised about.

Wayne says sternly, "Get your stuff, Heather."

"I don't want to go to Amarillo, Daddy."

"That's what we agreed!"

"Who agreed?" Opal says.

"*I* never said," Heather says.

Joy appears in the living room. "Well, well," she says.

"Joy," Heather's father says. Joy is still wearing tap pants. Heather's father gives her legs a look. *This* look, also familiar, says: I'm never surprised at what you do.

"Do I have to?" Heather asks her mother. "Do I have to?"

"She's nearly fourteen," Joy says. "Shouldn't she be able to make up her own mind?"

"When she's fourteen she can decide," Wayne says. "She can come live with *me* if she wants."

"I don't want to," Heather says feebly.

"What?" Russell asks, just out of the bedroom. The phone rings and he grabs it. "Tannyyy!" he shouts.

"I'm about to lose my patience," Wayne says evenly.

Tanya rushes to the phone. "Yes?" she says. "Just a minute." She tells her father, "It's Hector."

"Take it in the bedroom," Opal tells her.

"Mom and Dad are in there," Russell says.

Tanya looks desperate.

"Tell him you'll call him back," Opal suggests.

Tanya starts to cry.

Imogene comes in from the bedroom. "He's asleep."

"So go on in there," Russell tells his daughter. "He won't know from ice cream." Tanya runs into the bedroom; the door swings shut with a bang.

Wayne says coldly, "I have never been in this house that it wasn't a zoo."

"Nobody asked you," Opal says.

"*I* sure didn't!" Joy says, and leaves.

"Daddy?" Heather says.

"What?"

"Could I go over for dinner, but then come back? And not go to Amarillo? So I can—I can go to the sales tomorrow?"

"The *sales*?"

"It's the best time at the mall."

"They have sales in Amarillo, young lady!"

"But you won't want to take me."

Her father considers this. "They poison your mind here, Heather. You've got a strange sense of values, growing up in this house."

"Now, look here," Russell says.

Clancy, risen from the couch, says lazily, "Let's make bread pudding with the leftover rolls, Mama. I can't remember where I saw bread pudding lately; it's on my mind. With those golden raisins, and cinnamon?"

Wayne says, "Christ. You're all certifiable."

"You know your wife doesn't want me around," Heather says, crying. Her father steps over, stands right beside her, and speaks just to her, as if it really matters to him what he is saying. "My mom has made a turkey *and* a ham. My sister and her kids are there. Mom really wants her grandkids around. Joanne wants you with us. It's Christmas. You're my daughter. I never see you."

Heather sets the bottle of cookie decorations down by the bowl of icing, now crusted. "I like ham," she says. She wipes her nose on the back of her hand. "But I want to come home after, Daddy."

Tanya emerges from the bedroom. "Hector is coming over with Georgie," she says.

Wayne says, "Who's Hector? Who's Georgie?" He doesn't ask like he cares to know; Heather can tell he is being sarcastic.

"How many places does that make?" Opal asks.

Tanya gives Opal a glaring, narrow-eyed look. "Nobody said we was going to eat here."

"I'll be back after while," Heather says. She follows her father out the back door. Nobody says good-bye. Nobody says a word about her not wearing a coat. Probably Opal would rather she didn't wear the new one to the Ronnanders', anyway.

7

O pal sits up in bed, creaming her face. Russell sprays his nose with mentholated Afrin and hops in bed. He says, "Whew." It has been a long, hectic day, and nothing especially awful happened, he seems to say. To him, the hardest part was hauling his father home. Papa Duffy has had several small strokes and is confused and frail. He probably didn't realize it was Christmas.

"It just breaks my heart to see Joy like this," Opal says.

"Like what?"

"You mean you don't see it plain as anything? For over a year Mick Jasonbee eats here day and night, sleeps with Joy, like he lives here—"

"I haven't minded," Russell says. "Mick's okay."

"Yes, and now he is going to be *done*. He is going off to med school, and he is going to leave Joy here on her little heinie."

"No shit. What does she say?"

"She doesn't say anything."

"How do you know all this?"

"Russell! Are you deaf and blind? This was Christmas! He didn't give her a present! I wouldn't be surprised if we never see his face again."

"Poor kid."

"At least Tanya's back with Hector." Opal puts the lid

on the cold-cream jar and sets it on the headboard of the bed.

"I thought that all went okay, didn't you?" Russell asks. "That little Georgie all spiffed up, he was real cute."

"Yes." There isn't any use in pointing out that a white suit is an Easter outfit, and not for Christmas, not above the border, anyway. Of course Hector stayed. For sure, *he* wasn't making Christmas dinner, and his parents live in El Paso. At least things settled down; even Rosa more or less behaved herself. And it was a relief to see Tanya out and Clancy in the front bedroom, where she can shut the door when she wants.

Clancy looks like she is carrying a sack of stones around—hunched, listless, dogged. Opal wonders if she *wants* to feel better. One thing Opal knows for sure: A good time does not come looking for you.

"You have to admit, ole Hector's done all right for his-self." Russell affects a little extra drawl, maybe to tease, or to be charming.

Opal knows that Russell means that Hector is now manager of the nightclub where he has worked for years, a nightclub with a salsa band all week and hard rock on Saturday night. "You don't think he'll leave Tanya, do you?" she says, although Russell wouldn't see a bird till it lit on his nose.

"Oh, Lord, girl. Knock on wood. We don't want Tanya and those kids around here on a permanent basis."

Opal is glad to hear Russell say this. She says, "Anytime you want, you can give my kids notice. It is your house."

"Honey, you know I don't feel like that—" Russell scoots over to her and cups her breast with his hand and gives it a jiggle. "Mine, yours, ours," he says.

Opal arranges herself against the pillows and lies back.

"I'm about whipped, Russell. These varicose veins, my hemorrhoids—I'm going to have to have surgery sooner or later—and my thumb—"

"You poor thing." He reaches for a Kleenex tissue and blows his nose loudly.

Opal sighs.

Russell sighs, too. "All right, listen. They're gonna be starting up a new pipeline down by El Paso sometime soon—maybe the end of January—"

"What about school?" Opal doesn't want him saying she made him quit, although he was fool-stupid ever to begin. Not long after they married, Russell sold his station and, consulting no one, plunged nearly twenty thousand dollars into the stock market. He had hunches. He had been watching certain stocks. Interest rates were then at a record high. In T-bills he could have doubled his money in six years. In the market, he thought he could make that much overnight. All around them, the oil industry was teetering, but Russell knew that far away, in New York, there was money to be made, if you quit thinking like a hick. He had plans. He would finish his degree in petroleum engineering—he had one semester, twenty years ago—find a job in Houston, and give Opal a fat retirement. Opal's mother lived long enough to say I told you so.

Now Russell puffs up like one of those poisonous fish, in fear.

"I've sorta been waiting for the grades to come out," he tells her, "but, Opal, honey, it's an awful long grind. Maybe I'll work a while, like you say—"

"*I* say!" They're all her dependents. Russell, too, unless he gets off his college butt. "I'm worn out. I can't work forever." She turns on her side, away from Russell.

"I could be gone five or six months," he says.

There is a long silence. Then she turns and puts her head on his chest. "I'd drive down on weekends. I'd come stay in the trailer with you, leave all this mess for the ones who make it—" She speaks softly, lays a hand across his belly, shuts her eyes.

"That'd be nice," he says. He slides his cheek along her greasy face, and kisses her lightly on the lips. "We could get a real nice trailer, where everything fits together neat."

"I'm sorry I got fat," she whispers.

"Shoot, I don't care about that, except for you not feeling good."

"I'm always thinking about Mother, and her stuff in the flood." Everything had been marked with masking tape: JOY on the bedroom chests from the farm, CLANCY on a butter churn. "So much of it ruined, and the rest waiting for—" She can't finish the sentence. *Waiting for me to take care of it.*

"I know you miss her."

Opal wishes Russell wouldn't say anything. He can't know what it's like. Like having your heart cut out. He sees his dizzy mother more than he wants.

But he is here, he is the only one here, and she hurts. "I hadn't talked to her in two days," she whispers.

Russell takes his hands off Opal and falls back on his pillows with a soft thud.

"Sorr-ee," says Opal.

"Hell, she didn't know what was what those last weeks, Opal. She wasn't getting enough blood upstairs."

"Jesus, Russell!"

"You have just got to get yourself together and *sell that house.*"

Opal falls undefended into grief and anguish, the morass of her mother's death. She can't quit thinking of her mother facedown in floodwaters on her own kitchen floor. Opal let them talk her into a closed casket; a drowned body swells. It was a mistake. As they lowered sweet Greta into her grave, Opal was horrified at the image of her mother in the casket, laid out like a flounder.

"You hear what I say?" Russell is nearly hollering.

"She wanted me to have that house!" Opal says back.

"That's exactly right. She wanted you to leave my house and move into hers. And that's why you hold on to it, isn't it? So you can do that if you want to! So you don't really live here!"

Opal climbs off the bed and slips on her robe. She makes herself take several long, deep breaths. She hears Russell behind her, panting. She says, "I'm going to heat up a cup of milk. I'll never get to sleep." She walks quickly to the door before Russell can make a move. "Don't get up, I know you're *tired*."

"Honey—" Russell says plaintively. She turns to him. "Wasn't that something?" he asks. "Hector helping me wash the pots? There aren't many Meskin men would do that!"

Opal shuts the door.

She pours herself a cup of milk. She puts the carton back in the refrigerator and takes out the plate of battered asparagus Swiss rolls. A few were handled, but she doesn't think anybody actually ate one. She brushes them into the trash compactor. She opens the fridge again and tears off a strip of turkey from the carcass for the cat, Chocolate. She lays the meat on the counter.

She looks in the dishwasher and turns it on. The cabinet rattles, the water roars. The dishes, stacked every which way, clang. It wouldn't surprise her if everybody stormed out of their beds in a fury, and she doesn't care if they do.

She warms the milk in the microwave and sits at the table sipping it. She thinks about leaving her mother, to go with her first husband, Joy's father, to Florida. He was an airman. Greta said, "You'll be back, Opal Mae, he isn't worth his uniform." Oh, she hated her mother for saying that, and, oh, she was glad to come home, Joy in her arms. And then, it was like a miracle, meeting Thatch so soon after. It was a blind date, doubling with an old girlfriend from high school and her fiancé. They all went dancing. Thatch wanted to go out the very next night, but Opal had to say they could only when her mother was able to watch Joy. Thatch said, "That won't matter." He found things they could do, taking the baby along, or they left her with his mother. The day they got married, Thatch told Opal, "That girl is mine now," but if anyone mentions him, Joy leaves the room. She acts like she doesn't know him. Joy hates him, when Opal doesn't. You'd think Joy got the divorce.

"Chocolate," Opal calls. She carries the tidbit of turkey around. Chocolate is Russell's cat, a leftover from his first marriage. Opal has complained often of the food dish in the laundry room and the litter box in the garage. Years ago Chocolate had a scare, on the busy avenue that crosses their street at the corner. Now she ventures out fearfully, full of false starts and rapid retreats, and sometimes not for days. She never goes six feet from the porch. She does all her business inside, sitting way up high, as if she minds the bother.

Opal stands for a moment, a phantom in her threadbare pajamas, caught in the luxury of nothing more to be done. The back-porch light comes through the windows where the curtains are still drawn open, and in the yellow glow, patches of her skin shine like slick spots on a road. Chocolate comes padding from her place behind the couch, to purr and rub against Opal's ankle, begging love in the middle of the night.

Opal settles in the recliner upright. The cat arranges herself along Opal's thigh and nibbles at the bite of turkey, then stretches out and purrs. By day, Chocolate avoids Opal's presence, darts at a glance, spends weekend hours in the laundry room or one of the girls' rooms across the house. But sometimes, on nights like this, she shows she knows how false is Opal's coldness. She moves in with the easy confidence of children. She warms Opal's flesh with her thrumming body.

Fibrillations

8

Joy is dreaming of caresses.
She went to bed early, weary and alone, but now she feels
the fine comfort of a light hand over the slope of her shoulder, along the bony ridge of her spine, around the curve of
her buttocks. She murmurs softly and stretches; her feet
move into a spot of chilly sheets, and she pulls her knees up
again, toward her chest, like a child. She dreams not of
Mick, or others, forgotten, but of affection and solace.
Sleep suspends bitterness. She throws the quilt off, turns
onto her back, and flings out her arms.

A shrill burble pierces the stillness. The phone. The cat,
curled on the bed near Joy's thigh, yowls and digs her
claws through the sheet into flesh, then leaps away, out of
the room.

Joy sits up suddenly, violently, sucking in her breath,
waking just before she would scream. The room is stifling.
Opal keeps the heat on all night. The windows do not
open—Russell has sealed the house with nailed-down
storm windows—and the only way to cool Joy's room is to
prop open the door to the patio, off the hall across from
Heather's room. She did so earlier, but now she is damp
with perspiration. The door has been shut, probably by
Opal on her rounds before bed. Even though her daughters' rooms are separated from her own by most of the
space of the house, she would make sure *their* comfort
conforms to *her* ideas.

"Heatherrr!" Joy hears her mother's shrill voice as Opal stomps down the hall and throws open the door to Heather's room. "It was for you."

"What do you want?" Heather shrieks.

"What is this about?" Joy comes up behind her mother into the doorway of Heather's room. Already her daughter's face is contorted with rage. There is so much hostility between Joy's mother and daughter, usually contained in sullenness and seething, that the least leak threatens an explosion.

Opal stands, hands on hips. " 'Hello,' most people say. Your friend giggles like a girl. 'Is Heather there?' he asks, and he giggles, like it's not a quarter after midnight."

"Who? Who called me?" Heather is up on her knees on the bed. She wears a large bright pink T-shirt that says ASK ME. Her hands are clenched into angry fists.

"I said, 'Heather is in bed, and so are the rest of us in this house.' " Opal has taken on an even, tense tone.

"I was *not* asleep. You could have called me! It was *my* phone call!" Tears spurt onto Heather's cheeks. She is shaking with fury. Spying her mother behind Opal, she shouts, "It was my call!"

Opal smirks. "He said to tell you Blaise called. What kind of name is Blaise?"

"Only the name of the cutest sophomore in all of Lubbock High! Only the name of the boy who just broke up with Penny Thomas and isn't dating another girl yet." Suddenly Heather's countenance takes on a stunned look. "Calling me. And I'll never know why."

Opal's shoulders quiver. Her pajamas rustle with the odd movement. Her voice crackles slightly as she says, "You tell your friends that people in this house go to bed at night. Tell them to call you by nine o'clock." She twirls around and almost steps on Joy's foot. "I was asleep!" She pushes past her into the hall.

Heather screams. "She hates me! She doesn't want me to have any friends. I hate her! She's a stupid old witch."

Joy closes the door and then sits on the bed and puts her arms around Heather. Heather collapses, sobbing, against her shoulder. Her chin-length permed hair sticks out wildly in a woolly tangle. "Shh, shh," Joy says, brushing Heather's hair out of her eyes. She knows there isn't any use in saying more. She would like to run down the hall, across the living room, into Opal and Russell's big bedroom, to pull her mother's hair right out of her head. It is true that Opal is mean to Heather. It is a repeat of history, the way Opal always looked for the wrong in everything Joy did, as if her awful father was showing up in her all the time and no one would put up with it. Now poor Heather has her own worthless, spiteful, know-everything father, and Opal thinks it's somehow Heather's *fault* she's here in their laps, instead of in Amarillo, where Wayne's *new wife* would be answering the phone.

Heather pulls away and blows her nose on the sheet. She rubs her eyes. Below them are black smears of makeup. She has gone to bed without washing her face, as usual. She looks like a raccoon—a pretty, unhappy, thirteen-year-old raccoon. She is too young for high school. Joy should have kept her back a year starting school, instead of pushing to get her in despite her Valentine's Day birthday, but she was so smart. When she was four years old, she could read from the back of cereal boxes. She could retell the plot of any story you read her, any show she saw on TV. She would ride down the street calling out words. She would ask the saleslady, "How much is the sales tax?" At *four*.

Heather sniffles. In a small voice she whimpers, "I don't even know him."

"Who?" Joy says sharply. She is remembering her chemistry teacher asking her where she would go to college. She was going to secretarial school, a six-month course. The teacher was dismayed. "That's a waste," he said. Joy was flattered. She told her mother. Opal said, "How nice."

"Blaise. He's never said one word to me."

"So what is he *calling* you for?"

A cry starts somewhere in Heather and turns into a baby's long loud whimper. She throws herself flat-faced into the bed covers.

"I can't understand what you're saying, Heather Ronnander. *Lift up here and talk to me.*"

Heather does lift her head slightly, to peer at her mother. "He only called me because it's too late to call anybody else. He'll never call back." She sounds limp and woeful.

"Maybe you ought to go call *him* right back. Maybe you ought to let *his* mother answer the phone at this time of the night."

"You're on her side!" Heather yells, scrambling away and huddling against the headboard. "We live in *her* house, and *she's* the fat *queen*. Why don't we have our own house? Why don't we live someplace of our own!"

Joy stands up. She feels sorry for her daughter, but she doesn't have the slightest idea how to help her. Heather might as well complain about dust and wind. Control of their lives is not in Joy's hands, nor anyone's, really. Destiny is cosmic; some people are never going to get ahead.

"I was asleep, too," she says, and leaves Heather to her weeping.

She opens the door to the patio and stands there a moment, enjoying the slap of cold air, thinking of Mick. If she calls him now—he is in his dorm room—he will fumble for the phone, cursing, and as soon as he hears who it is, he will say, "Shit, Joy, give it up." He is young, much younger than Joy. She does not think he has another girlfriend. She thinks that this semester, the last of his undergraduate studies, has been harder than any before, and that his future is suddenly near. He is going to medical school at Baylor in the fall.

Never once has he been mean to her, except to leave and not come back, and she thinks he only did that because he is young and inexperienced and ashamed and sorry. He didn't know what else to do. She aches to think of going back to her bed alone; she misses the smell of him when she curls against him and puts her face on his back. She is almost forty years old, and cannot imagine her own future brightened by the slightest happiness, but she does not hate Mick Jasonbee. He never slammed his hand against her face. He never called her names and accused her of unspeakable acts. Her husbands did those things, but not Mick.

She will settle for the comfort of the cat, who has surely gone to hide in the laundry room.

She pads slowly down the hall to Clancy's room.

"I'm awake," Clancy says from her bed. A sliver of moonlight falls like a white branch across her face. The cat lies stretched out between the wall and Clancy's leg.

Joy sits on the edge of the bed. "Mother had one of her fits."

"She's all strung out, with Russell in El Paso. He did what she wanted him to do, and now she's by herself."

"Why does she have it in for Heather so?"

"Because she's here."

Joy sighs. "I miss Mick."

Clancy snorts. "Men," she says.

Joy laughs. "Mothers."

Clancy pats the bed. "Want to sleep in here?"

Joy considers her sister's long body. Clancy never turns over, lying still as a log all night. Hers is a sister's flesh; she understands. "I better sleep with Heather," she says. She stands up. "I want to move."

"Okay." Clancy yawns noisily. "This weekend. We'll trade bedrooms." Both of them laugh, even though it isn't funny.

O pal is up extra early in the morning, making banana nut muffins from scratch. She sets them on the counter with a tub of margarine, takes out orange juice and milk from the refrigerator, and makes a pot of coffee. On the other side of the house, Clancy, Joy, and Heather scurry from room to bath and up and down the hall. Heather has MTV on, but not too loud. Every once in a while she sings along for a line or two. It is a wonder to Opal that she can understand the words.

Joy follows Clancy into her bedroom. "I really need for you to take Heather to school this one time," she says. Usually Heather goes with Opal, who works in the same general area as the high school, and who can go in a little later than Joy. If Heather arrives at school early, she has to stand around in the cold, because they keep the buildings locked until right before classes begin, and it makes her look stupid, as if she doesn't know when school starts.

"This isn't a good morning," Clancy says. "It's my turn to pick up doughnuts."

"She doesn't want to go with Mother."

Clancy shrugs. "The bakery is in one direction, the school is in another, the bank downtown. I should already be gone. I can't." She doesn't say she's sorry.

Joy tells Heather she will have to go with Opal or take the bus. Heather is in the bathroom, sitting on the counter with her feet in the basin, lining her eyes. "Maybe I'll walk," she says to her mother. She has never taken the bus in her life; she wouldn't know what bus to take. The school is four miles away.

Joy goes into the kitchen without speaking to her mother. She pours coffee in a cup and Coke in a juice glass and takes them both into the bathroom as Heather exits.

"There's breakfast out here!" Opal shouts aggrievedly. She is sitting at the table reading the morning paper, drinking her coffee with extra milk. There is a special feature, the fifth of a six-day article series, about a Lubbock man who has finally been convicted of murdering his wife six years ago. He electrocuted her with a radio in the bathtub. They would never have caught him if the wife's parents hadn't worked to bring him to justice, and if he had kept his mouth shut instead of bragging to people about what he had done. Opal takes a deep, satisfied breath, glad to see someone get what he deserves. Evidently he did it for the insurance—he had a girlfriend—and you can bet that money is long gone, and what good did it do him? Tomorrow she will find out what his sentence was.

Heather prances through the kitchen, pours a glass of Coke and leaves the bottle on the counter with the cap off, puts a piece of bread in the toaster, and stands with her back to Opal. She wears what Opal is sure is a brand-new pleated skirt, and one of Opal's part-angora sweaters. Opal has not seen that sweater in a long time; she wouldn't be able to get it on anymore. Probably it was in Joy's closet all along.

"I did make muffins," she complains.

Heather slathers margarine on her toast, sprinkles it with sugar and cinnamon, and carries it and the Coke into the bathroom, where her mother is. She has managed never to look in Opal's direction. Tears well up in Opal's eyes. The phone rings, and she welcomes the distraction, although it is only seven-thirty. It is her mother-in-law, Imogene, wanting to know when Opal will be home in the afternoon. Opal considers lying and making it later than it will be, but she would not put it past Imogene to park up the street and check on her story, so she says she will be home some time before six. Imogene has her hands full, with Papa Duffy mute and hardly mobile after another small stroke, but she is lonesome and restless, too, especially with Russell out of town. "I could pick up some barbecue," she offers.

"Whatever," Opal says. Imogene will bring a quart of beans, a pint of slaw, and a puny serving of stringy beef, although she knows there are four of them in this house who have to eat. Isolated and rejected this morning, Opal adds, "I can fry up some potatoes. I set some Jell-O last night, with bananas. Cherry Jell-O?" She goes back to the table.

Joy returns to the kitchen—without her or Heather's dirty dishes—and picks up the phone. It is soon obvious that she is calling Wayne, although she doesn't speak his name. The call to Amarillo will appear on Opal's phone bill and never be mentioned. "Your check is late," Joy says, and, to whatever is his excuse, "You aren't supposed to mail it on the first, I'm supposed to *get* it on the first. And I need it. Also, it is nearly your daughter's fourteenth birthday, if that makes any difference to you." She is gripping the phone so tightly, her knuckles are white. He says something, then she says, "It is none of your business where *my* money goes," and slams the phone back on the hook. She looks at Opal, makes a face as if Opal were in league with her delinquent ex, and makes another pass across the wide central area of the house.

Opal wonders if Heather would like a pair of those acid-washed jeans you see all over.

A moment later, Clancy comes in and pours half a cup of coffee, drinks it in two gulps, pinches off a piece of muffin, sniffs it, and nibbles a tiny bite before throwing the rest into the sink. She wipes her fingers on a dish towel.

"A whistle could blow you away," Opal says.

"Big lunch at work, Mother. This is stew and cornbread day." The bank serves lunch to its employees for a little fee, automatically deducted from their checks. Opal thinks this is very nice of them, but Clancy has said it's like paying the company store. She wouldn't protest, though. She wouldn't call attention to herself that way.

"Oh, good!" Opal watches Clancy go out the garage door and then rises, still in her slip and robe. "Twenty minutes, Heather," she calls, as cheerfully as she can manage.

Joy appears, followed by Heather. "She's going with me," she says hatefully. There is a morning ritual all worked out—Opal always takes Heather to school—and there is no reason to violate it now, just because of a little fuss from which Heather could learn something.

"There's no need," Opal says. She feels a rumble of gas in her lower bowel; last night she ate tacos, when she ought to know better by now.

"From now *on*," Joy says. She gives her daughter a light shove on the shoulder and sends her ahead to the door. Opal farts loudly and long; there is nothing she can do about it. "Oooh!" she squeals, in embarrassment and relief.

"Till I can get her a *car*," Joy adds before she slams the door.

"My Lord," Opal declares to the empty room, "that girl

can't drive until she's sixteen years old!" She walks away from the bad smell she has made and takes out one of her muffins from the pan. It split on top as it baked, and there is a thumb-sized soggy spot of wet banana mush. She doesn't know what has happened to her cooking lately. She leans against the counter and eats slowly, then puts the juice and milk away. She goes to her room to dress for work. Coming back through, she shakes the muffins into the trash compactor.

Barbecue, she thinks, will pump me up like a helium balloon. She remembers a cow she saw on the farm as a girl, so bloated her grandfather had to stab it in the belly. What an awful sight, an awful smell.

That poor cow, she thinks.

10

J oy unlocks the doctor's of-
fice and goes around turning things on. She tries to arrive
half an hour before the others; she likes the feeling that
it is her office, that she is in charge. She likes the empti-
ness, and the hum of fluorescent lights and machinery coming on.

Doctor will be late this morning; he has a court date
with his soon-to-be-ex wife. Joy is sure he would much
rather be in surgery, removing some woman's uterus. He
refers to hysterectomies as the "bread and butter" of his
practice, but they could be better described as caviar, since
he doesn't do obstetrics. It is nice, though, once it's over,
never to have a period again, Joy thinks. She had her op-
eration when Heather was three years old. The doctor had
told her everything was drooping. She supposed it would
one day fall out. Her mother came to help while she was
recuperating. Her husband started screwing a lab techni-
cian where he worked. Her dog died. All those things
seemed related, at the time.

She sits right down to see what to do about the February
billing, which is already late. Doctor put in desktop computers, but he tried to save money on software. When there
is the slightest deviation, the system isn't able to accom-
modate it. Joy finally talked Doctor into calling in a consultant to do some reprogramming, and to teach Joy how
it all works. They have had two sessions so far, and Joy

found them amazingly fun. The consultant says she has a natural aptitude for computers; not everyone does. For patients of long standing, she wants to delete the chiding line at the bottom of the bills, the one that points out the number of days they are overdue; only, she doesn't know how to tell the program to identify those patients. So she has been plowing through the bills one by one and, in doing so, has found errors of other sorts. She wants to determine if they are the fault of the billing clerk, the program, or the doctor. At first she was frustrated, but she finds the tasks intriguing, like puzzles, and they block out other matters from her mind.

When the receptionist, Kay Lynn, comes in and goes to start the coffee, Joy remembers she meant to call the district attorney's office, and that is the end of her pleasant absorption. She has been telling Kay Lynn about her ex-husband's delays with the child support payments, and Kay Lynn says that her sister got *her* ex-husband's ass in a sling through the D.A.'s Program of Support Compliance. It is possible, says Kay Lynn, to attach the father's check directly, and that will put an end to this game-playing.

After Joy is put on hold, then directed through three different people, she finally gets someone on the line who knows what she is talking about, but it does not go well.

"Are you on welfare, Mrs. Ronnander?" the woman asks. Joy says she is not. "We give priority to welfare clients, in order to recover funds due the state."

"That sounds smart, but what about me? I'm not asking for anything from the state except a little help in goosing my daughter's father." She goes on, tries to explain that for four years Wayne has been tormenting her by sending checks when he feels good and ready, by making them ten dollars short, or thirty; once or twice, fifty. Sometimes he skips a whole month and sends two payments together.

"How much in arrears is your husband?"

Joy cannot believe Wayne is being called her husband. If he were her husband, he would have to pay her bills, and he would have to do something about the furnace in her house in Amarillo, which is about to go out. "Four hundred dollars," she says.

"Oh!" the D.A.'s person says in a puff of exasperation. "Mrs. Ronnander, just what is your monthly support payment?"

"One-fifty."

"So he is less than three months in arrears."

"That's how he does it. He deducts things. At Christmas he bought Heather new tennis shoes and then took the cost out of my support check. He said I sent her up there half naked. He forgets she *grows*."

"You must be angry with him," the voice says soothingly.

"I just want my four hundred dollars." Her brakes need a new lining, her clutch is about to go out.

"I can certainly understand. But Mrs. Ronnander, we have clients owed four *thousand* dollars. We have delinquent fathers who have never paid anything at all. You can come in and fill out some forms, but until Mr. Ronnander is six months or a thousand dollars in arrears, I can tell you nothing will happen. It's not that we don't sympathize, dear. It's a question of staff."

"He's an engineer at Pantex. He makes forty-five thousand dollars a year."

"You should get more child support."

"How?"

"You need a lawyer, ma'am. I'm sorry. You need your own, private lawyer."

Kay Lynn sets a cup of coffee down in front of Joy. She has been standing there a couple of minutes. "How did he ever get you to agree to one-fifty?"

"I got the house," Joy says. "The big expensive unsalable white-elephant house." The phone rings.

"You got screwed, sweetheart." Kay Lynn answers the phone.

At three Joy takes her usual "lunch" so she can pick up Heather and drop her off at home. Back in the office galley, she nibbles on Saltine crackers and drinks a Tab. Kay Lynn pops in for a few minutes to pick up the conversation. "It's a big colonial job," Joy tells her, "with an upstairs, and a Jacuzzi and barbecue, all that stuff. We put sixteen thousand down seven years ago, so all that ought to be mine, you know? I never intended to stay in it as long as I did, two years; I couldn't keep up the bills. I had to borrow money from my mother, and then my grandmother. But when I put it on the market, it sat there like a humongous slug. Practically all we paid is interest; I still owe nearly a sixty-thousand-dollar mortgage. Now the agent tells me I ought to sell it for sixty-five. I could pay off the bank, and her, and I'd have nothing left. Zip. He knew. The lawyers knew. Only I was too stupid to know."

Kay Lynn clucks her tongue. "So now you're making payments down a rat hole?"

"I've had four different renters. One couple I had to evict, and that cost me; then they were so mad they stole my doorknobs. What I get paid in rent is less than the mortgage, and that doesn't count insurance."

"Maybe you should bail out."

"I thought I had!" Joy moans, referring to her marriage. She doesn't want any advice about taking what she can get,

which is nothing. The equity has become a ghost ship floating off the horizon, and Opal and Russell have been telling
her to give it up for the past two years, but *it is not fair.*
With sixteen thousand dollars she could buy a decent car,
get an apartment, live her own life. She could start over,
she could move to Atlanta, Seattle, anywhere. If she sells
the house and gets nothing, Wayne has the last laugh, the
bastard. "I let her have the house," he says.

"You wear your big tits like announcements," he told
her. What did he expect her to do? Cut them off? She
would if she could. They tug on her bra straps, they're
tender, they remind her there's nobody who touches them.
There was a time he thought they were four-star breasts.
Now he has a wife with no breasts at all.

Joy and Kay Lynn talk again at the end of the day. "My
mother and Heather don't get along," Joy says. They are
almost whispering. Doctor has been on a rampage all day.
Joy thinks: I bet he would not be sympathetic about my
house. It's almost funny. "I need my own place, but I can't
swing it."

"How much more a month would you need?"

"A couple hundred, I guess. Three would do it."

"I have an idea. If you're not interested, that's perfectly
okay, but we've got to find somebody, so why not ask you
first? Listen, Joy, what do you know about snow cones?"

11

Opal arrives home at a quarter to six and right away the place is hopping. Imogene's car is parked in the driveway, blocking Opal's access to the garage, so Opal pulls in beside her. Russell's son, Buddy, is driving Imogene's car, and Imogene is in the backseat. Papa Duffy is in the front, staring at the garage door as if it were an outdoor movie screen. Buddy oozes out of the car while Opal opens the garage door. She and Buddy steer Papa into the house by his elbows. Imogene brings up the rear, carrying a big white sack of take-out food. They plant Papa in the lounge chair facing the television, and Imogene says, patting him on the shoulder before they leave him to go sit in the kitchen, "He wanted to see trucks. We went out on the highway and drove in and out of the equipment yards."

Opal starts right in peeling potatoes. She has peeled three and begun to cut them up when the phone rings. Buddy is squeezed into the corner at the table, looking at one of Russell's car magazines. Imogene answers the phone, hollering as if the equipment is failing, "For you, Buddy."

It is Buddy's wife, Leeanne, wanting to know when he is coming home for supper. He tells her, "Just a minute," and lays the phone on the counter. He is out of breath from the effort it took to get out from behind the table and over to the counter where the phone hangs. Opal pushes sliced potatoes into a pan of hot Crisco. Buddy says, "Does somebody want to run me to my house? Or I can stay here until Gran's ready to take Papa home, so I can help." He is trying hard these days, with Russell out of town, to be a more grown-up son, and Opal wants to admire him for it, but, turning around from the stove, she has a moment of fresh surprise and revulsion at the spectacle of his big belly hanging over his pants.

"Who's supposed to take you home?" she says testily.

"I guess I can, while you finish supper," Imogene suggests weakly, looking to Opal for a decision. She gets up slowly and peers around to check on Papa. The TV is blaring the news. "Papa's asleep."

Buddy says, as he picks up the phone again, "I guess Leeanne could come get me." "Leeanne" would, of course, include Leeanne's wild eight-year-old son, Jimmy, who always acts crazy and puts Opal's nerves on edge. She doesn't know what his life was like before Leeanne married Buddy, but that was three years ago, and somebody ought to be able to settle him down a little.

Imogene likes this new idea. She plops right down into her chair and sighs. "What can I do, Opal, honey?" she says, without the slightest hint of energy. Buddy tells his wife, "I'll call you right back." He is the most patient person in the whole constellation of Thatcher-Duffy families; he hardly burns any calories at all. He works in his father-in-law's printshop, running a photocopy machine all day. There's no telling what Leeanne does all day.

The minute the phone is on the cradle, it rings once more. "I'll get it!" Opal snaps. It is the real estate agent in Amarillo, wanting Joy. She says she has a firm offer. Opal tells the woman that Joy should be home any minute, and she'll have her call back. "Sure, I'll encourage her to get it settled," she says when the agent asks. "But I can tell you my opinion doesn't count for much around here." Joy owes Opal nearly three thousand dollars, and Opal has already decided that when Joy sells the house, Opal will forgive the debt and tell her to use the money on a better car. Russell is always working on Joy's Bronco, and what will she do while he is gone?

Clancy, home from work, winds her way through the kitchen with a grunt of greeting, and goes straight to her room. Opal can see her in her mind's eye, kicking off her shoes, unbuttoning her skirt, and lying down like a big stick on the bed, staring at the ceiling. She must use it all up at work, thinks Opal.

"We-uhl?" Buddy says. He is probably hungry, but his big round face is calm as a pie plate.

Opal scrapes the edges of the potatoes where they are sticking in the pan, and turns the burner down. There isn't enough food for Heather, Clancy, Joy, Buddy and his two, Imogene, Papa, and Opal. She feels like banging her head against a cabinet door. Instead she holds the pancake turner out to Buddy. "Can you manage to watch these potatoes while I go to the store?" He looks amazed. Imogene jumps up and says she will do it. "So tell them to come on," Opal tells Buddy. She can see that that's what he wanted her to say. Leeanne is not much of a cook, and Imogene says Buddy is always stuck with the dishes.

"I am going to the *bathroom* first," Opal says. She will buy a sheet cake at the store bakery, and Neapolitan ice cream.

Opal tells Joy about the real estate agent's call, and suggests she talk on the phone in the big bedroom. It doesn't seem she is in there long enough to conduct business, and she isn't telling her mother anything. Opal is putting supper on the table when Joy, Heather, and Clancy saunter through the kitchen and out the back door. "Hey, we're eating!" Opal protests. Heather, last in line at the exit, turns and grins maliciously. "We're going to the cafeteria," she says.

Buddy eyes the potatoes and barbecued beef. Leeanne has not yet shown up. Opal has also boiled hot dogs—a whole lot more than she needs, evidently—and cooked some frozen mixed vegetables in cream sauce. "Go on," she says to Buddy.

Imogene is staring at the garage door. Opal, annoyed at the criticism implicit in Imogene's expression, says, "Oh, don't mind them."

"She's such a sour one," Imogene says. "When I was a girl, my mother would have boxed my ears for talking to a grown-up like she does."

Opal sighs. "Don't I know? When I was Heather's age, I was living with my grandmother on the farm. If I looked cross-eyed, she sent me to the yard to pick my own willow stick. I had *some* welts on my legs, I tell you. Once she locked me in the cellar for something I didn't do." Opal thinks Heather doesn't have any idea how lucky she is. Tears bubble in her eyes. "My mama was off cooking for a railroad gang after my papa died," she says softly. "She couldn't take us all." She remembers bitterly that Laura got to go. She remembers how close she felt then to her brother, Amos, when he's crazy and hostile as a rabid coyote now. She hasn't seen him since their mother's funeral, and he wasn't speaking to her then.

"Those were hard times," Imogene agrees, and the sound of her whiny voice jerks Opal right out of her reverie. Besides, Leeanne and Jimmy burst in just then. Jimmy is wearing a holster with toy pistols on his hips. "Not at the table," Opal says, steering him to a chair. The boy lays his weapons on the table, beside his plate. "I'm thtarving," he lisps.

When everything is said and done, when the Duffys have all gone home and everybody's eaten what they are going to, the pile in the kitchen is disheartening. Nobody touched the coleslaw, the uneaten hot dogs look like big grub worms, the ice cream sat out too long and melted a stream on the cabinet before Opal saw it. Her head aches.

She does the dishes. She is wiping the table when Joy, Clancy, and Heather return. They are carrying assorted sacks from the mall. Clancy has brought her mother a little carton of black-eyed peas. "I know how you like them," Clancy explains. "You never make them anymore."

Opal, touched, nearly bursts into tears, even though the peas are cold by now. "Put them on the counter," she says. "I might have a snack before bed." She can't keep from asking Joy what went on with the agent in Amarillo.

"I have to think about it!" Joy says. She is still mad at Opal; Opal can't remember why.

Opal carries the peas in a cereal bowl into her room. She clicks on the little TV Russell bought her before he left—so she wouldn't be lonesome, he said—and finds a Goldie Hawn movie in progress. Goldie plays a woman who falls off a boat and wakes up not knowing who she is, and this fellow convinces her she's his wife. He does this because he is up to his ears with kids and housework and cooking. Goldie looks bedraggled. Opal thinks, Sometimes I feel like that. Fast on the thought, she considers whether Russell might feel like *he* just came up out of the water and there were her kids.

Of course, Joy and Clancy are grown. Russell's the one

with little kids around so much of the time. It's just like the cat: She ends up taking care of them all.

While she is thinking all this over, he calls.

"It's awful late for you, isn't it?" she asks. Usually, when he's working, he goes to bed not long after dark.

"I tried to call you earlier and the phone was busy. When I woke up to go to the bathroom, I thought I'd try again."

"Joy might be able to sell her house."

"Hot dog!"

"If she will. Sometimes I think she would rather send her money off to that bank than give me two dollars for groceries."

"How's my cat?"

"I haven't seen her all evening. I think she is in Joy's bedroom. Or Clancy's."

"It's sure lonesome in this skinny little bed," Russell croons. He is living in his father's old travel trailer, sleeping on three inches of decaying foam.

"Here too," she answers. Her heart is doing one of its jerky dances. It doesn't have to do with Russell, it has to do with life. It would be so simple, she thinks, if it were just the two of us. The trailer would be a tight squeeze, though.

"You know, I don't even have a picture of you."

"Oh, Russell, what would you want one for, anyway?"

"I like the way you look."

"I'm fat."

"Sometimes when I touch you when you're not expecting it, you open your eyes like a startled doe."

"Russell," she says softly.

"You've got a heart as big as Texas, Opal, honey. You're so good to your kids, and my kids."

She feels small-spirited and mean. Sometimes she thinks

that when her mother died, bulbs went out in her, diminished her wattage. "I just do what has to get done," she says.

"If I was there, I'd make your eyes get gre-at big," he says.

It's hard to think about sex, with him so far away and all these pounds crowding her bones. Deep in her bowels she feels a dull tugging pain. Diverticulitis.

She can feel him waiting; a man has feelings, too. "Only 'cause it's so scary when it's so swoll up," she teases. He laughs and makes a kissy noise into the phone. "You better come down here soon and check on me," he says. "Some things I can't do by myself."

12

The computer consultant's name is Bill Tweed, and in his own way, he is cute. He has sandy hair that is dark on one side and blond on the other, and he has one blue eye and one brown eye. Tweed is a good name for him. Joy would like to pat his head, to feel the rough brush of his rowdy hair. She tries to concentrate on the program he is teaching her.

While they are working before lunch, there are two calls about Joy's house. The first is from her renter, who says that the heater broke down, and it will cost three hundred dollars to get it repaired. He and Joy agree that he will pay for the repairs and take the money out of the March rent. Then she will have to worry about how to make her mortgage payment, and right now, when she is hoping to move. Next, the real estate agent calls. She is anxious to wrap things up. Impatience rises in Joy like indigestion, but the woman has a new offer. "More money?" Joy asks eagerly. The buyers have offered sixty-three-eight; how do they come up with these figures? They won't budge, but the agent has talked it over with her boss, and since she is making the sale herself and has no fee to split, they are willing to split it with Joy instead. "Meaning what?" Joy asks.

"Meaning I take three and a half percent instead of seven. You walk away with nearly four grand, Joy."

Joy takes a long, deep breath. "Okay." She figures she's only getting screwed about fifteen thousand dollars' worth. It's not the agent's fault; it isn't even Wayne's fault. It probably has something to do with Arabs and oil, and greed and fear. Maybe it's Nancy Reagan's fault.

The agent is overjoyed. "I'll FedEx the papers right now, you FedEx them back. Can you come up for closing, or do you want to do a power of attorney, or send stuff back and forth?"

"I'm not coming to Amarillo," Joy says.

"I'll send papers for you to sign. Don't spend the money yet, Joy, it'll be a few weeks. But these buyers have a good downpayment, they're not going FHA, it'll all come together. You better give your renters a month's notice."

"Whoopee," Joy says.

Bill Tweed asks her to lunch. She explains about having to go out at three. Another time, she could go anyway, but Doctor is in a foul mood. He told Joy this morning that his wife wants child support, *and* the house, *and* half his practice as alimony. Her argument is she put him through medical school. "Like what was *I* doing all those years?" he snarls. "And what about the twenty-nine-thousand-dollar debt I'm still making payments on?" Joy feels weak with jealousy; now, *that's* a settlement, she thinks, although she doubts Doctor will let it happen.

Tweed leaves and then reappears with a huge sandwich cut in half. He pulls a chair up to Joy's desk. "Turn it on," he says, pointing at the computer. "That way, we can eat and work at the same time." He grins. "If anyone asks." The sandwich is corned beef and really good, except for having Swiss cheese on it. Swiss cheese smells like baby throw-up to Joy, but over the mustard and the meat, she doesn't actually taste it all that much.

He is wearing a wedding ring. At least he *does* wear one. Wayne never would. Probably he just means to be friendly. But Joy feels a pleasant gurgle of interest, a sensation that makes her feel alive and pulsing. She hates sleeping alone, although, married, she longed for it.

Tweed shows up again at the end of the day and says, "Now think of a good excuse or else come have a beer." She laughs and says she'll take the beer. At a smoky little bar where bankers and lawyers hang out after work—she's never been in a bar with men in suits before—he tells her she ought to take some microcomputer courses. "You can make more money," he says, although there's been no discussion of what she makes managing Doctor's office.

"Guess I better be going," she says. It irritates her that he offers her advice, as though she can't figure out that you get paid more if you know more.

"Don't go," he says urgently, and puts his hand over hers. His hand is hot.

She taps his wedding ring.

"I'd like to see you."

"Does it look that simple?" She means *easy*. He might be ten years younger than she is.

"You're grown up," he says. "I like you. I won't lie to you. I won't make promises." After a moment, he adds, "We can follow new rules; it'll be safe—you know what I mean. You're a health professional."

Health professional? She smiles. She isn't tempted. She ought to be mad, but it is faintly flattering to be propositioned. It reminds her that she ought to be looking around. "What did you have in mind?" she asks. He blushes, which she likes. "I mean, where did you think we would go?" If he says a motel, she thinks she will spit in his face.

"Your place?" he says.

Her hand is free now. She leans back in her chair. "I live with my mother."

He stares at her for a moment, then laughs loudly; people turn to look at him.

"What's so damned funny about that?"

"Shoot, nothing," he says, still laughing, "except that *I* live with my mother-in-law."

"And your wife," Joy reminds him, but she is laughing too.

Opal is cooking Big Spring Goulash, a family favorite. It is called that because she made it up when they lived in Big Spring, when Clancy was a baby. It's sort of like spaghetti sauce, but with cabbage and carrots finely grated, and over big macaroni shells instead of noodles, then baked with french-fried onion rings on top. Heather likes it a lot, too. "I've got to run another errand," Joy tells her mother, "so don't wait on me."

Opal holds a wooden spoon out in the air in front of her. "So I'm cooking for nothing?"

Clancy, halfway across the room, says, "I'm eating. It was deli day at work, ugh."

"I'm eating too," Joy says. "But not for an hour."

"It's not ready yet, anyway." Opal looks up at the clock. "I am going to put this meal on the table at seven, no matter what."

Buddy has parked Jimmy with Opal while he and Lee-anne meet with an agent about life insurance. Someone has been whispering in his ear about these things. Joy thinks he doesn't have enough brains to be a grown-up, let alone a father to somebody else's child. He does dote on Leeanne, though, and he treats Jimmy as if he were his own.

Jimmy nearly knocks Joy over as she heads down the hall to Heather's room. He is on a little scooter he is too big for. "Take that thing outside!" she yells. Outside it is dark and cold.

"Opal thays I can too ride it in the houth," he says back. His tongue is halfway out of his mouth. Don't they work on those things at school? Joy remembers when they tested Heather in fourth or fifth grade and declared her "gifted." Joy had to sign consent forms for the tests, and she received endless pieces of paper, but she can't see that it ever did Heather any good at all.

She tells Heather she has an errand to run.

Jimmy drops the scooter with a bang. "I want to go," he pleads.

Joy opens her mouth to say no, but Heather says yes. Her look, to Joy, says, Oh, why not?

"Where're we going?" he asks in the car.

"Riding around," Joy answers.

Heather huffs. "I wish this car had a tape deck."

"What for?" Joy asks. "You don't have any tapes."

Heather can't take a joke. "I wish I had my own tape player. I'm the only teenager in the whole world who doesn't have any *music*."

"We might get a car with a tape deck," Joy says. Something maybe a year old, she thinks. Maybe a little Pinto.

"Oh, sure."

"What'll you play?" Jimmy asks from the backseat. He is breathing down Joy's neck, his breath slightly damp, and hot. "John Denver?"

Heather turns her head to give Jimmy a look of contempt.

"I'm serious, honey," Joy says. "I sold the house today."

Heather pays attention. "Do I get any of the money?"

"Honestly, Heather. It's *my* house."

"It was Daddy's house before."

"It was *our* house. *Before* is right."

Nobody says anything for several miles. Joy pulls up into the parking lot of the Meadows Apartments complex. She won't have a mortgage payment anymore, she'll have maybe three hundred dollars a month from selling snow cones at Kay Lynn's flea market concession, and she'll have money from the house.

"What are we doing here?" Heather asks suspiciously. She looks like she thinks Joy might leave her here.

"They got a thwimming pool here?" Jimmy asks.

They get out and walk around the grounds a few minutes, then find the manager's office. Joy tells him she's in a hurry and can come back, but she would like to peek inside one of the units. He wants to know how big.

"Depends," she says.

He knows all about it. "One-bedroom's two-seventy-five, two-bedroom's three-forty." He has a spiel, spoken very fast, about utilities and washers and dryers and pool rules. By then they are standing in an empty apartment. The kids run around it. Heather comes back in a moment and says, "The bathroom is pink and white."

"Give me your card," Joy says. "I'll call you in a day or two." She would love to get the rest of her stuff out of storage.

"We've got four vacant, somebody coming tomorrow," the manager says, but Joy knows there are a lot of apartments all over town. She can take her time and find something nice.

"Don't say anything to Mother," Joy says in the car. She wishes she hadn't brought Jimmy along.

"I love pink and white," Heather says.

"Me too," says Jimmy. "Can I come over when you move?" He sounds perfectly normal when there aren't any *s*'s.

13

Doctor has surgery in the morning and a court appearance in the afternoon, so Joy says to herself, This day has been a long time coming, and she goes out for two hours to look at apartments. The best deals are frame houses, but then you have a yard to worry about, and there's a sad feeling, like people got better off than you and even the house feels sorry about it. Some of the apartment houses look noisy, but if she stays away from the university, that should take care of most of it. She narrows her choices down to the Meadows and one other place that's a little more expensive but has two stories. She'd love to have stairs again. Before she makes up her mind she ought to try to talk Clancy into moving with her, although she doesn't think Clancy has the energy to carry her toothbrush across town, and she won't want to leave Opal while Russell is away.

Of course she doesn't have money for the deposit and first month's rent, but she figures she can skip the next mortgage payment while the sale is pending, and she will tell Kay Lynn she needs to borrow against the first month's work. Kay Lynn will feel important and generous. Both Joy and Heather are going to work all day Saturday and from noon to five on Sunday at the flea market, although Heather doesn't know it yet. Kay Lynn is going to pay Joy seventy-five dollars a weekend for the two of them, straight cash, no deductions. She explained to Joy that it would be a "contract for services." She said, "It's up to you to report it and pay taxes." She winked at Joy.

Joy is locking up the office when Doctor comes in a little after five. His face is splotchy red, as if he's been running hard. "Are you okay?" Joy asks.

He can hardly speak. "Can you stay a while and cancel all my appointments?"

"You have to go back to court tomorrow?" she asks, her heart sinking. She wanted to take another look at those town houses.

Doctor says, "I don't mean tomorrow. I mean all of them. All my appointments."

Joy is completely baffled. She wonders if Doctor is drunk. "Till when?" she asks weakly.

He plants his hands flat on her desk and leans against it. "I don't suppose you can call everybody in one night. Call next week's appointments. Then get a card printed tomorrow for the rest of them. For everybody."

"You're not going to see your patients?"

He snaps up straight, as if to attention. "I joined the navy this afternoon," he says. "See what she does about that."

Joy sits down heavily in her chair, nearly swooning.

Doctor is agitated. "She got what she asked for, the bitch. Half my practice for eight years. I'm going to spend all day every day with my fist up—" He catches Joy's expression and smirks. "She'll get the house. She'll get child support. But if I'm in the service she can't get alimony. I won't *have* a practice. And I'll get my loans forgiven." He slams his hand against the desk top. "She won't believe it!"

Joy remembers the soft gray carpet in the apartment; she thinks of herself standing on the little balcony overlooking the pool. She realizes she would have asked Bill Tweed up some time.

She opens Doctor's appointment book. "What do I tell them?" she asks. "What do I say?" She looks up at Doctor's sharp-nosed face. "What about the nurses? The office help?"

"Tell the bookkeeper I want her in here tomorrow at eight o'clock. I'll give everybody two weeks' pay but you and Kay Lynn. I need you to wind everything up. I'll pay you a month, even if you get done faster." He is pleased with himself. "It's not you I'm mad at."

That night, Joy takes Heather out to the mall and buys an expensive shampoo Heather has been wanting, and a pair of midcalf boots. Heather is no fool. In the car coming home, she asks, "What's going on? Do I have to go to Daddy's?"

Joy explains about the snow cones. She expects Heather to make a fuss, but in fact she is oddly acquiescent. Weekends are boring. "I'll buy you a tape player, like you've been wanting."

"Yeah?"

"It's like an enlistment bonus, when you join the army."

"With earphones?" Heather asks. "With two decks, so I can copy tapes?"

Opal
on
Dry
Ground

14

Opal says, "Drive by real slow."

Real slow is not one of Russell's gears. With a snort of exasperation—he has been patient for half a day of travel —he stops dead in front of the house.

Opal whimpers. Russell has driven onto the edge of the yard, parallel to her mother's house. She stares out the truck's front window, down the street, not looking at the house yet. The street has gone to hell in the past ten years. It is full of potholes and cracks. Here and there is a tidy yard, cared for by aging owners who, like Opal's mother, Greta, were once thrilled to move onto Grant Street, when it was only blocks from the city limits. Now, for the most part, the yards have been eroded by neglect, starved for water, and allowed to die by careless renters. One lot, four houses away, has high grass and weeds, as if an underground spring fed it.

"I don't know if I can do this," Opal says.

Russell reaches over and tries to pat her clenched hands. "There's not much you have to do, Opal, honey," he says. Opal jerks her hands away, twisting her thumbs and wincing. "We'll come to the sale and see how it goes. Or stay at Elizabeth's, if you want, and collect after. They don't need you, do they?"

She gives him a look like a snarl, then turns and gazes out the side window at the house.

*   *   *

Her mother built her house on Grant Street in 1953. At that time it was the last house on the street. You could stand on the back of the lot and look across prairie at open sky. She bought plans and construction at a deep discount, and at that price could make no changes. "I'll add a sleeping porch later," she said—because there would always be family there, for visits, and sometimes for extended stays—but she never did. They made do, all of them, on visits long and short, on cots, twin beds in the larger bedroom, an extra mattress stored, when it was not in use, against the wall behind her bed. In time she built a storage shed in the backyard; she needed it, for Laura's things, when she died, and later, for her mother's. She built it on a slight rise in the yard, and on a solid, high foundation; thus it was that some things were saved in the flood.

She willed the house to Opal. She left a note tucked inside the will: *Who knows how long you'll stay in his house?* She wouldn't write Russell's name. Men were always generic to her: *he,* and *him,* and even *that man.* Could she have thought that, in the worst of times, Opal would ever move back to Wichita Falls, to this decaying street, this dilapidated house? She knows no one here anymore, except the old neighbors and her ex-husband's mother. The house is cramped, poorly insulated, pitifully furnished. It is stained with damage from the flood, although repairs were made. It is not much of a house, a place Opal could not bear to see her mother live in, in these last years, but Greta was fierce in her determination not only to live, but to die there.

And she meant for Opal to have it. She might better have left it to Opal's brother, Amos, who has never managed to make a go of it. That she did not made him act crazy; he challenged the will and added to the anguish of Greta's death. Opal said she would sell the house and split the money with him, but even that didn't satisfy him. The day came when she said she would *give* him the house, but he only grew angrier, so unreasonable that his own lawyer threw up his hands and withdrew. It was months before Opal realized: Amos would have lived in the house. He would have been glad to have it, but his mother left it to Opal, and now he would not take it in a hundred years. He only wanted to be sure it went to strangers. Even he must have thought Opal would live there eventually.

"Such spite," Opal whispers. She has not seen Amos since the funeral. She remembers how, as children, she and Amos were close, as orphans might have been, as they half-were. After Papa died, Greta left the two younger children on the farm with her parents, and took Laura away to New Mexico, where she cooked for the railroad. "We want to go!" Amos cried. Opal knew better than to ask. "I'm going to live in boxcars," Greta wept. "You're better off here."

She took Laura. Amos clung to Opal and came to her bed at night—he was seven when they were left behind—and sought a give-and-take of comfort when there was mighty little comfort to summon. And now he hates her, hates his mother, forces this house and its goods to sale, although the last public act Greta performed was to go to the bank and pay the $2,731 outstanding balance on the loan she had cosigned for Amos.

I'll feel better when it's done, Opal tells herself. The matter of the will has been settled for months; she agreed to sell everything and give Amos half. Her mother has been dead a year to this very week.

She stares at the house and thinks: I'll never step inside

it again. It is a box of a house, with salmon-colored aluminum siding and a tiny concrete porch. The bushes have been cut back and the yard carefully trimmed and tidied, perhaps watered, although it is yellow and brown and stiff. Greta's little Nova sits under the carport, freshly washed, checked and tuned and priced to sell. It would be a decent car for Joy, Opal thinks, but she knows it would hurt too much to see it day after day in her driveway.

"Should I call Amos?" she asks. Russell closes his eyes and opens them again slowly, as if she has just come into view. "He wouldn't talk to you," he says as patiently as he can. "And it's all set. You wouldn't want to hold it up now." He scoots toward Opal a few inches. "This time tomorrow it will be *over.*"

She starts to cry, and then feels the terrible burning in her intestines that tells her they had better hurry. "I've got to go," she says.

"Sure," Russell says, starting the car immediately. "To Elizabeth's?" Elizabeth Thatcher is Opal's mother-in-law. *Ex*-mother-in-law.

"To—the—*bathroom,*" she says, struggling with the pain and urgency. "Oh, hurry!"

They are only two blocks from a service station and, mercifully, the bathroom is unlocked. Opal reaches it in time. She is racked with cramps, but the routine of her distress is familiar and distracting, and for both reasons not so terrible. Only the smell is awful.

She rummages in her purse for matches. There are half a dozen or so still sticking up in a book, and she strikes one and uses it to light the rest, then holds the flaming matches aloft, gently waving them in an arc, to burn away the smell. She wouldn't want to be the next woman to come in the rest room. She can't help thinking of that.

When she comes out, she looks up and sees the sky. She thinks: Why, it's a lovely May day. She is amazed. It is so wrong. This is tornado season, and she wishes one would come this very minute. She would rather see her mother's things ripped and hurled and smashed about than sold in the yard like a poor person's castoffs. But the sky is clear, a limpid lovely blue, and, swallowing her anger, which she knows to be irrational, she looks straight up and, for the slightest moment, blocks out everything except the clean, bare beauty of space where, now and forever, her mother's soul floats free.

15

Elizabeth has prepared a cold supper of baked chicken and tomatoes, macaroni salad, and potato rolls. Opal shakes her head. "You shouldn't have baked."

Elizabeth says an old lady has a lot of time to fill. "I was awake at four this morning," she says. "That's when I made the rolls."

Russell gapes at the food laid out on the counter. Elizabeth tells him, "Have some," although they haven't been in the house five full minutes. He helps himself to several rolls and a chicken leg, and walks through the kitchen and out to the backyard. Opal is embarrassed, but Elizabeth is too gracious to show any reaction to Russell's greediness. Besides, she is of a generation that deferred to men.

She is a tall, elegant woman with beautiful white hair. Her house smells of lemon polish. Her father was a Presbyterian minister, which was probably how she learned to be a lady. Opal's mother always called her Mrs. Thatcher; when Elizabeth insisted she call her by her first name, Greta simply stopped saying any name at all in Elizabeth's presence. To Opal she called her "your husband's mother." Opal understood. For years after she married Thatch, Opal felt defensive when she was around Elizabeth. She felt vulnerable to criticism: Her father was dead, her mother packed flour. Her mother's house was a crammed stucco box. Her own housekeeping was tolerable but uneven, and

Joy was a fretful, messy child. In time, Opal realized Elizabeth was never going to criticize her. For one thing, Thatch's parents weren't in the young couple's home (*homes,* over years of oil-field moves) half a dozen times. Elizabeth preferred to entertain her family visitors a few times a year—nothing like Greta, whose own home and Opal's home and, some of the time, Laura's, were all interchangeable. Elizabeth and James Thatcher had lived in an unincorporated section on the edge of town, not far from Greta's house. They too had dirt roads, funky neighbors, roaming dogs, but their house was like a little Tara, gleaming white against a bright green lawn. In the summer there were grandchildren, and they had their own playhouse outside. In the evenings, or in rainy weather, the children were gathered in a room off the kitchen where the chairs were old and the carpet thin, and they would not be scolded except for hitting.

This newer, smaller house came after James retired. It is near the college, so to keep it up Elizabeth takes in a student, who cleans in return for her room. There have been four or five girls, and they all learned to please Elizabeth, and to love her. She is always so collected.

"I wonder if I'll ever take a breath again without missing her," Opal tells Elizabeth at the table. Through the alcove window Opal sees Russell sitting on a bench, his elbows on his knees, bobbing his head, as if he might be singing a slow song. He must be very bored.

"Maybe not," Elizabeth says calmly, surprising Opal, who is expecting a mildly religious sentiment, something like "God will help you in His good time." "As we get older, our bruises don't heal so fast; why should our psychic pain?"

Psychic pain? Opal wonders what Elizabeth reads these days; she has always read the Bible, *Reader's Digest,* church bulletins, knitting magazines, but certainly not psychology. But, then, *Reader's Digest* has these topics now. It is sobering to think of millions of readers, in how many languages, all over the world, absorbing American culture, learning about personal space and the inner child.

Opal presses her chest with the flat of her hand. "I don't feel I got to say a proper good-bye," she whispers. She has been dying to say this, she realizes, to someone.

Elizabeth has done an odd thing with her food. She has carefully separated out the ingredients of her serving of macaroni salad into neat piles—with space between—of olives, walnuts, green peppers, the small shells. As she speaks, she seems to be studying the arrangement.

"My mother died when she was only sixty-four," she says. "My, that seemed old then, and now it's so young! She was sick for a long time; her sickness was like a mood in the house, for months, and then she slipped away. We all knew it was coming, but it was so hard."

"I remember. You drove back and forth every day." The old woman had lived in Seymour. It wasn't long after Opal and Thatch married. Opal remembers thinking, although her own mother was young: I hope Mother will be near me when the time comes. Was that so much to want? So wrong? Greta told her on the phone, "Lord, child, it's mine to do." Opal pretended not to understand. "Do what?" she said. "Do what?" stupidly.

Elizabeth nods and pushes at a mound of macaroni with her fork. "I couldn't believe she was dead. I dreamed about her every night. She always wore a white dress and slid down the banister to me. The dreams became less frequent, but they went on, year after year. I had that dream again, when I heard that Greta was dead."

Opal has an almost irrepressible urge to eat from Elizabeth's plate. She wonders if it offended Elizabeth to watch her sons eat as they were growing up. Thatch likes gravy poured over everything. Not now, maybe; he's had two heart attacks, had his arteries scoured. He can't be eating so much grease. Clancy harks back to her grandmother, toying with food instead of eating it.

"I could have taken care of her," Opal says. "I could have made it easier."

Elizabeth's eyebrows lift. She lays the fork down. "Dying?"

"On her floor!" Opal squeaks. Lately, her voice has become unreliable.

"She had a heart attack; it was fast," Elizabeth says gently.

"In three inches of water." The doctor said her heart exploded, she would have felt nothing, she was dead before she hit the floor. The water. *Was he there?*

Elizabeth rises and clears the plates.

"Let me," Opal says.

Elizabeth gestures for her to stay seated. "I can't drink coffee this late, but I have a nice herbal tea."

Opal nods, although all such teas taste, to her, of grass and licorice.

The time it takes for Elizabeth to heat the water and brew the tea gives Opal a chance to get hold of herself. She knows she has no business bringing this to an old woman who, herself, seems to be moving toward death through evaporation, growing ever thinner.

Both of them make a fuss with spoons of honey, much stirring and blowing and sipping. The tea, grassy as expected, but not unpleasant, tastes faintly of peppermint. It is soothing, with its minty vapors rising in tendrils above their cups. Opal smiles a little, suppressing the thought that this is the kind of moment she wished for with her mother, and seldom had. There was never this peace between them; neither of them had Elizabeth's serenity.

"I'm surprised Clancy hasn't called," she says. From her seat she sees into the living room, where a quilting frame is wrapped with a white cloth against which Elizabeth is stitching pale intricate flowers. "She wanted to come with me, but they didn't want to let her off work."

"There's Russell," Elizabeth says blandly.

"She hates to be alone, and this is Heather's weekend in Amarillo, and Joy will be out somewhere."

"Maybe Clancy has gone along?"

"Joy goes to bars," Opal says. It probably doesn't matter to Elizabeth. "So it's just Clancy and the cat." Clancy has been coaxing the cat out from under beds and from inside closets. She has cushioned a cardboard box with a plush towel, to make the cat a bed in her room. She says the cat has needed someone to pay attention.

"I asked her to come and live with me, you know."

Opal hopes Elizabeth does not see how surprised she is. She takes a drink of her tea. "Mmm," she murmurs.

"It was some time ago. She came to see me just after she filed for divorce. I offered to send her to college in return for living with me. She wouldn't have to do anything, I'd still have one of the girls to clean."

"She never said," Opal says. She thinks of Clancy sitting on her bed, her legs stretched out, the cat draped crossways on her lap. The years she has been away have disappeared; it is as if she has gone from fourteen to thirty overnight, still a girl, needy and quiet and sad. It must have been very difficult for her, acting like a wife. That would be hard for Elizabeth to understand. Opal wonders if Clancy would want to talk about it, sometime, about her married life. *Lives.*

Elizabeth appears to be waiting for some sort of reply, so Opal says, "She should. She should go to college." The truth is, she feels a kind of burning at this news, resentment, perhaps. At the same time, she thinks: Maybe Elizabeth will leave Clancy this house.

"It wasn't for her, of course, it was for me. For the company. I don't mind living alone, it isn't that, but I want to be able to stay here. I'm afraid of being moved."

"Who would do that!"

"My sons, if I grow feeble." She has three: Thatch in Norman, Oklahoma, and two more in Houston. She leans toward Opal and speaks softly, "You have daughters. Sons are different. They find someone else to do their laundry, and they're gone." She sits up straight again and laughs oddly. "I understand Greta," she says in a deeper voice. "She wanted to be in her own home that she worked so hard to have."

Opal starts to cry. Elizabeth ignores this. She says, "I went to see her the week before she died. I had a nice visit. She seemed very peaceful, Opal. She was tired."

Opal thinks this is something Elizabeth has invented to soothe her feelings. In the last months, Greta was quarrelsome and agitated, sharp-tongued when she spoke, and downright stingy with words. Opal remembers her desperation that Greta was taking all the unspoken words with her, that they were at the point of no-more-chances; and she was right, there were no more words, no more opportunities. The last time Opal phoned her, her mother said, in a low, suspicious voice, "There's someone on the line."

Opal wipes her eyes carefully with the tips of her fingers.

Elizabeth says, almost dreamily, "I was sitting in this very chair the day James died. He wasn't well. He had said to me, a few days earlier, 'I wouldn't want to go to one of those rest home places, Lizbeth.' The very idea was absurd, of course. Just then the phone rang. It turned out to be the minister's housekeeper, inviting us to lunch. I learned that many days later. James said he would get it. He was over by the glass doors, talking about the garden we used to keep, and he walked toward the phone—" She points to the wall above the counter, where the phone hangs, speaking deliberately, as if this were the scene of a crime and she a witness. " 'I'll get it,' he said, the last words he ever spoke. He reached for the phone and fell—not hard, the cabinet broke his fall—and he slid down—" Her hazel eyes, brimming with tears, look old and cloudy.

Opal doesn't know what to say. She doesn't understand how they got to talking about James instead of Opal's mother.

Elizabeth takes Opal's hand and squeezes. "Clancy said, 'I wish I could, Grandma, I'd like living with you, but I have to be with my mother.' I saw she intended to go back to Lubbock, though it was months before she did." Still holding Opal's hand, she says, "My heart went out to her just then. She seemed a lost creature. But I could see what was holding her up: She knew she had you.

"Children are a burden; you don't think about how it will go on and on, how you'll feel their pain, but don't you doubt it, Opal dear, you've loved your girls. And they know it. I'm sure that's been a lifeline many a time." She pats Opal's hand, then lets go.

Ashamedly, Opal feels gratified to hear this. Clancy, she knows, belongs with her, for now, for a while, until—well, until she's strong enough to be on her own. It's not a matter of age, it's circumstance, and times have been hard for Clancy, and for Joy, too.

She shakes her head slowly. "Well" is all she can think to say. For some reason she remembers Mr. Braithauser, the man appointed by the judge to act as executor of the estate. She hopes he was careful with her mother's things.

Elizabeth clears her throat.

"Yes?" Opal says.

"I don't know if I can say this just right, Opal dear, or if I should. But—well, you can't save them from hurt, you know. You can't make it up to them when they've been hurt, no matter what you do for them."

Opal nods her head sadly.

"And then you have your own pain—"

Opal's throat constricts. She can't make a sound.

"Your mother talked a little to me that last visit. About that time in your lives, after your father was killed in an accident—"

"A dust devil," Opal says. It sounds like such a small thing.

"She said she never really got over having to leave you while she worked that next year—with your grandmother, wasn't it?"

"Oh," Opal moans. She and her mother never spoke of it, not once. Opal always knew her mother did what she had to do.

"And now it must seem she has left you again."

Opal's chin trembles, tears spill onto her face. She wishes her mother had spoken to *her*.

"When I think of heaven—" the older woman says, "I do believe in heaven, you know—I think of seeing my mother again. I don't think of God."

Opal knows just what she means.

16

Russell comes inside and turns on the television too loud. Elizabeth excuses herself and goes to her room. Opal wonders if she has made her feel bad.

She decides to call the number Mr. Braithauser gave her, although he probably thought she would be in town earlier than this. He answers, however, and is courteous. It seems he has two boxes of Greta's personal possessions Opal should have, he says. Perhaps it would be better if he brought them tonight, and not to the sale site?

It is dusk, the sky going from pink to navy. Opal's heart surges, then sinks. The opportunity to hold in her hands something that belonged to her mother is both irresistible and frightening. "These are things one does not sell," Mr. Braithauser says. She gives him Elizabeth's address.

They can hear him coming up the long driveway, and Opal rushes Russell out the door to help. The two men return, each carrying a new white carton strapped with tape. Opal tells them to set the boxes in the living room against a wall. She finds it hard to take her eyes off the boxes, as if they contained something live scratching to get out. She thinks it is nice that Mr. Braithauser bought new boxes for her mother's things, instead of using old ones from the Piggly Wiggly. Of course, it will all come out of the estate proceeds. She can't remember how much Mr. Braithauser is to be paid, but she is relieved to see he is a gentleman. He has worn a suit and tie on his errand.

Elizabeth emerges from the hall, wearing a long burgundy velour dressing gown, looking rather warm on this May evening. Opal remembers that Greta was cold that last summer; Opal had come into her house and found it hot as a barracks on the border. She warned her mother, "You'll have heatstroke. You'll fall over from dehydration." Of course she did not; she died quite wet.

"Mrs. Thatcher!" Mr. Braithauser says with delight. "I didn't make the connection."

Elizabeth says, "Mr. Braithauser is a member of Grace Presbyterian." She peers at Opal, seeing something that disturbs or perplexes her. "My dear," she says, "your mother's estate is in good hands." She smiles. "Honest, Christian hands."

Opal is fighting tears. She agreed to all this, almost eagerly; she had not known how she might manage to dispose of her mother's things; but now she bitterly resists the notion that a strange—albeit Christian—man will hand them out to the highest bidders. Who will offer what for a battered bureau? A butter churn? A boxful of pots and pans?

She says, "Elizabeth is my first husband's mother. This is my husband, Russell Duffy." She gestures toward the place where Russell was standing a moment before, but he has gone into the kitchen. She hears the refrigerator door open and close.

"I could make tea," Elizabeth offers.

"Thank you, no," Mr. Braithauser says, to Opal's relief. "I only wanted to give Mrs. Duffy her mother's things. There are Bibles—one in German, very old—and photograph albums, some packets of letters." He speaks slowly.

"The pictures were all off the walls. I trust you took them when your mother died."

Opal cannot tell if this is some sort of transgression. Can Mr. Braithauser, in the name of the court, make her give them back? Photographs of her grandparents and parents, pictures amateurishly painted by her mother in her few years of avid art study, after Laura died? "Mother had me take them that last winter," she lies, and Mr. Braithauser nods solemnly.

"How prescient," he says.

Opal turns from the neatly trussed cartons. There will be time enough to look at the contents, time enough to break her heart. While Russell watches the news, she takes a long bath in Elizabeth's guest bathroom. She dresses in a long cotton gown, one she gave her mother years ago, later left at her house who knows when. She rubs the front of the gown where it is pleated, thinking of her mother's body inside the fabric. Greta was always a thin woman, except for dapples of flesh under her upper arms, but in the last couple of years she went soft and sprouted a round spongy belly that made all her trousers too small. She wore pull-on knit pants with stretchy waistbands after that, like other old ladies. She wouldn't let Opal buy her anything nice.

Russell comes to bed. He has splashed his face and brushed his teeth but has not bathed. The guest room has no shower. She feels clean as a nun, and a bit offended by her husband's carelessness in Elizabeth's house. She would like to go to another bed, but in the third room Elizabeth's college girl lives. She came home while Opal was bathing; Opal saw the light under her door. She is probably studying. Opal considers how pleasant it might have been to have her children in college, tucked in at night in bed with books, but when the girls were that age, they did other things, took other training. It was never discussed. She can't remember why that was.

"You know, if you told me what you want me to pick up, I could go by myself," Russell says.

She isn't sure she understands; it isn't possible that he means she might not go to the sale of her mother's things. She feels so suddenly angry, so hot and sullen and sad, she doesn't dare reply. He is up on his elbow, waiting. She arranges herself under the sheet, her back to him, and feels him sink back onto the bed. Don't touch me, she thinks. Don't you dare do that.

She wakes toward morning—it is not yet dawn—amazed to find that she has slept. She tiptoes into the kitchen, thinking she will make coffee, but Elizabeth is already there in her pretty velour robe. "Dear Opal," she says. It seems a theatrical, although not a false, thing to say.

They stand side by side at the sliding glass doors, studying the oncoming morning, while the coffee perks. Opal's body is so heavy, she wonders how she will move out of the house, to the car, to the sale. She does not remember a single reason for her brother to be angry, nor Joy, nor Joy's husband, nor Heather. . . . She feels like a nappy fabric, attracting anger as lint. She is mired in dread, sticky as molasses. She could stay in this calm, clean house forever. Her own life is far away.

The coffee bubbles and stops perking. The room is suddenly quiet. Opal and Elizabeth turn back, and Opal takes cups from the cabinet. When they have their coffee and are seated, Elizabeth says, "I'm very happy that your divorce didn't include me, Opal." Opal's cheeks burn with pleasure. She is acutely aware in this moment that there are very few people left in her life who are older than she is. Elizabeth is really the only significant person in front of Opal in the last line she will ever stand in.

She can't think what she should say.

"You must know that now I'll be—"

As Elizabeth hesitates, Opal tenses with apprehension. For one terrible moment, she thinks that Elizabeth is going to say she will be her mother now. As if such a thing were possible.

"I'll be glad to go out to the grave in reasonable weather, and you'll always stay here, whenever you like."

Opal is staring so hard into her own thoughts, her eyes lose their focus. Elizabeth asks, "Are you all right?"

"No," Opal replies. "Of course not."

"How lucky Russell came with you. What will he eat for breakfast?" Elizabeth is suddenly on her feet and busy.

"It's too early," Opal whispers. "He won't wake up for hours."

Elizabeth laughs. "Of course." They are bound by old shared experience, husbands heading out to oil fields in the dark of night. She sits down and leans toward Opal. Opal longs to lay her head in her lap. Instead, she inches her hands along the table beyond her cup. Seeing the gesture, Elizabeth covers them with her own hands. "It's good you're not alone."

Opal thinks that it is a generous thing for her ex-husband's mother to say. And true.

"I don't think I could stand it," she says.

17

Opal and Russell are on Grant Street by ten till ten. There is a large sign in the yard that says NO EARLY SALES. At least a dozen cars are already parked in front and across the street. Russell, however, sees an opportunity to nose onto the edge of the yard, between two cars. It is Opal's instinct to scold him—the people in the cars turn to stare at him hostilely—but she does not want to have to walk far to the car when she is ready to go. "Don't let anybody block you," she tells Russell. He says, "Don't you worry." He is at his best when he has something to take care of.

At ten, although there is neither bell nor announcement, a tide of folks washes onto the lawn; suddenly there are currents of motion. Tables from the house have been brought out—the yellow Formica-top kitchen table, a side table from Greta's bedroom, her sewing table—and card tables set up, all their surfaces piled with things. Many are priced to sell, with bright orange stickers: three dollars for a stack of kitchen towels embroidered (Sunny Sunday, Mild Monday . . .) by Opal and Laura as children, too precious to have been used; one-fifty for a butter dish that was Greta's mother's; how did it last so long unharmed? One dollar each for a tin cake dish with a lid, a scuffed jewelry box, a pen-and-pencil set that is probably twenty-five years old. It is heartbreaking to survey.

Objects piled on the kitchen table are meant to be auctioned rather than sold outright. There are a couple of kerosene lamps, a chamber pot, other items from the farm. It seems sad that all Greta had "of value" should be old things skimmed from the past, when they were objects of utility. Opal understands that these objects will bring a higher price *because* they are old—they are "antique"— but why is a chamber pot—and you can be sure it was used, filled with you-know-what at night and emptied in the morning—worth more than those towels, or any of a dozen other things handled by Greta over the years, or, conversely, stored lovingly? How can they put a price on these things? She turns back to a card table and picks up the cream-colored ceramic bowl Greta used to mix biscuits. The lip is chipped in two places; an orange sticker offers it for seventy-five cents.

She wants to buy everything. No one else should have these things.

As if by telepathy, Russell appears beside her and says, "I've got a couple of boxes in the truck." She nods, and points to things, filling her arms and Russell's, then pays a pert young woman who stands by the front steps, wearing an apron that says DEITER ESTATE SALES. This round comes to twenty-two dollars. "Let's just call it twenty," the girl says, hurting Opal even more with her irreverent nonchalance.

Opal spies two rows of old Mason jars, and remembers suddenly, vividly, the way they looked lined up on shelves along the cellar wall at her grandmother's farm, filled with ruby-red tomatoes, bright peaches and apricots, dilled beans and onions. She remembers lying on the tiny cot in the cellar all one terrible evening—so long ago!—staring at the shelves, looking at each jar, one by one, to hold down her panic as it grew darker and darker, so that even the slivers of light through the cracks were gone and the faint gleam on the glass disappeared.

A woman in pedal pushers—now, there's something old-timey, thinks Opal—buys the jars from under Opal's nose. She hears someone behind her say, of something else, "Why would anyone save those old things?" She has to shut her eyes for a moment, squeeze the tears back in, take a breath. The ache in her is bottomless.

She walks over to the washer and dryer she bought her mother a few months before she died. She doubts ten loads were done in them; they look brand-new. Russell, behind her, says, "I still think you should have taken them." Mr. Braithauser would have agreed—Opal had receipts—even though, technically, the appliances belonged to Greta, and gifts are not returnable at death. Opal had wanted them and not wanted them; she wanted to *show Amos*, to be scrupulously fair, to let the whole process go as far as it had to go. Forever she would say, "He made me give everything up." "What do you think?" she had asked Mr. Braithauser, and he, perhaps sensitive to her peculiar set of conflicting needs, had said, gently, "They'll fetch a nice price, Mrs. Duffy."

"I'm going to buy them back," she says now. Russell makes a snorting noise and says, "Why would you want to go and do that?"

"I bought them for my mother!" The shiny white tops of the washer and dryer reflect the bright sun and hurt her eyes.

"They ain't exactly sentimental thangs," Russell drawls.

"Never you mind!" Opal snaps. He shrugs and walks away. She tells herself that Clancy can use them, when she has a place. Joy has her own in storage.

Nearby is the old spinning wheel from the farm, still in

good condition, missing only a spindle. She wants to turn to the crowd and shout, "This was once real!" but they'd laugh at her or pity her. Her grandmother liked to spin; she said it calmed her nerves. She kept a few sheep, peculiar in that county. And canaries. It was canaries that got Opal into such trouble.

On the front door is a sign saying SEALED BIDS FOR THE HOUSE ACCEPTED UNTIL 1:00 P.M. SPECIFICATIONS AVAILABLE. Russell says, "Neighborhood like it is, they'll be lucky to go over ten thousand," and Opal pinches him hard, just above his wrist. Her mother's house. It will go as a rental, of course; it will house a succession of welfare families, fly-by-nights, dogs and cats and children with snotty noses, men who drink and spit.

"Sorry, honey," Russell says. "But it *is* just a *house*. Greta's gone."

She looks at the sky, and wishes for a tornado.

The auctioneer is a sprightly man in his sixties, wearing a bright plaid Western shirt with a string tie. Mr. Braithauser, who hovers, is dressed formally, as if for a funeral. As they get ready for the auction to begin, Opal looks around for Russell. He is leaning against the truck, smoking. Whatever stupid thing he'll think to say, she wants him with her, knowing all the while he'll be no help. There is no help for this.

The auctioneer starts with furniture, a heavy walnut dresser that came from the farm. Opal turns to look again at the spinning wheel, which, at any price, she means to have. She runs her hand along the top curve of it, and at that moment sees a red pickup pulled along the yard behind another car, its tail stuck too far into the street. Her heart lurches; she knows in an instant who it is, but she has to move a few steps away from the spinning wheel to spy the driver. There is Amos hanging out the window as if he were gawking at the setup of a circus. He wears a cowboy hat that hides his eyes from her view. She doesn't think he sees her, not yet, and she is torn for a moment between her desire to run to him and beg him to stop this terrible proceeding, and her frantic wish not to be seen at all, to disappear into the spokes of the spinning wheel, never to see her brother again. *She lay on the cot in the cellar, saying prayers. He came out of the house in the night; he banged on the cellar door. I'm sorry! he cried. They'll come in the morning.* And of course he was. Of course they did.

Russell trots to her from his truck. "You sick?" he asks in a loud stage whisper. She supposes she looks pale. She feels contorted with sheer frustration: This is happening; she agreed to it; there is nothing she can do.

"Uh-oh," Russell says, spying Amos's truck. He reaches for Opal as a fat woman steps between them and bends to look at the spinning wheel. His hand brushes the woman's stiff sprayed hair. The woman turns the wheel slowly.

"Don't!" Opal shouts, and clamps her hand on the top of the wheel. Heads turn in her direction. "You stop that!" She feels her heart fluttering out of rhythm.

"Mrs. Duffy," Mr. Braithauser says from a few yards away. The auctioneer has ceased his droning. There is the rumble of voices; she thinks she hears Amos's laugh. Russell says, "Whoa, Opal," and pushes to get to her. She steps back, escaping Russell and Amos and Mr. Braithauser, but the yard is clogged with tables and goods and people, and there is no place to go, certainly not backward. Her leg knocks against the butter churn and she jumps aside, bumping a table piled with Laura's good dishes, rattling cups and saucers. Panicked that she will have broken them, she tries to turn and right a cup and hold in place a stack of dessert plates, but she feels her heart skipping and her face feels numb, and she stumbles into her sister's dinner plates, pulling them down with her as she plummets to the ground, her arms in front of her, her heart wrenched in its cavity.

18

Opal is in a hospital room, hooked up to an IV, and there beside her, inexplicably, is Clancy. She blinks and sucks air and cannot find a word to say.

"Shh, Mama, it's me, you don't have to talk."

The ceiling of her room has a muted, recessed light. She has no idea how long she has been here. If it was a long time—if she were really in trouble—she would be in ICU, wouldn't she? She would be attached to machines, there would be bleeps and beeps and the soft rustle of efficient nurses. There would be more light.

"Russell?" she whispers. She tries to feel the beating of her heart, and thinks it is steady.

"He's gone to get something to eat." Clancy squeezes her mother's hand.

"They called you?" Opal asks. She doesn't understand how Clancy can be here. She doesn't know what time of day it is. Maybe, if Clancy has come from Lubbock, it is serious.

"I was at Grandma's," Clancy says. "Joy was going to the flea market, and then she was going to have a date—I couldn't stand it there by myself. I'd just arrived when Russell called."

"I don't remember very well," Opal says.

Clancy waves her hand vaguely. "Whatever they gave you—"

The door swings open. "You poor baby," Russell says from the foot of the bed. A doctor comes in with him.

She closes her eyes. She's not ready.

"It doesn't seem to have done any damage," the doctor tells her. What can he mean? She broke dishes, she wrenched her knee, she *fell*. Her *heart*.

"Fibrillation can mean a lot or a little; you need to see a cardiologist when you get home. I'm making some calls for you. I talked to your husband." He is one of those prissy young doctors who tolerates patients because he likes what he can do for them. She thinks she is probably not very interesting. Her heart twitches now and then; she knew it did that. It seems minor; obviously, it's over now. It comes when it comes.

"We thought you ought to spend the night," Clancy says. She looks worried. Opal still doesn't quite understand how she got here so fast.

"We'll go home in the morning," Russell says. He has been eating fries; there is catsup on his shirt, between the second and third buttons. Or blood. Could it be blood?

"Was there blood?"

"Oh, naw, Opal, you just fell, honey."

"Want me to stay the night?" Clancy asks. "The chair sort of lets down, like a cot."

"You don't need to."

"We could go out to eat," Russell says. Clancy rolls her eyes. "Or pick something up on the way back to Elizabeth's."

Opal can't keep her eyes open. "Y'all go on," she says. "I'll be all right." She is sure she senses the IV dripping into her vein. It's a cool sensation, almost pleasant.

She dreams.

She sees herself at a table, perched on a hill like a bird at a feeder. The barren hill floats between sky and water. She dials a phone again and again. She looks out across an expanse of dark lapping water. There are no edges to the dream.

She sees her mother. Greta is in her house, making her bed with new sheets. She shakes them out and smooths the creases. The sheets billow above the bed and float down slowly. The sheets have a pattern of roses. Rain splashes on the windowpane. Greta crawls on the bed, between the flowered sheets.

"Did you think you would die in your sleep?" Opal asks in her dream, but Greta does not hear. "Were you afraid?" she asks in Greta's ear, and a current washes her away. "Mama!" she calls, swimming helplessly against the current.

The roses swell and drift, then settle again over Greta, a comforter of roses. She sleeps, she wakes. She goes around the house, turning on the gas heaters. For a moment, she is clear and present and real, and even in sleep, Opal's heart aches.

From her hill, Opal sees the house, across the water. The rain pours; waves splash against the foundation of the house. The house rocks slowly.

Greta opens the front door and steps out onto the tiny concrete porch.

"Careful!" Opal cries. Her mother is both near and far— the house is *over there* and yet her mother seems close enough to touch. Opal puts out her hand, but her mother is out of reach. Opal is both inside and outside the dream, inside and outside her mother's house. She understands that it is a dream, and she draws back her arm, not to interrupt, not to wake up and lose her mother. She retreats, to save the dream.

Greta peers out over the lake of the yard. There is a man at the edge of her lot. "Who are you?" she yells. The man shouts back, "Help is coming, don't be alarmed."

"Go inside!" Opal calls.

"Go inside!" the man calls. He sloshes closer. "Get up on a table," he tells her. "You can float."

She closes the door with a thump. Water is seeping in, her feet are wet. She takes off her shoes and socks and dries her feet carefully, especially gentle across the corns. She puts on a heavy sweater. Each movement is liquid; her very edges are watery. She takes a quilt off the bed. She goes to the kitchen and opens her quilt on the table and climbs on top. "Dear God," she prays. She hugs her knees.

Water laps in the kitchen.

"Mama, Mama," Opal cries. She dials and dials.

The table is a raft. Greta seems to drift in the loss of light.

"Hold on!" Opal cries, as if the dream is another chance, as if she does not know it is a dream, it is too late.

The water rises in the kitchen, stranding Greta on the table. She pulls the quilt tight around her. She gargles gravel bubbles nobody is around to hear, then crumples. She slips like polished stone, miles and miles toward the green linoleum, the ocean floor.

And there is Opal, sitting now in her own kitchen, sitting at her own table in Lubbock, the phone in her hand away from her head a little, failing to connect. Opal, on dry ground. Her face has a long sad look, her eyes are blistered over with loss. "Mother! Mother! Don't leave me behind!" she pleads into the phone, into the dark, her cries a long shrill unfurling, like a strip of paper before a fan.

19

When Opal opens her eyes, it is morning. Clancy lies under a rumpled blanket on the chair, which is let down like an airplane seat. Pencil-thin stripes of light from between the window blinds play on the wall across from her bed. When the nurse comes in to check on her, she can see how routine it all is. There is nothing to worry about. Her mother is dead, and she is alive. She isn't even wet.

"I've got a surprise for you," Russell says when he comes in. Clancy goes on ahead to Elizabeth's, to bathe and eat.

"What?" Opal asks.

"It's at Elizabeth's."

"Just tell me."

He smiles smugly. "Remember the fat lady who was looking at the spinning wheel?"

"Of course I remember." The thought of it makes her chest flutter, which does scare her, a little. She has to tell Clancy where she'll want to be buried—by her mother. Russell won't like it, but he'll forget soon enough. She should write it all down. She wishes her mother had written something more personal than a will.

"She's an antique dealer," Russell says.

"I guess it was her lucky day."

He smiles broadly. "I tracked her down and got the wheel back."

She is amazed. "Thank you, Russell," she says.

In the truck, he whistles tunelessly, probably a song of his own invention.

"I'm anxious to get home," she says.

"We'll pick up our stuff and be on our way."

"I thought I was going to die."

Russell pats her knee, then speeds up and recklessly passes another truck.

"What did Amos buy?"

"I never actually saw him. That red truck?" He frowns. "I'm not sure that was him in that truck."

"Who do you think it was, a ghost?"

"There were some of them around, weren't there?" he says, giving her a sly look.

"Drive by."

"Aw, honey, you don't want to do that."

"Don't tell me what I want. I said drive by."

Huffing, he does as she says, slowing to twenty so she can take it in by not blinking. The lawn has been cleared of all signs of yesterday's sale. The house, empty now, looks as old as it is.

While Russell is packing the truck, Elizabeth mentions Mr. Braithauser. "He felt so bad," she says.

"I don't understand why he does it."

"If he didn't, it might be somebody crude and hurried," Elizabeth says. "Instead of a churchgoing man."

Opal nods. She knows Elizabeth is right.

She wonders if Elizabeth and Clancy had a long talk this morning while they waited for Opal, and what they talked about. Maybe Elizabeth offered again to let Clancy live with her. She puts her hand to her chest. Clancy won't leave her now.

"It was such a kind thing for him to do."

Opal looks up. "What was?"

"The spinning wheel. He explained about it to the lady who bought it, and gave her her money back; she was very nice, he said. She didn't realize who you were, at the sale."

Opal laughs. "So it was Mr. Braithauser!" she exclaims. There is a second of irritation—Russell is a clumsy liar—and then she feels lucky that his foolishness is so often acted out on her behalf, with good intention.

Elizabeth beams. "His daughter is a doctor." Opal's continued laughter bothers her. "Are you all right? Are you up to this drive?"

Russell appears. Clancy is in another room, calling to the cat, who came with her from Lubbock. "Chocolate, oh, Chocolate," she calls, her voice tender and seductive and patient.

"Ready?" Russell says. He glances at Elizabeth nervously. "Everything okay here?"

Opal is grinning. She gets up. "I didn't really need the appliances," she says. She kisses Elizabeth on the cheek. "Of course, if I did, Russell would have seen to it I got them."

Russell mumbles good-bye. He is blushing.

The cat is sleeping in its box on the backseat.

Russell helps Opal into Clancy's car. "I'll drive behind you. If you need me, just turn on your blinker and get off the road."

"We'll be fine," Clancy says. She leans over the seat to tuck an edge of towel over Chocolate.

Russell ducks in awkwardly and plants a kiss on Opal's forehead. "You'll feel better at home in your own bed."

"Oh, stop," Opal says irritably. "I'm fine. Let's go."

On the road, she says to Clancy, "I can't believe the cat would come."

"She was asleep in the box. I didn't know if Joy would look after her. Why not? I thought. When she woke up, she was on the road. At Grandma's, she hid the whole time. When she went out, it was about ten whole inches from the back step. There wasn't a chance she'd run away. She's a scaredy-cat."

"I dreamed about Mother."

"I don't know what I dream. I never remember."

"The day she died. I wanted to help her, but there was nothing I could do."

"I think dreams are cruel, like that. If it's a dream, why can't it work out?"

"It would be crueler to save her, then wake up."

"Sorry, Mother. I miss her, too."

Opal snuggles down in the seat and puts it back partway. "When I was pregnant with you, I used to dream we were floating in a big warm ocean, like we were both inside some giant womb."

"Did it hurt?"

"Being pregnant?"

"Having me."

"Sure, for a little while. It was worth it, silly."

"I don't think I could do it. I'm scared of hurting that much. Besides—"

Opal tries to pat Clancy's arm, but her own arm feels so heavy she doesn't quite reach it. "There's still time," she says weakly. "And other men. The right one for you." She realizes, though, that it isn't likely, not anytime soon. And maybe Clancy isn't up to it, anyway. Babies, marriage. Clancy has enough to take care of, getting up every day and going to work.

"You might as well take a nap," Clancy says. "There aren't any men along *this* road." It hurts Opal to hear her speak with such bitterness.

"Oh, shit!" Clancy says, a little later. Opal is dozing.

Something brushes Opal's shoulder and face. She yells.

"It's the *cat*," Clancy says. "God *damn!*"

The cat jumps back over Opal's shoulder, then to her lap and onto the floorboard, where she crouches, her back up, her ears flat.

Opal feels the car slowing. Clancy pulls off onto the shoulder. "You okay?" she asks. "Bad cat!"

The cat slithers onto Clancy's lap and pushes against her ribs. Now she is purring. Clancy lays her hand on her head.

"I'm sorry, Mama. It was dopey, bringing the cat," she says.

Russell runs to the car and jerks open the door by Opal. "What? What?" he shouts.

"Calm down, for heaven's sake," Opal says.

"You come in the truck." Russell tugs at Opal's wrist. "I can go a lot faster and Clancy can catch up."

"It's not an *emergency*. Nothing's *wrong*." Opal still feels disoriented. She has gone in and out of sleep too many times in the past twenty-four hours.

Russell has leaned inside, his face nearly up against hers. "I'm taking you straight to the hospital when we get to Lubbock."

She shoves his shoulder away. "You are not. It's not me, I told you. It's the cat."

As if one cue, Chocolate catapults out of Clancy's lap, into the box in the backseat.

"We ought to go," Clancy says.

Russell pats the top of the car. "You don't want to come with me?"

Opal shakes her head.

"You ought to come with me to Farmington," he says. He's got another pipeline job coming up, five months in New Mexico.

"I've got a job," Opal says.

This time he bangs the car, and Opal jumps.

"Baby, I think it's time I took care of you!" he says enthusiastically. "I think it's time you retired."

"I can't even do that," Opal says, "unless we get home."

Laughing, Russell goes back to his truck.

"What do you think?" Clancy says when they are on the road.

"I think," Opal answers, "he's going to be surprised when I agree."

She thinks her life has become a full-time job.

Club

Dancing

20

Sometimes while she is at work, for just a moment, Clancy imagines herself a dancer in a glass cage. She sees herself writhing to sensual and pulsating music while she runs her fingers lightly up and down her torso.

The bank's music, packaged by a company in Houston, is mostly sentimentalized Beatles and show tunes, so pale and dull you forget that it is playing. It is not the music that provokes fantasy in Clancy; it is the space where she works. A mezzanine juts out over the lobby, and here she sits at her desk, facing Mr. Riddler's office. Behind her an elaborate wall, three feet high, shields her from the direct gaze of customers below, who would otherwise look straight up under her dress; and on top of that is a panel of glass that is, when she is standing, exactly eyebrow-high.

It is nearly noon, and she is lightheaded after a single cup of coffee and no breakfast. Today is deli day, and she is looking forward to cheese and meat, a dab of mustard, and the brown bread, which no one else ever touches. She has worked steadily through the morning, and her desk is tidy. Mr. Riddler has a long meeting at another branch after lunch, so she'll be able to finish everything by the end of the day, and she likes the idea of coming in the morning to a bare desk. She likes the idea of starting over.

She swivels her chair and looks out over the lobby just in time to see Travis Murphy enter the bank and lope across the floor. He glances toward her, sees her looking, and grins. At least he doesn't wave. She turns back to her desk briskly, pulls a memo up on her computer screen, and checks it for punctuation. She is scrupulous about punctuation.

By the time Travis is at her desk, her ears are burning and her toes are cold. She wants to smile, she wants to hide, she wants him to go away, she's glad he's there.

"You can go on in," she says prissily, pointing to Mr. Riddler's door. Travis Murphy and his dad are prize customers. They've been putting cotton money in this bank since it opened in 1970. Travis has been in lately, discussing some land for a vineyard, negotiating a loan the bank will be glad to make. He says he'd like to try something a little different, besides the cotton. He wants to diversify. Clancy doesn't know anyone who drinks wine.

Travis leans his elbows against her desk. "Does he have a couch? A cot? A soft, soft carpet?" In that position, the nice curve of his rump is all too obvious. He is wearing tight, faded jeans and a yellow plaid shirt. He smells faintly of perspiration and aftershave and sunshine.

"He's *in there*," she answers, suppressing a giggle.

Travis straightens up. "In that case, we better go somewhere else." He reaches for her, and before she can think, she has extended her hand and he has pulled her to her feet.

She makes a face like someone growling, but without a sound, then laughs. "You'll get me in trouble, Travis Murphy."

He lets her go, steps back, and says, "Let's tell Clive Riddler you and I are going to discuss investments in the comfort of a room at the Best Western."

"Travis!"

"I'm turning over a CD today. They sent me up to you."

"They have officers downstairs who can do that," she says.

"But it's a big CD, and you're the president's *girl*."

She has to stop and think. She knows he's teasing her, but the joke is studded with insult she doesn't think he intends.

"Travis, presidents don't have *girls*."

"But I do," he says, and slips his arm around her waist. She jumps back like someone stung. "I'm at work!"

He taps her watch. "It's noon, lady; we're going to lunch."

She gets her purse out of the desk drawer.

He takes her to an apartment complex near the university. "Who's here?" she asks when he stops the car.

"My friend's out of town," he says. "It's you and me." He tosses a ring of keys in the air and catches it with a flourish.

She does giggle when she sees that he has bought a tray of delicatessan food: white and orange cheeses, bologna and ham and roast beef slices. "We could have had this at the bank," she tells him. Actually, she's impressed. She would have guessed they'd have hamburgers out of a sack.

"But could we have had it *nekkid*?" In no time at all he has taken off every stitch of clothes. She watches, stupefied, as he throws his arms out and cries, "Here I yam!"

"I haven't had one bite this whole day," she says, and turns her back to him, to construct a half-sandwich of American cheese and ham, and find her wits. She feels close to fainting. "I've got to eat something."

He presses up behind her. Through her gabardine skirt, she feels his hot body, the bulky pressure of his—*thing*.

"Give me a bite," he whispers. One night, not long ago, he showed her how he could flip pennies with his penis. He made a big show of warming them in his hands before he set them, one by one, in place.

She is flush against the counter, so that if she turns she will be caught against his body. She tries to chew a bite of sandwich. Her stomach hurts a little; she knows she's starved, but she doesn't feel hungry anymore.

He pulls up her skirt and clasps her hips. "Mmmm," he says.

She has never made love at lunch before.

She thinks he is pushing his luck. Maybe he is making fun of her.

Maybe he thinks he can do whatever he wants.

She makes a sudden break and slips away, along the side of the counter, and ducks around to the other side. "I guess I can get myself a glass," she says, as if it were an issue. He has that silly grin plastered on his face. He likes seeing her surprised and embarrassed.

"Eat up," he says.

"What about you?"

"I have something else in mind," he says, and then he's there again, behind her, breathing on her neck.

When Clancy ran out of Elavil, the doctor she went to see said he thought she ought to have her medication evaluated. "I've been taking it for months," she pointed out, but he wanted her to see a psychiatrist. He wondered if this drug was the most efficacious. "There are new ones now," he said. Obviously he thought he could tell by looking that she wasn't all right. All she could manage was to shake her head. "A therapist, at least," he said gently. She had made a mistake, choosing a young doctor, one who had ideas about treating the whole person.

Probably he would have given her a prescription if she'd stuck to her guns, or another doctor would have. Everybody knows that doctors give out antidepressants and tranquilizers and painkillers like crazy. He wanted to gouge her a little, make her grateful, remind her who was in charge of her depression. She felt defenseless, naked, although she was dressed. She felt invaded.

She walked out of his office and didn't even stop to pay.

She waited to fall into a deep hole. She was scared for weeks, but she didn't really feel any different when she stopped than she had when she was taking the medicine. She cried a little more easily, and she went to bed an hour or more later—so she read more, that wasn't so bad—but she went right on, just the way she had been: fairly even, a little sad, resigned. It was a great relief to realize that she was really okay after all. She was over what Jeeter had done to her; she could hardly remember what he looked like. She couldn't remember any of his shirts, only his Jockey shorts, because he wore them in bright colors, and she didn't care then or now about that. Maybe she was depressed some of the time, but mostly she went along on an even keel. Things didn't make her cry the way they did when Jeeter had just left her. This was life, and she was going to live it. At work she thought about work; at night she read or watched TV. She bought a felt ball and played with Chocolate; she carried her in her arms out to the yard and showed her how nice it was there, but didn't put her down, because she didn't like it.

Then she met Travis. He teases her, says that when he came in the bank and saw her up on her glass pedestal, he thought she was on display, waiting for him. He made excuses to see Mr. Riddler. He found ways to have her do bits of business for him, handle papers, give him things to sign. He took his time, so that she was wondering when he'd be in and if he'd talk to her. One day he announced, "Saturday's the night, right?" and she had said yes before she realized how rude he was.

In two months her life has swung up and down and back and forth. He is silly and lusty, an overgrown, spoiled boy. She feels precariously poised on a teeter-totter. She waits for him to jump off the other end and send her flipped and sprawling. She has been thinking of telling him she doesn't want to see him anymore; she's scared he's going to say it first. On their first date he took her Western dancing, and she remembered how much she loved to dance, and that she was good at it. When other women at the club simpered and smiled and sidled up to say hello, she told herself his being popular made it all the better. On their second date he took her to see clog dancing at the Opry, and it was a lot of fun. He introduced her to his parents and some other old couples as his "new girl." Part of her was tickled, and part of her was annoyed, but his saying it didn't make it so unless she wanted it, so what was the problem? Their third date he took her to his house and fed her spaghetti made with sauce from a jar, and rubbed her back and played records, and then took her home. He was so quiet, she thought he must be mad at her, except he hadn't acted mad. He just hadn't acted silly; he hadn't made jokes. Maybe he had a serious side.

The next date, the next night, they ate spaghetti with leftover sauce, and went to bed. He simply stood up and put his hand out and led her from the room. She must have had a bewildered look, because he said to her, standing by the bed, "It's okay, Clancy." She *was* a little scared, and unprepared, but he had a condom all ready on the nightstand, and as much as she wanted to protest—he'd taken a lot for granted—it was easier to make love, and she realized she didn't care that he'd known she would. He took a long time; it worried her, she thought something might be wrong. Both her husbands had been fast lovers, and she'd been glad of it. Every time she thought Travis was about to ejaculate, he'd slow down. He seemed to be holding his breath, then he blew softly in her ear, and started up again. She heard his Dobermans on the porch, howling and scratching to be let in, then forgot about them. Afterward, she lay in the crook of his arm, her eyes wide open. The dogs had lain down on the porch; she could hear them whimpering. Travis called them his "pals."

His bedroom smelled musty; when she was getting dressed, she saw a sea of dirty clothes. She couldn't see the floor underneath. She asked him if he ever picked up. He said when he ran out of clean clothes, he took everything to the laundry. He said he didn't bring women to the farm. The implication was that she was special, but later she thought it might just mean that all his other girlfriends have places of their own. Only she lives with her mother.

He asked her if she was on the Pill. She said she had a diaphragm; it embarrassed her to admit it. She had never slept with anyone before except husbands, and she wanted to tell Travis, but if he believed her, she'd just sound dumb. And it would make him more special than ever, not just because he was tall and athletic and smooth and blond, but because he'd caught her when she wasn't thinking. He had rocked her boat. She thought it was amazingly responsible of him to bring it up—men were embarrassed about that sort of thing—but then she realized he was protecting himself, not her, and the more she thought about it, the more she thought he was the sort of man who thinks a condom will cut off the blood flow to his penis, or deaden the sensation, the sort who wants the full effect.

He kissed her in funny places: under her nose above her lips, on the sides of her breasts (holding each arm up in the air), on the backs of her knees.

"You must have had a lot of practice," she told him. He pounded his chest. "I mean it," she said.

"I'm very, very careful," he said.

She hadn't really thought of being careful—being scared was what it meant—until he said that. She hadn't wondered about the other women, except that they'd been before her; she wasn't good at sex. She had always just lain there, except that with Travis, she kept jumping and twitching and twisting and moaning, and maybe all those involuntary movements could seem intentional, could make her look, well, *competent*.

"Besides," he told her, just last weekend, "I've been saving up a while. I was really tired of fucking around."

Timidly she said, "I don't really like that word, Travis."

He didn't say anything about that. He said, instead, "I'm thinking about being thirty-two years old and alone out here on this old farm—" As far as the eye could see, cotton was poking up in his tidy fields. His house, which was the old farmhouse his parents had left to build a snazzy new one a quarter mile away, was a disaster. It was dirty, it needed paint inside and out, it smelled of cooking and his two brute dogs. In the living room he was working on a dismantled dirt bike.

"And I like a lady," he said, sweet as melon, and ran his tongue slowly, gently, around her lips. "I like a lady a lot."

*   *   *

"How come you laugh when we're making love?" she asked him.

He said, "Didn't you ever hear of *joie de sex?*"

And she asked, "Do you have a lot of girlfriends?" She wanted to get it all out in the open.

"Hmm. One who likes to ski—we go to Ruidosa. A couple who are good dancers—"

"I'm a good dancer."

"—and one who can cook."

"I don't care all that much about *food*." She was surprised at herself, trying to be funny. Next she'd be batting her eyes.

"And one who's really smart; she's getting her master's in education." He stuck his tongue out at her the littlest bit.

That stung, although she knew he was teasing her. "I'm thinking of going to college," she said. "The bank wants me to take a class at night."

He tried to tickle her feet. "All my other girlfriends are ticklish." She jerked her foot out of his hand. "And then there's one who's nice and tall and skinny—" and he grinned at her. "You're not jealous, are you? You're not—"

"I was *curious,*" she said. "What I was doing was, I was *making conversation.*"

"So let's talk about your boyfriends."

"I married them."

"Talk about your husbands."

"Dead meat," she said.

"Hey! The girl's pretty funny!"

She relaxed a little. "I wasn't making a joke," she said.

They are on Travis's friend's bed now. It is king-sized, covered with an embossed spread. Clancy has taken off her skirt and hose and panties, but not her blouse. "I only have an hour," she whispers.

Travis gently pushes her down on her back.

"We don't want to make a mess on his bed—"

"Shh." He kisses her, then slides down and kisses her kneecaps and the tops of her feet. Then he puts his face between her legs.

"Travis, uh—" She's not sure what to expect, but probably she won't like it. And what if he wants her to put her mouth on him? Jeeter told her she was as much fun as a fish when she said she wouldn't. She couldn't. It made her gag before her lips ever touched. It made her sick to think of it.

She reaches down to push him off. He burrows. He holds her hands away. It feels very funny to have someone's face down there. She squirms. "Oh, boy," Travis says. "Yum, yum." She wriggles once more, then thinks, what does it hurt? There isn't time to make a fuss and make up and start over. He's bigger than I am.

And amazingly, it feels very nice.

She is thinking: How can he stand it? What does it taste like? And then she isn't thinking at all. She lies quietly, and her vulva seems to have grown large and moist and quite alive, almost apart from the rest of her. She hears the sound of his slurping, his silly exclamations, and she hears herself moan, and notices, then forgets, her legs stuck up in the air like safety pins undone. Until she says, "Travis, Travis, oh, oh," and tugs and tugs at his shoulders. "Come up here," she says. Whatever it takes to make him stop the other, and the feelings that are washing over and out of her, that make her face tingle and her chest hot under her impossible blouse. "Just *do it*," she whispers.

He crawls up beside her. His face is all wet. "Fuck?" he

whispers. She doesn't answer. "Fuck?" he says again, and she answers, "*Fuck.*" Then he is inside her, and moving, and her great swollen vagina clasps him. He is panting. He wipes his face against her shoulder. "You are one sweet lady," he says.

She can barely find her breath. "Don't do that, Travis," she manages to say. "Never again."

21

Joy is drinking her fourth cup of coffee and soaking her left hand in a pan of ice water. The house is quiet and empty and unaccusing. Even the cat is nowhere to be seen.

She has been trying to read the morning paper—although it is no longer morning—but she can't concentrate. She keeps thinking of the night before and wondering who she ought to be mad at. She wonders if her little finger could be broken.

If Heather had been home, she wouldn't have stayed out as late as she did. She had gone to a bar with a nurse from the old office, and when she went home—*she* had another job now—Joy didn't want to go back to the quiet house, where Clancy would be huddled in her bed, reading or sleeping, and there would be nothing to do but watch television on a night when all the programs are stupid. There was a man in the bar she knew a little, from other times she had been there. Miller. She didn't know if that was his first or last name. Miller said there was a little party getting together at his friend's, and she ought to come. She had an idea a party on a weeknight wasn't going to make the papers, but she didn't have to be anywhere in the morning. She sat there nursing a beer while he went off to call the friend and say they were coming. She was feeling sorry for herself, and Miller is the sort who is full of jokes, okay jokes that aren't mean and derisive, like he's memorized them out of *Reader's Digest*. She followed Miller's pickup across town to a little frame house. From the street she could see the glow of a television and the pale amber of a single lamp near the window. It didn't look like a party to her. There were a couple of cars in the driveway. "I don't know," she told Miller. "Maybe I better get on home." She was standing by her car. Miller came over and sweet-talked her. He said he'd been wanting to get to know her better for a long time. He said it was only nine-thirty, what was the rush? He said his friends had some nice grass, if she was into that. She said she wasn't. He said that didn't matter, to each his own. He spoke to her softly, without a trace of that good-ole-boy arrogance she hated; she could almost believe he had been thinking about asking her out. Probably, she wanted to believe it. A bar wasn't the best place to meet men, but where else was there, when you got right down to it? And the bar—Sweeney's—was a comfortable place, old and well kept. She liked to think of it as a kind of Lubbock "Cheers."

Inside the house there were two more men. They were watching one of those programs that tell about unsolved crimes and terrible deeds yet undone. They acted happy to see her. "Oh, yeah, *Joy*," one said from a BarcaLounger. "Here, here," the other one said; he hopped up and left his warm spot for her on the couch. She sat down and he pulled up a kitchen chair nearby; Miller sat down next to her, not especially close. The two who had been in the house started filling her and Miller in on what was happening on the program. She couldn't follow the story line, if there was one. She was a little worried about a party with three men. "Who else is coming?" she said. She stood up. "I think I'll go home," she said. She wasn't comfortable, although the house wasn't half-bad inside, not the living room, anyway. The couch was lumpy and fat and deep, and the floor looked swept. From where she was, the kitchen didn't look bad, a few dishes on the counter but nothing piled up and disgusting that she could see. Men could be such pigs.

Miller said, "Isn't Betsy coming? I thought Sue Ann would be here?" and the other guys said they didn't know, it wasn't for sure. "Hell's bells," one of them said, "stay a little while, we just ordered pizza." They were friendly. They didn't give her any kind of nasty once-over. It wasn't a party, but it was people. Television and pizza. All three men wore jeans and polo shirts, like they were some sort of singing trio. While she was trying to decide, another woman did show up, the Sue Ann they had predicted, a pretty blond woman about Joy's age. The men were a little younger. Aren't there any men my age? Joy wanted to ask the world. In less than twenty years, she'll be her mother's age. She doesn't want to be alone.

She took a beer and sat back down. They cheered. There's something really good at ten, they said, stick around. She laughed and relaxed. She was hungry. Pizza sounded good.

While her stepmother, Joanne, is at the pediatrician's with brat baby Andrew, Heather has her first opportunity to take a close look at her daddy's new house. She knew he was getting a house; he's been married nearly a year, and they've adopted Andrew and need more space. She didn't expect her daddy to live forever in an apartment, but she hasn't ever been in a house this nice. The carpet in their bedroom is so lush it feels to her bare feet like soft summer grass. There are pictures on the walls in sleek chrome frames. The switches on the walls are ceramic instead of plastic. The closets are full of clothes. And the baby's room! Oh, whoa, take another look! The walls are papered with colorful zoo animals, and the crib sheets match. There's a special table just for laying him on to wipe his butt. The furniture is a *set*. Her bed—of course it isn't really hers, but the baby's when he gets big enough—is high, with a big deep drawer that pulls out from underneath, already half-loaded with toys he can't even have because he's not big enough, and it has the softest, nicest comforter she's ever touched, which she loves for its feel and hates because she knows it's really for *him*.

When Wayne told her he had bought a new house, she anticipated a room of her own. She hoped he might buy her her own little TV for it, like at Opal's; if Joy could afford a TV for her, *he* sure could. She wondered if she would get to pick anything out—a nice bed, maybe, and a little chest to keep some clothes in even when she isn't there. He is always saying, "You live here, too, Heather." Usually he says it when he wants her to run the vacuum or take the dishes out of the dishwasher, but she thought for a while that maybe he did mean she has two homes, one for each parent, and since neither of them are really hers— which is to say, not her mother's—when you think about it, it seems her own father's house ought to feel more like hers than her grandmother's. He *is* her *father*. But the third bedroom, which she thought would be hers, has no bed-room furniture. It is a rather bare room, with big double windows, a small desk, and a large table completely taken up with a model railroad. And she, the daughter with two homes, sleeps in a room with a farting, hiccuping, whining baby *who isn't even her daddy's flesh and blood.* Wayne likes having a boy; he picked him out, didn't he? But she doesn't think he especially likes having a baby. Joanne rushes around and fusses to keep Andrew quiet when Wayne is home. Last night, in the absolute middle of the night, he set up such a howling, Heather was afraid they would accuse her of biting him. Joanne rushed in to get him, and said, "Why didn't you pick him up!" *Pick him up!* He smells bad. He's ugly. He's *their* baby. Joanne said, "Your daddy needs his sleep." Like he needed the last piece of peach pie Heather had dished up for herself after supper. Like he needs whatever TV program *he* wants, and needs it to be turned off when he's through watching. She feels like she is walking around carrying something she is afraid to spill. Her father always knows exactly how things are supposed to be done. He used to come in the house after work and complain if things weren't picked up, although Joy didn't get home more than half an hour earlier. He used to lecture them at dinner about nutrition, and tell them who ought to do what while he watched the evening news. Heather thinks the divorce was more his idea than Joy's, and that it was meant to include Heather in the amputation. They never seemed to please him. He said Heather had all Joy's faults: sloppiness, bad temper, an ignorance of national events. He used to send Heather to her room and then start lecturing Joy in this hateful soft voice, until Joy would get so mad she'd start yelling. Heather never saw him hit her mother—and he never hit *her*, he just sent her to her room again and again—but she did see Joy hit *him* once. Joy had bought a toy poodle at a pet shop, and he took it back. He came home during the day, while Joy was at work and Heather at school, and took that sweet little dog and returned it like a pair of shoes that didn't fit. Joy screamed and called him names, and when he said she didn't know how to manage the house or her life or her daughter, she punched her fist into his stomach. He grabbed her by the wrist, and he said, "Someday somebody is going to want to kill you, Joy."

She wonders if he has ever been that mean to Joanne. Maybe he warned her; she's like a mouse. You can tell she wants everything to be *nice*. The other night, she sat down on the couch by Heather while Wayne went to buy some ice cream. From out of nowhere, she produced a book.

"I got this for you," she said. She thrust it at Heather, who saw that it was actually a journal, fancy, with a cloth cover of printed flowers, and lined pages.

"For *what*?"

"I know you must have a million thoughts inside."

Heather rolled her eyes. Did Joanne think her thoughts were on her *nose*?

"And it might help—you might feel better if you wrote them down."

"You want to know my *thoughts*?"

Joanne laughed softly. "Oh, heavens, no, I didn't mean that. I meant, if you kept a diary, you could tell it things you didn't want to say to us. It helps if you express your feelings." She laughed some more. "I'm sounding really awkward, but I bet you'll see what I mean." She is always coming up with ideas to make Heather a happy girl. Not two days ago it was "Let's go get your dead ends trimmed." It made Heather feel so *observed,* she hated walking in front of Joanne the rest of the day—like, what else would she find to *make better?* Heather sat lumplike with the journal in her hand. She thought Joanne was undoubtedly the dumbest woman she had ever met, dumber than any of her teachers, and that was bad.

"I know it's been hard for you," Joanne said. *It?* What's *it?* Heather wanted to ask. Having parents who hate each other? Having a grandmother who thinks you're loud and dumb and in the way? Having no friends in a school as big as a whole city? Having a stepbrother with his *own room*? She glared into space; no way was she going to look at Joanne's *concerned* face. Joanne said, "I know your parents were very unhappy"—and Heather couldn't help herself, she *snorted*. Like, what do people get divorced over, *having a good time?*—"but your father and I get along very well."

"Oh, congratulations," Heather said. She had to say something.

"Sometimes, in an unhappy home, a man isn't the father he could be," Joanne went on. "That doesn't mean he doesn't want to do better. It doesn't mean he won't." She had the kind of voice, you could imagine her teaching kindergarten.

Heather jumped up and turned on the TV. The journal fell to the floor. On TV, one car was chasing another, and the first car turned a corner and the driver saw it was a dead end—you saw this look on his face, *Oh, shit*—and he swerved and smashed into the side of a building and the second car smashed into him. It was tremendously, satisfyingly loud. Heather finally looked at her stepmother. Joanne had this look, a Won't you please like me and give me a chance and *believe this is so much better than what you had before?* look—and Heather said, "What kind of ice cream will he get? He didn't even ask me what kind I wanted. I like chocolate chip mint, and he'll get Rocky Road, won't he? I don't want any. I'm not hungry anymore. That chili stuff we had is making my stomach hurt. *I want to go home.*" Joanne got this sappy, disappointed, patient look, and she said, "Wayne will take you home Labor Day, that's the agreement." Then she *smiled*, like there was something to smile about. Now, *that* was the kind of look Heather could imagine hitting.

Heather wanders into the train room and looks over the envelopes and papers on the desk. A tray holds a neat stack of bills marked "Paid," lots of bills from department stores and gas station companies and credit card companies. On the surface of the desk is a neat pile of personal letters, most of them addressed to Joanne Ronnander. Joanne Ronnander. She can't believe Joanne has the same name as her. The same name as her mother. The same name as Aaaaandrew Waaaanndrew. She picks up the top envelope. The return address is Houston. Who does Joanne know in Houston? The name is Wilson. What a boring name. She thinks about reading the letter, but she realizes that she isn't really interested in what adults say to one another, especially adults she doesn't even know. She wonders if anybody writes her father. She has never written him, or received a letter from him. All the arrangements for her visits are made between her parents, as if she were still a little girl. Her mother says, "You better do what he says, Heather Lee, or he'll take it out of the child support." She acts like it is terrible every time Heather goes, but that there's nothing she can do about it. Maybe it's a relief not to have her around.

She sees that stupid journal lying on the desk, too. She could not imagine what Joanne thought she would write. Letters nobody would read? "Dear Diary" entries like some dork from a book? Well, she has an idea what to write. She takes it and a ballpoint pen and sits down at the desk. "Model train," she writes. Below that she writes, "pictures (art)." She means to make a list. She gets up and moves through the house, stopping to lean the book against a wall and write: "TV, toaster oven, blender, fancy lamp, exercise bike, *four phones*." She goes back upstairs to their bedroom and throws open the closet door. She starts counting Joanne's dresses and skirts. She can see it will take quite a while. And she doesn't want to forget: king-sized bed.

When the phone rings in Lubbock, Joy is sitting at her computer, tapping with one hand and one finger of the other hand. She has a manuscript to type: *The Contrarian Entrepreneur,* by a college business professor. This—it's hard not to laugh, *ha ha,* she thinks—is her new career. Unless you count selling shaved ice at the flea market. With the proceeds from her house sale, she bought a computer and printer, had her engine overhauled, and gave Heather a hundred dollars for tapes. She doesn't even have enough left to pay all the taxes she will owe at the end of the year. It was Bill Tweed's idea. It sounded so good, the way he described it: In a college town, with a business community, there's a lot of typing to do. You can be your own boss, set your own hours. When she hauled all this home, her mother went into a tizzy rearranging the alcove by the door to make it Joy's "office." She crammed her sewing machine into a closet, along with Russell's ex-wife's sewing machine. She kept asking Joy, "Is it fun?" and "Do you want to get some cards printed up?" She even said, "Maybe I could learn to use it; I could help you when you're busy." It took Joy weeks to learn how to use the word processing program, and she still feels lost in an impossible labyrinth. She has promised this manuscript by the last day of August, and time is passing fast. Her hand hurts with every movement, hurts even more with any pressure. She is going to have to type the damned book with one hand. She wonders if her mother has some Darvon somewhere in the house.

They started watching a show about cops, eating their pizza and making a lot of stupid jokes. She could tell that Sue Ann had been sleeping with one of the guys, Todd. She had that look of ownership, but Joy would bet she was not his top girl. She was a secretary in a real estate office. Joy's impression was, if you do that very long and don't learn to sell houses yourself, you probably aren't very smart.

On the television, this very earnest policeman was telling about driving down a city street somewhere in Ohio and seeing something looking fishy about an office building. It turned out a really crazy guy had his girlfriend hostage inside, and the story—which was supposed to be true— was all about how the cop talked the crazy guy into coming out, no gunfire, no blood, nobody hurt. He told about it in a flat, dumb voice while actors acted the whole thing out. Not only was it not believable, it was boring. And she said so. She said cops always exaggerate. They exaggerate the danger they are in, they exaggerate the part their wits and courage play, instead of luck, and they exaggerate how modest they are when it's over. While all the time they are in love with their guns and cars and authority. It was like somebody turned on a radio and Joy's voice came out; she could not stop talking. She felt hot and nervous. "I always thought cops are the guys who'd be making trouble if they didn't have cop shit to do." Very quietly, Miller asked, "Now, what gave you that idea, Joy?" and she realized they were all staring at her like she'd just grown snakes out of her head.

"I guess I know," she said defensively. "I used to be married to one of the sons of bitches." (It's been fifteen years since she divorced him, and he still makes her furious.) When they didn't say anything, she leaned forward and said, "He took to wearing his gun to bed." She didn't say he also took to swatting her like a late-summer fly too slow to get out of the way. She didn't say he used to cruise by her apartment after their divorce; that sometimes she thinks she married Wayne so fast just to get away from him.

She'd had several beers by then, and the program got to her. Her ears were burning, her face felt numb across the sinuses. It took her a few minutes to realize *they* were all mad at *her*. Nobody looked at her or said anything. She shut up and tried to sit still. The next segment of the program was livelier, if not more believable; it had a robbery, a chase, an exchange of gunfire. Joy felt pushed; she couldn't help herself. She said, "I wonder how many people they kill every year just because they're in the way when they're playing cops and robbers." She's heard they're always having wrecks.

Miller turned his head slowly and said, "This is a true story; they're not playing."

"They're *acting*," she said.

"Most cops never use their guns," Miller said. "Most use their wits."

"Oh, right," Joy went on, digging herself in deeper and deeper. "Their wits on the end of a nightstick."

Todd got up and said, "In sixteen years, I never shot nobody," and stomped off to the bathroom. The house was so small you could hear everything he was doing, even with the TV on. Sue Ann turned, and with a pleased smirk, said, "Todd's an officer with the Lubbock Police."

"Big wow," Joy said, blushing.

"Me, too," said the other guy, whose name she couldn't remember. He held his beer can up like a toast, but he kept looking at the television and not at her.

"Piss on cops!" Joy said, and jumped up. One of the pizza boxes was next to her knee, and when she got up it went flying to the floor.

"Hey, come on, Joy," Miller said. Evidently he wasn't a cop; he didn't look like he wanted to kill her. He had a different look on his face. He said, "Here, help me pick it up," very calmly, and she realized *he felt sorry for her.* She made a show of looking at the cold pizza on the floor, the box, Miller, letting them see her contempt. She was shaking.

"Thanks a *lot* for a *good* time," she said. She reached down for her purse, and Miller reached up for her arm. "Hold on," he said. He had caught the sleeve of her shirt. "You've got something to do here first."

She had turned to take a step away, and his tug at her sleeve, the slightest restraint, infuriated her. She turned back to him, the momentum of the movement a furious impulse, and she jerked her arm away and, without a second's consideration, swung it out in an arc across her chest, then back at him with all her strength. He ducked, and she hit the wall behind him with a startling thud. She screamed; she thought for a moment her hand had shattered; she was actually surprised to pull it back against her stomach, cradling it with the other hand, and find it whole. *And nobody did anything.* They looked at her like posts. They thought she was crazy, and worse, they knew she couldn't do a thing to hurt them. And then, to make matters worse, she had to ask Sue Ann to move her car so she could get out.

*   *   *

"You've got to come get me, Mommy," Heather says in her littlest-girl voice. "I can't stand it here, and Daddy won't bring me for another week."

Joy's hand is throbbing. She remembers her mother keeps pill samples in the drawer by the stove. "Okay, okay," she says without even thinking. "I have to get dressed."

"You will?" Heather asks. "Oh, thank you!"

"You didn't think I would?" Joy says. "You didn't think I'd know what it feels like to be in somebody's house where you don't belong?"

"I hate them, Mom. They won't let me play my music. Joanne wants to get my hair cut."

"I'll leave in ten minutes," Joy says. She doesn't mind at all. She goes to look for some Darvon.

22

When Joy calls Clancy at
work to say she's going to pick up Heather, Clancy is
momentarily bereft. They won't be back before nine, and
she will have to go home to that empty house. She had
hoped she could talk to Joy; she wanted to talk about
Travis. She wouldn't tell what he did today, that would be
too embarrassing, but she wanted to ask Joy what she
thinks: Is it too soon to like someone again, and is Travis
too wild anyway? Isn't she better off reading books?

It's a relief when Irene, a teller from downstairs, asks if
Clancy would like to go after work to the hospital to see
her sister's baby, and then they can eat in the hospital
cafeteria and talk a while, or they can go to the mall and
walk around.

As soon as they step onto the maternity floor they can
hear the cooing and fussing of babies. Walking down the
hall, Clancy sees plastic carts on rollers in the rooms. She
goes into Irene's sister's room and admires a baby so fu-
riously red, he is almost purple. She puts her finger into
the baby's palm, and the baby instinctively grasps it. It is
delicately pleasurable to feel the tiny fist around her finger. Irene's brother-in-law shows up, and Clancy tells
Irene she'll go look in the nursery and wait for her in the
lounge.

There are spaces for the missing carts in the nursery, and

a half-dozen babies in ones left along several rows. Clancy stands at the window, studying the infants, not thinking anything, enjoying their scrunched-up faces and wiggly toes. In the corner, away from the windows, a baby lies in one of the plastic beds with a wire taped to his chest. Smaller than the other babies, he is sleeping. She watches him for several minutes, until the nurse, noticing her gaze, points to him, smiles, and lifts him gently from the crib to show her. Clancy feels foolish—the nurse must think she is a relative—but it is easier to smile and nod and wave than to try to convey her irrelevance.

"I spent many an hour rocking that baby while he was in the preemie nursery," someone beside her says.

She turns to see a woman, older than her mother, wearing a short hospital jacket over her street clothes. A mask dangles around her neck.

"I come in and rock the preemies, as a volunteer. They need lots of touching, you know. It helps them grow."

Clancy smiles. "I don't know the baby, I was just looking."

"They're miracles, every one," the woman says. "They can save babies now who're what? A pound or two? It's a miracle."

Clancy turns again to the window. The nurse has tucked a light blanket around the baby and come down to pick up another baby nearer Clancy. She rests him on her shoulder. A hot swirling sensation pours through Clancy. She longs to hold one of the babies herself. The nurse is dressed in a crisp white uniform; she moves briskly but, Clancy thinks, happily. Why wouldn't you be happy, holding babies all day?

I could do that! Clancy thinks fiercely. In a rush, she

wonders so many things: whether she is smart enough, whether she can afford the schooling, whether everyone will say she's not the right type. She's happy when Irene comes along and suggests they go downstairs to the cafeteria. They both buy coffee and slices of banana bread, and Clancy shyly tells Irene what she's thinking. Irene says encouraging things. She says Texas is still a place where you can get an education cheap. She says she read that older students do the best. She says, "The bank's not much of a career, is it?" and shrugs. She is young, maybe only a few years out of high school.

"What about you?" Clancy asks.

Irene grins. "I have a boyfriend. I hope—well, I'd like to have my own baby soon, you know? I'd like to get married and have a family."

"Not me," Clancy says. "I tried being married. I just like the babies. I never thought of nursing until this evening. It never crossed my mind; my sister and mother both worked for doctors and hated it, so maybe I was always thinking of the doctors instead of the patients." She thinks of tiny, tiny babies lying across a nurse's palms. It's so amazing, never to have considered it.

"Want to go to the mall?" Irene asks. She thinks the conversation about nursing is over. Clancy wishes she could talk about it some more. She wonders what Travis would think. Probably he'd think she was hinting that she wants a baby. He ought to know better; she always uses a diaphragm.

"Oh, shit!" she exclaims. She is putting her cup and saucer in the bucket by the kitchen and she lets go too soon and makes a clattering racket. Irene touches her arm. "Are you okay? What's wrong?"

Clancy tries to smile. "Sorry. I just forgot something."

Probably, it doesn't matter; it was just this one time.

She ought to be on the Pill, she thinks, but she knows she isn't going to see a doctor. She'll be more careful; she won't let Travis spring any more surprises on her.

23

Opal has been staying with Russell in Farmington for three days, and she thinks one more may kill her. It is hot as the bottom of an iron, and dusty, and there's nothing to do all day but play the little TV he's got hooked up, and read—her eyes get to bothering her before too long—and work on projects. She's making a landscape out of painted Popsicle sticks. She follows directions from a craft magazine, painting sticks two shades of orange, blue, white, and green, then laying them out to form a picture of a Southwestern mesa against a bright sky, with three cacti in the foreground, like little dancing children. She glues them to a board backing.

"You done with that?" Russell asks when he comes into the trailer. He's been in the shower house, and with his hair wet and his face scrubbed, he has an appeal she forgets at other times. He looks over her shoulder. "It's real pretty, honey."

She stands up, too, to get a better look. There's barely room for both of them to stand at the same time; they have to squeeze back away from the table. In a while she has to put everything away and raise and prop the table, pull out the platform that goes across the two seats, pull down the cushion that's strapped behind one of them, and make her bed, if you can call it that. She sleeps in it catty-corner and still can't quite stretch out without sticking her feet into air. Russell, at the end of the trailer, has a too-short bed, too, but he has the better cushion—a foam pad—and, of course, he works hard every day and needs a sound sleep.

She longs for her bed at home. She wishes she had gone to the camp office and called Clancy before they locked up for the night. She knows how lonesome Clancy gets.

"Did you get some beer?" Russell asks. They have a refrigerator the size of a small cardboard box. He likes for her to cook on his two-burner stove. He says he lives on soup when he's there alone. She can manage eggs, chili, spaghetti sauce on macaroni, other simple dishes, but she would much rather go to the café up the road. It's a lot of trouble, in that small space, and she has to take the dish bucket to the shower house and wash it there, where the water is hot.

"I forgot," she says apologetically. "I bought milk and stuff for your lunches."

"It's okay. If I drank one I'd have to get up in the middle of the night anyway." He sits on his cushion and starts clipping his toenails. She wishes he would catch them in his hand instead of letting them fly every which way.

"Guess I'll go home tomorrow," she says.

"Aw, I wish you wouldn't."

"I have a checkup." She's on medication, doing fine; he won't argue with a checkup.

"I thought when you stopped working, you could stay with me."

"Where're you going next, Russell? You call the union today?"

"There's a gas line in New South Wales, starts up in October."

"That's Australia!"

"Wouldn't that be fun? You could go."

She slaps her chest with her palm. "In my condition?"

"You're not an invalid, Opal. And they have doctors in Australia."

"Where else?"

He looks sly. "Nigeria."

"Go on!"

"Terrebonne Parish, in Louisiana."

"That's a little closer to home."

He whistles a few notes, then says, "Mineral Wells, in six weeks or so."

She knows where he'll go. And what excuse is there not to go with him? "I can't live in this little space, Russell. You're gone all day, but I'm cooped up. And I worry about my girls."

Russell has pulled off his jeans. He wears only his boxer shorts. His arms and face and shoulders are burned a deep red tan.

"You ought to be wearing a shirt with sleeves, Russell Duffy," she scolds. "That much sun is poison."

"It's summer."

"Suit yourself, it's your skin." She carefully picks up her glued-on-Popsicle-sticks picture and lays it on the counter and across the sink. "Don't forget this is here," she says.

He has moved to stand behind her. He puts his hands on her hips. His burned skin, his thighs, put off heat. In her pajamas, she feels fat and awkward. He says softly, "You come stay with me in Mineral Wells, we'll leave the house to them. It'd be a great arrangement. You know I wouldn't throw them out. I just want *you* with *me*."

Clancy would be upset. "It'd be like living in a closet."

With one hand, he strokes her hair at the crown. With the other, he fondles her breast. "Maybe we could fit on my bed."

She turns around, astonished. "If we took shrinking pills, maybe we could!"

He laughs and lays his arms over her shoulders. "Kissing's good enough, if that's all the room there is."

She hopes he remembered to brush his teeth. "You'll be home in a couple weeks anyway," she reminds him. He nibbles her bottom lip. The smallest of chills darts from the base of her skull to the middle of her back.

"That's a long time away," he says, but after one damp kiss, he goes to his bed, and she to hers. Lying there, waiting for sleep, she thinks about her next project, when she visits him at the next site. She'd like to make a trivet, for hot dishes. Something out of blue tiles. She'll make one for Clancy, too, for when she has her own place.

 24

When Joy arrives at Wayne's house, she pulls along the curb and honks twice. Her hand is discolored and swollen, and the pain, even with Darvon, is constant. She certainly doesn't have the energy to be nice. The garage door is up and she can see a Toyota parked inside, surely Joanne's car, since Wayne doesn't believe in buying Japanese. If he is still at work, she won't have to deal with him; that's a relief.

Heather comes flying out the front door, followed, more slowly, by Joanne carrying her baby in a hip sling. Heather throws her bag into the backseat, jumps in the front, and slams the car door. "Let's *go*," she says.

Joanne is waving and hollering. Joy could pull away, but her hand is sending up fresh messages of pain, and she has to breathe deeply and let some of it pass.

"*Mother,*" Heather whines.

Joanne runs around to Joy's side of the car and taps on the window. Joy rolls it down.

"He'll be home in half an hour," Joanne says, out of breath. The baby is sleeping soundly, his body tucked around hers. If they had those sling things and backpacks when Heather was a baby, Joy didn't know about it. She hauled Heather around like a sack. "I know he wants to talk to you," Joanne says. They both know who "he" is.

Heather is making growling noises.

"I can't wait," Joy says.

"*Joy.* There's not a problem here," Joanne says in her bossy, let-me-spell-this-out voice.

"Heather seems to think there is. *Joanne.*"

"She doesn't want to talk to us. She doesn't want to help out. I don't know what she's mad about. It's her attitude." Joanne leans down so close, the baby bumps the car door. "We want her with us. You understand that, don't you?"

Joy looks at Joanne directly. "If she doesn't want to be here, why would you want her? It must be such a worry to you."

"I wish you'd wait."

"I wish you'd move." Joy shifts gears, and as Joanne takes a step back, pulls away. "Prissy bitch," she says.

"I'm not on their side," she tells Heather in a while, "but I can tell you, you could be a little nicer."

"Daddy has this whole room just for his toy train."

"I guess he makes it run on time, huh?" If Joy gets started on complaints about Wayne, she will just get angry, and she doesn't want to be sidetracked from her point.

"And they've got four phones."

"I guess that's what you call 'lifestyle.' "

"And I'm just in the way."

"They didn't want you to leave."

"They didn't want me to have my way."

"Kids don't get their way, that's why they're kids. Otherwise, who would grown-ups push around?"

"Mom. You're joking, aren't you?"

Joy sighs and raises her left hand to the roof of the car, thinking that if the blood drains down, it won't throb so much.

"What're you doing that for?" Heather asks.

"I hurt my hand. In the car door."

"Oh," Heather says. "Mom, I'm hungry; can we get a hamburger?" She slumps down to wait.

They find a drive-in north of Canyon and eat hamburgers in the car. Joy hands Heather her trash.

"Huh?" Heather says.

"I told you, I hurt my hand."

Heather takes the sack to the garbage can. Joy watches her daughter's sulky movements and flicks away her urge to call out: Is it really too much trouble? There's a certain satisfaction in thinking of Heather at Wayne's, defying his mandates for order and the right attitude. She always needs a day to recover from a visit, time to shed her defensive resentment. She has no reason to be mad at Joy, though. When she's buckled in again, Joy says, "You know I'm on your side, but I'm not the one who's got anything. You want to go to college? You better make your daddy see the light. If you count on me you'll get bus fare to your first clerk's job, Heather."

"Suck up to him, you mean?" Heather says sarcastically.

"Not the word I'd choose. Listen, he's an asshole, I divorced him, right? But he's the father you've got and we need him. It could be worse. At least he's got a job, and we know where to find him."

"Take what you get, what else can you do with parents?" Heather says bitterly. "You can't trade them in."

"You're not mistreated. I could tell you about parents."

"You don't have to, we live with her, remember?"

"When I was a little older than you, she kicked me out."

"I don't believe you."

"Well, she did. Not forever, maybe, but it was bad enough."

Heather groans. Evidently the conversation is boring her.

"I'll tell you a little story," Joy says. She rests her left hand on the seat by her thigh. "You think you've got it so bad." She gets back on the highway before she starts to talk. She doesn't know why she never told Heather before. Heather is old enough to hear a lot of things. They study about Indians and Mexicans in school now; why doesn't anybody tell them their own mothers have stories? They should tell them to ask.

"I can hardly remember being little. My memories all start when I was about sixth grade. My mother was at me all the time: I didn't help enough, I was lazy, what was wrong with me. Maybe I was happy before that, I don't know. Maybe I was just a kid. But all of a sudden I was hired help, and I was the one Mother bitched to about everything. Daddy was never home. He worked all over Texas and New Mexico, sometimes Oklahoma. Mother worked at the hospital, about five blocks away. She worked late, but on the other hand, she could slip away sometimes and pop in at home and check on things. When she did that, I was always doing something wrong. I was sleeping, or watching TV, when I ought to be *helping out*. Clancy was little; she stayed with a woman a couple houses away. Mother would come home and say, 'Why didn't you go get Clancy? I pay someone to watch her, when she's your sister.' God, I was a *kid*.

"By the time I was in high school we hardly ever spoke to one another. I can remember Mother coming back from Odessa on a shopping trip. She'd have bought all this shit for me, and she'd come and just *dump* it on my bed. 'I suppose you won't like it,' she'd say. She'd pick out the clothes she wanted me to wear, and then be pissed off if I wasn't all excited. I remember one year I begged her and begged her for a mouton coat—"

"A *what*?" Heather's interruption startles Joy; she has almost forgotten she is there.

"A kind of fuzzy fake-fur coat, short. I don't have any idea what they cost, but she didn't say anything about them being expensive, and lots of girls were wearing them. She said she'd think about it, then ordered me a coat from the Sears catalog. It was a tartan plaid. Plaid!"

Heather sighs.

"One day, right after school was out—it was already really hot—Mother came home after work a little late. Daddy was home, working on the car out on the driveway. Clancy was out there with him. She'd set up all her dolls on the paving, and was telling Daddy a story about them. I remember it because I thought it'd be fun to get down with her and play, but I knew I ought to make supper, so I left them and went inside.

"By the time Mother got home, I'd made spaghetti; I'd taken the laundry out of the dryer and laid it on the couch to fold later on. Mother comes in and looks around kind of crazy. She runs down to her bedroom, then back to the kitchen. She's in this hospital uniform with her name on her pocket. And she starts yelling at me. *There's no salad.* She rushes to the refrigerator and starts chopping tomatoes. 'There's tomatoes in the *sauce*,' I tell her. It made me furious. She *slams* this salad down on the table and says, 'Go tell him it's *ready*.' She's mad at all of us. We all get to the table—Clancy has to have her hands washed, all that—and Daddy starts serving himself some spaghetti, and there's Mother, eating salad *standing up*. It annoys him, and he says, 'For God's sake, Opal, take a load off,' and that makes her mad, so she rushes over to the couch and starts folding laundry. Daddy gets up from the table and turns the TV on really loud. Clancy starts crying.

"I start crying, too, and yelling: 'What'd I do? What's wrong with you?' Daddy gets up and leaves the house. He drives away without paying attention and runs over Clancy's dolls in the driveway, so later there's *that* for Mother to yell about. I screamed at her, 'I hate it here, I wish I lived someplace else!' Clancy was hollering like she'd been smacked, and Mother was suddenly busy trying to calm her down. She sent me out to look for the dolls. Later, when Daddy came home, Mother lit into him about it. 'It could have been Clancy, for all you cared,' she told him. 'You just wanted to leave, you didn't even look.' He said she was being stupid. Clancy was in her chair at the table. He wouldn't answer Mother when she kept on talking. He could go for days without saying a word to her.

"I was on my bed, still dressed, still mad and my feelings all hurt. She came in and stood at the foot of my bed. I remember it because for a minute I thought she was going to say she was sorry. I wanted her to hug me.

"What she says to me, though, was, 'If you don't like our house, maybe you could go live at your *other* parent's.' I didn't know what she was talking about, but I had this awful feeling; without even thinking, I knew. I mean, things made sense, little remarks from Granny, from Mother."

"Can I get a *Coke*?" Heather asks, in a voice that makes it clear she is tired of Joy's story. "I'm still thirsty." Joy pulls off at the Happy exit, makes the loop across the highway, and pulls into a Dairy Queen. Her skin feels hot and prickly, as if her limbs were all asleep and are just waking up.

"Wait," she says, her hand on Heather's arm. With a sigh, Heather sinks back against the seat. "I want you to hear this. *I want to tell you this.*"

Heather says, "We never see Grandpa. When was the last time we saw him?"

Greta's funeral. Everyone was there. Joy pushes away a slap of sadness; when her grandmother died, she lost one person who was on her side.

"That's what I'm trying to tell you! He's not my father. *Listen* to me, Heather. Mother was married before. My real daddy was in the air force. I don't know if he sent her money; I don't think so. I don't know anything about how she kept track of him, I just know that the day I didn't make a salad, she informed me that my *real* daddy was an air force colonel living in Arkansas, and if I didn't like *her* house, maybe I could try *his*. Two days later, I was on a bus to Arkansas, crying all the way."

"Gah," Heather says. "This is too weird. Can I get a Coke now?"

"Go in and get it," Joy says, thrusting her wallet at Heather. "Get me one too." While she waits, she leans her forehead against the steering wheel, weak with old anger. It feels like all the blood in her body has gushed to her head, which is pounding. A pain in her hand shoots up her arm insistently, in the rhythm of her pulse.

Heather hands Joy a paper cup of Coke, and says, "Joanne says Daddy thinks I should live with them. She says it's important for me to see how she and Daddy *are* together, how a marriage *works*. You know what she thinks, don't you? She thinks they're normal and we're not. They think you're a bad influence."

"Shit, Heather, I don't want to hear about Joanne! I was talking!" *How a marriage works!*

Heather shakes her head. "I don't get it, Mom. I know you're trying to tell me something, but what? Why don't you just come out and say it? And then can we go?"

Joy clasps her hand against her chest. "I just want you to understand that I've had my turn too. As a girl. That's not even talking about the rest of my life. My husbands—"

"Mom—"

Joy takes a long drink. The cold makes her head pound. She stares out the window at the cars on the highway. She wonders why it wouldn't work to make highways into big conveyor belts. Why does everybody need to buy gas? It'd be great: You'd just get on, and then you could read or sleep, like on a bus, but not with smelly strangers beside you.

"Mom—"

Joy breathes deeply. It's important, she thinks. She can't remember why. "We were strangers," she says.

"Well, sure."

"His name was Lloyd. He had two kids, a boy and a girl, maybe ten and twelve? Everybody sort of hopped to. You could tell he was a military man, you know? Everything was so damned tidy. Everybody had their chores. The table got set a certain way, and cleared. But it was a nice house. They had a swimming pool. The kids would get up in the morning and right away go out to swim. I can't remember their names. I haven't thought of it in so long. Can you believe that? They were okay; they must have thought it was really strange, but they didn't say anything. During the day some of their friends came over and they just said, 'This is Joy,' and nobody talked to me. I guess that was better than 'Hi, this is my dad's kid from a long time ago'; that would have been great. The first night, Lloyd sat down with me on the couch. I don't know where the others had gone. He told me this was how my mother had wanted it, she wanted to go and forget all about him; she took me away, he said. He didn't sound sorry, he was just explaining. And then he started in on this long speech about how everything ought to be. Stuff like studying hard and keeping your room neat and being polite; it was bizarre, all this shit about being *good*. He said he was glad he had this opportunity to give me some advice. You could tell he thought Mother would never get around to it."

"He sounds like Daddy," Heather says wearily.

"I got sunburned. I was there three days. I spent all day at the pool. I thought I'd die till I got to leave. At first I'd catch them looking at me, trying to figure it out, I guess, and then, by the third day, it was like I was invisible. Like I wasn't there. I was odd, but there wasn't anything special about me. I went home on the bus, and Daddy didn't ask about it, and Mother didn't either; it was like I was getting off a *school bus*. I don't think it was ever mentioned, except once I told Granny about it, and she said, 'I don't know what your mother was thinking.' " Joy tries to laugh; there's a joke in this. "I probably got my boobs from his side of the family. Mom's flat, Clancy's flat. From Lloyd I got *pectorals*. I never saw his mother, of course. I'm just guessing."

She wipes her cheeks with the back of her hand and looks at Heather, who is leaning forward against the dashboard. "Sit up," she says. "We better go."

That was my visit with my daddy, she thinks, but doesn't say. His kids have probably been to college and made something of themselves. She's probably turned out just like he'd have expected.

"I don't believe it," Heather says. "I just do *not* believe it." She is chewing on ice, making awful cracking noises.

"It happened just that way." Suddenly it doesn't seem all that important. Telling Heather has sent the memory up like vapor. It doesn't matter anymore.

"You didn't even *try* to like them? I could have had a grandfather with a *swimming pool,* and you couldn't get *along* with him?"

Joy presses the accelerator. Her hand is killing her. Her head hurts. All she wants is to get back to Lubbock and out of this car. "The only person more hateful than you, Heather Ronnander," she says, "is your daddy. And he's your *real* daddy, I promise."

"What about your mother?" Heather asks sullenly.

"Her too!" Joy shouts.

When they arrive home, Clancy is in the living room, reading a magazine with Elizabeth Taylor on the front. "You look awful," she tells Joy. Heather stomps past to her room.

Joy plops onto the couch. "I did something to my hand," she says. "It's killing me." She holds it out for Clancy to see. The little finger has swollen to the size of a hot dog; the side of her hand is a deep blue color.

"God, Joy, I think you've broken it; what did you do?"

Joy starts laughing. "I tried to smack someone and I missed." Then she starts crying.

Clancy takes Joy to the emergency room, where her broken finger is splinted and she is given a wonderful shot of something. By the time she gets home, she feels fine. She feels as if she is floating. She doesn't even care that she has fucked up her first word processing job. She hates the manuscript, which is all about making money by second-guessing everybody else who is trying to make money. She hates the professor, who gets a fat salary at the college and still has time to write books. She hates Lloyd, who never wrote or called to find out if she was dead or alive, and Wayne, who would probably have a preference about that. Oddly, she finds she doesn't hate Joanne. She doesn't know

Joanne. Joanne will pay plenty for marrying Wayne Ronnander without Joy hating her.

"I should go get us something to eat," Clancy says.

Heather, who has appeared at the sound of their return,
says dramatically, "I'm starving. I'd die for barbecue." She
looks at her mother, gauging the weather.

Joy feels pleasantly high. "She'd die for barbecue," she
says, and smiles at her daughter.

In a booth at a café, eating baby-back ribs in hot sauce,
Joy feels happy for the first time in days. Her finger hurts,
but the pain is muted and far away. "I could tell you
more," she says to Heather airily. She has nothing partic-
ular in mind at the moment.

Heather licks her greasy fingers and says, "So Thatch
isn't really my grandfather." She has been thinking it over.

Clancy looks at Joy quizzically.

"It's okay," Joy says pleasantly. "I'm sure he never thinks
of it." She slides her beer over to Heather, who always
wants to take sips. "Nobody's watching," she says affec-
tionately. She considers topics for further discussion, something besides her mother and Wayne. There doesn't seem
to be anything else to talk about. It's not quite time yet to
talk about sex.

25

To bring the new trailer into the backyard from the alley, Russell has to dismantle half the fence. He works on the fence all one Sunday morning, whistling and hopping around. Opal keeps looking through the window to see what he's doing.

She says, "I wonder if it's legal to open up to the alley like that." She is making an apple pie. Right now she's peeling apples on a contraption that screws onto her countertop. She bought it on Saturday, when she went out to see how Joy was doing at the flea market. She was so excited, finding it, the pie was really just a demonstration of its utility. She can't stand to peel apples by hand anymore; it hurts her thumb too much.

"Why would anybody care?" Clancy says lazily. She is making her way through a stack of brochures and fliers from the college, showing no expression, making no comment at all. She flips pages but doesn't really look at them.

At first, when Clancy mentioned the idea of being a nurse, Opal was horrified. She said, "Haven't you been listening all these years?" and Clancy went off to pout in her room. But the more Opal thinks about it, the more it makes sense. There's always a nurse shortage. Nursing is better than working in a bank, and nurses make friends with one another. Clancy could use some friends. Opal went to the college to ask about the program, and they told her a new graduate willing to work the off-hour shifts could make thirty thousand a year right away.

Why *she* never went back and got a nursing degree, she doesn't know. All the years in doctors' offices, she did a nurse's work for a lot less pay. Of course, she had a family; she had responsibilities. She couldn't let everything drop while she got an education. Clancy has the whole world open to her.

"What do you think?" she asks Clancy, who barely manages to lift one page and put down another. You'd think she had weights tied to her wrists.

"Of what?"

"Of nursing, honey."

"Oh, Mother."

" 'Oh, *Mother*' thought you were so interested—"

"Thanks for getting all this," Clancy says without fervor, hardly a real reply. She shoves the literature away from her and props her elbows up on the table, resting her chin on her fists. "Did you know that Elizabeth Taylor has lost three hundred pounds in the last ten years?" she says. "Or six hundred; I forget."

Russell opens the patio door and says, "I'm going to get it right now!"

"Be *careful,*" Opal urges. She had nothing to say about the trailer; it was all Russell's idea, although she can tell she is supposed to be excited. She hasn't seen the trailer, and doesn't even want to. What she wants is to get Clancy interested in something. Employment, education, and love: If you don't have children, that's the menu. Clancy has a dull job where she can't wear pants even if they look like Nancy Reagan's; she's got maybe one semester of college credits; she's got herself hooked up with another funny man who'll probably turn out to be unreliable.

For Opal's money, education would be the best bet. And if Clancy does go to nursing school, it probably *will* be Opal's money.

"Choc-o-late," Clancy calls. The cat has slithered along the periphery of the living room, as if the center of the room is mined. Now she hugs the corner by the laundry room, looking at Clancy. "Choc-o-late," Clancy calls again, and the cat takes the long route, along the wall and to the end of the table, by Clancy's feet. Clancy scoops the cat up and moves away from the table. "We're going for a walk," she says. She takes the cat to her room, puts her in the towel-lined box, and carries her out the back door. "Don't worry, I've got you," Opal hears her say; for a moment she watches her walking in the yard, talking to the cat. They disappear around a corner.

"Dear God in heaven, what did it *cost*?" Opal says after Russell has backed the trailer into the yard. "How are we paying for it?"

"Don't you worry." Russell is so pleased with himself, he looks likely to pop the snaps on his Western shirt.

"It's as big as a house," she says.

"Twenty-four feet. Bed, bath, dinette, galley, sofa. And that's a *double* bed. Home away from home," Russell says. "Come on." He opens the door and pulls her inside. "Look at that!"

Inside, the trailer is decorated in beige and navy. "It's so clean," she murmurs.

"It's new, darlin'."

She slides onto the dinette seat and pats the cushion. Russell sits beside her, bumping her hip to move over and make room.

"Like it?" he says.

On the wall, just above her shoulder, hangs a small fire extinguisher. "Look at that," she says. "They think of everything."

"See! I knew you'd love it!" Russell says. He gives her cheek a wet, loud kiss.

"Wow, it's great," Clancy says from the door. Her arms are wrapped around the box in which Chocolate rides like a cat princess, peering over the edge. "You could *live* in here."

"That's the idea!" Russell says, and laughs.

The cat meows. Clancy grins. "She'll have to get used to it."

As soon as Clancy is gone, Russell whispers, "No cats. No kids. Just you and me." He gets up, tugs her arm. "Come on in here."

In here is a double bed with a quilted bedspread. Russell sits down and crooks his finger and grins. Opal sits down beside him. Her chest feels fluttery, her head light. She lays her hand on Russell's thigh. When Russell leans over to kiss her, she is surprised by the nice smell of peppermint on his breath.

"You'll be lots more comfortable now," she says.

"I can work anywhere in the U.S. of A."

"Mineral Wells," she says. "When do you start?"

"The end of the month. And then maybe Utah, or Nevada."

She tugs at his shirt and two snaps pop open. She lays her hand there.

It's just like a nice motel in here.

He puts his arm around her. "Both of us, Opal Duffy. Didn't I have the right idea?"

The flutter in her chest, she decides, is actually quite nice. Why not Mineral Wells? Utah. Nevada. A house so small and compact and new has to be easy to live in. She won't feel guilty when he's gone, and she can visit him.

"The girls will take care of things here when we're gone," he says, pulling her down on the bed. "And we can leave our bedroom door open no matter *what* we're up to."

"Not now, though," Opal says. She wants to see Clancy starting school, Joy in a new job. Nobody eats when she's away.

"Well, no," Russell laughs, and closes the door with his foot. "This is too close to home to not close the door when we're doing what we're going to be doing right now."

26

Joy and Heather are minding
the Sno-Cone Kart at the Lubbock Old-Tyme Flea Market,
held in a defunct double-screen outdoor movie lot. Their
T-shirts say ICE IS NICE in cherry-red letters outlined in
purple, and their short shorts and socks are red, too.
Heather's shirt is a man's large, and it hangs so long that
when her arms are down, you can't see her shorts; but all
the time she is working, her arms are up as she scoops balls
of ice and squirts flavoring on hundreds and hundreds of
cones on this hot September Saturday. Joy's T-shirt is a
woman's medium, and it fits snugly across her bosom. At
the waist, she wears a tooled leather belt with a silver
buckle. Both of them wear dirty white running shoes with
fat soles.

All the vendors at the flea market know one another,
and during the weekend, Joy and Heather trade snow cones
for lunch (hot dogs) and drinks (they drink Coke con-
stantly as they work). Many of the customers are regulars
who come week after week, scouting for bargains, engag-
ing in endless haggles over prices, and, Heather thinks,
killing time when they have nothing else to do. In this
weather, everybody buys snow cones.

The sad truth is, she wouldn't have much else to do,
herself, if she didn't work, and although she complains,
especially about having to be at the market by ten in the
morning, the day goes by fast enough, and she gets to keep

twenty dollars a weekend to spend as she likes. She is amassing a substantial tape collection, which now includes just about every heavy metal band she's heard of, several of the new, folksy female singers, and tapes of all the Beatles albums. When it is her turn for a break, she puts on her earphones, takes a scoop of ice to chew, and listens to The Maggots while she sits on a bench under the awning by the hot-dog stand.

She returns from twenty minutes of hanging out, and Joy says, "If you can't keep track of time, maybe you better not go anywhere on your break." Heather hasn't taken off her earphones yet and she acts like she didn't hear what her mother said, although she's turned the music off. She smiles, flaps her T-shirt in front of her belly, and puts her earphones away in her yellow Gap bag.

"How hot do you think it is?" she asks Joy.

"Low nineties, I heard on the radio while ago."

"At school yesterday, everybody had soaked cloths or paper towels to put on their heads in class. The teachers didn't even tell us to put them away. If they want us to learn anything, why don't they get air-conditioning?"

Joy doesn't have time to answer. A man and woman with four little kids come to the cart clamoring for snow cones. Heather scoops up the cones while Joy tries to sort out what the flavors will be. As soon as a grape cone is handed down to the littlest child—a boy wearing an orange undershirt-style shirt with huge armholes, and tiny dotted boxer shorts—he drops it and begins squalling. Before they have to ask, Heather has already made another in a double paper cone. Instead of handing it over, she walks around the cart and kneels in front of the little boy. "Shh," she says. "You don't need to bawl, look, here's a new one." Instantly the child is silent, although his mouth hangs open.

He stares at Heather for a long moment, then takes the cone and turns toward his mother's bare leg, smashing ice against her; purple juice runs down from her knee to her ankle. She says, "Well, shit," not too angrily.

"Don't I wish I'd had six?" Joy says sarcastically when the family moves away.

"Maybe they wouldn't all have been as much trouble as me," Heather says in a similar tone. Joy reaches over and squeezes her above the elbow. "Silly," she says.

"Wouldn't you rather have a beer?" somebody says. Heather sees it's the man from four aisles over; he sells used vacuum cleaners and some kind of wooden carvings. He has eaten at least four snow cones today, hanging around sucking ice and making pointless comments about the weather.

"They won't let me," she says, knowing she's being silly. He laughs more or less nicely, like he's being friendly. She knows it's all a show for her mother, who can't possibly like a man who isn't any bigger than she is and wears a mustache.

"I can't leave," Joy says. She has a *busy* expression, her lips pursed slightly, her chin high.

"I could bring you one."

"Oh, go on," Heather says impatiently. The last thing she wants is to listen to this vacuum-cleaner cowboy flirting with her mother. She cannot imagine what grown-ups talk about, what *anybody* talks about. She truly wonders if there are people who talk like characters on TV, back and forth, with everybody getting something in. The only person she ever talks to is her mother, and you couldn't call what they do *conversations*.

It's nearly six, and the traffic has thinned out. Everyone is sticky and miserable in the heat, and lots of tables are already being packed away. "And then can we *go?*" she whines.

Joy shrugs and wipes her hands on a towel and moves on with the man. She doesn't look especially enthusiastic, more like she's going out to empty the trash. Heather starts cleaning up. She is hoping her mother will take her to a movie tonight. It's embarrassing to spend every Saturday night with your mother, but if that's all there is, at least she'd like to see a movie.

"I practically lived on those last summer," a girl says. Heather glances up and recognizes her from school. You couldn't miss her. She is the color of toffee, with hair of similar hue, done up in four-inch-long dreadlocks. If it weren't for the hair, she'd be pretty; she has the full lips and straight, thick eyebrows of famous models, and long legs and arms. But the hair is unbelievable. It's like a cross between rope and the stuffing of an old chair. Heather heard somebody in the cafeteria at school call her "maltomeal" once. She's always by herself, and she's always wearing something unusual. Today it's boxer shorts—a bigger version of what the crying boy was wearing—and a T-shirt that says BRONX ZOO and is cut off at her midriff. Her sandals have long laces that tie up on the ankle.

"So, do you want one?" Heather asks, and thinks she sounds snotty. To make up for it, she adds, "For free, I mean. I'm putting it all away."

"What kinds are there?" the girl says, pointing to the jars of syrup.

"Cherry, grape, lime."

"Oh. I used to get them every day in Central Park, right near the Met. They had papaya and kiwi and tangerine."

"I don't think that'd go over here," Heather says. The girl has some kind of accent. Wherever Central Park is.

"Give me a little squirt of each, if that's okay."

"Sure." Heather hands the girl a cone and makes herself a little cherry one. "Central Park. Is that San Francisco?"

"Manhattan." She slurps the cone loudly.

"Oh, sure." Heather has never been anywhere.

"Thanks a lot." She stands there watching while Heather wipes the jars and cart. In a few minutes she says, "My name is Jamaica. I've seen you at school. I'm a sophomore."

"Yeah, me too. I'm a sophomore. Heather."

"Well, see you—"

"Hey," Heather says. "Are you living here now? I mean, to stay?" Jamaica, she knows, is still another place she doesn't know anything about, not even where it is. She tries to imagine being named "Lubbock" or "Texas."

Jamaica shrugs. "Looks like." She smiles and walks away. Over her shoulder she waves her hand in a funny gesture, fingers together and folding over the palm, like she is working a puppet.

Joy returns and tells Heather, "That was Otis. We're going to go out after while; let's get this stuff put away." She doesn't really look at Heather, which makes Heather suspicious about what they did or said while having a beer. Is there something Heather might guess if she studied her mother's face? Is there something she isn't supposed to know? Or is her mother just embarrassed to be going out with the first man who comes along and buys four snow cones? She would love to ask her mother what men and women talk about, what they do with one another. She can hardly remember when they lived with Wayne. Mick was secretive and silly. And Opal and Russell don't really count; they're *old.*

"Do you *like* him?" she asks, as if it isn't possible.

"Heather, I hardly know him, do I? We're just going *out* and maybe have a little *fun*."

"And he'll be your boyfriend?"

Annoyed, Joy says, "Not *likely*."

"So why go out with him! If you don't really like him, why bother?"

Joy sighs. "I'll tell you when *you're* forty, Heather."

"I wanted to go to a movie," Heather complains, although she knows she's lost. She hopes when she's forty, she'll be better off than her mother is, but it's hard to imagine what's ahead for her. "I haven't got anything to *do*."

"Ask Clancy. Ask one of your friends. I didn't say I would." Joy is talking briskly while she's *doing* things; it's exactly what Opal does all the time, like this morning, when Heather was looking for her T-shirt in the laundry room, and Opal says from the kitchen, where she's making pancakes for Russell, "I put a big pile of clothes that have been in there for days on your bed, Heather Lee; don't you look?" and sure enough they were at the foot of the bed, practically on top of her all night, but she hadn't noticed.

She scowls. She can't think of one single person who would go anywhere with her, and her mother knows she doesn't have any friends. She's told her what it's like at Lubbock High, that she feels invisible around sticky masses of kids who already know each other and aren't interested in anyone new. "Don't bother about me," she says. "Don't think twice." She can see it isn't any use to say that; the way her mother is tossing her hair and sticking out her chest, you can tell it isn't Heather she's thinking about. She wants to say something else, though. What she does say is, "I wish Kay Lynn would get some new flavors. In New

York they have kiwi." Joy isn't paying attention; she doesn't say a word.

Joy is going out, and everybody else, except Russell, is in a bad mood. Opal says her thumb is killing her and she can't make supper, but when Russell says they could all go out, she gives him a look and goes to lie down. Clancy is in her room, the door closed. The awareness that a long night stretches ahead in this house brings tears to Heather's eyes. Then Russell says, "I guess it's just us young'uns have the energy to get around, huh, Heather?" and, stupid as he sounds, he's the only thing going on tonight. Together they go to the video store and check out *Batman,* which they've already seen at least three times, but which Russell dearly loves, and then they pick up fried chicken for everybody, whether they're hungry or not.

Heather would like to think life will get better when she is older, but she doesn't think it's better for her mother, or Clancy, or Opal, either. She doesn't see how you can live whole lives as bad as theirs.

Opal surveys the dance floor. Couples bob and twirl around in a shuffling circle, the men solemn and dandy, the women girlish and giddy. Her party has been at the Hi-Lo Western Dance Club for a quarter of an hour or so, but so far nobody has danced. First there was all the settling-in to do, choosing seats and arranging legs under and elbows on the table, then drinks to order and taste and remark upon. Now they're all gazing out on the dancers, as if some unspoken question were being answered in the pattern of their steady course around the floor.

She wonders what this is costing. Russell is as ever the big spender. A third wedding anniversary is not such a big thing, unless, of course, you're afraid one of you won't live for a fourth. Will she make it another year? Opal wonders. She has done well enough, although her medicine makes her burp and she sometimes feels herself palpitating, and her thumb and her knees just about kill her, and she's going to have to get new glasses.

Russell bought fancy outfits for Opal, Joy, and Clancy, and ostrich-skin boots for himself. Opal is wearing a white blouse with a red kerchief, a denim skirt with white leather fringe, white boots that pinch her toes, and a silver-and-turquoise link belt that must have been a pretty penny. It's hard to enjoy a pretty belt when you're nearly as big around as you are tall. The girls are cute, Clancy in a skirt and blouse with a fringed shawl tied at the hips, and Joy in a short flared skirt with matching panties, like a cheerleader. Russell's mother, sitting on his other side, wears a Western-style dress with ruffles around the neck and wrists and at three seams of tiers. She looks like a calico cake.

Russell is pleased as he can be, Mr. King of the Road. He sits with one thumb tucked in his belt, his fingers patting his belly. He leans over and whispers, "Three years, hon." She smiles and nods. She can't decide if it's been fast or slow, three years. It's *been,* that's all.

They're all grinning at one another. Travis leans close against Clancy, touching her hand and wrist, flicking a speck of something off the napkin on which her drink sits. Otis, one of God's small men, leans back in his chair, his drink held with both hands, looking happy. Clancy has her usual deadpan expression. Joy stares into her glass. Imogene, like her son, is going to have a good time. Who knows when she last went anywhere, except to the nursing home to visit poor Papa Duffy, or Furr's Cafeteria for supper, or Russell's house? She says loudly, "I thought Buddy and Leeanne were acomin'."

"They'll get here," Russell says heartily. "I bet they're practicing, what do you think?" he asks Opal. She smiles, the easiest thing to do since she has no idea if he is joking. Opal catches Clancy's eye, and fights the urge to ask her what's wrong. Clancy's face is drawn, her shoulders hunched. She pays no attention whatsoever to Travis's constant ministrations. Spying her mother, she does smile wanly.

"I reckon this calls for a toast," Otis says, holding up his glass. Travis lifts his glass next, and the others raggedly follow suit. Otis says, "To love at any age," which could be a nice thing to say or could be sarcastic; how can Opal tell, since he is a complete stranger? She doesn't know what to make of a man who carves faces out of pine knots. He does act good-natured.

Travis says, "Every age," and kisses the air beside Clancy's cheek. Clancy rolls her eyes at Joy, who mimics the gesture. Joy, however, joins the toast. "To love," she says.

"Well, then, drink up!" Russell shoves his glass into the air in front of him, clinking nobody's, and then takes a long gulp. Imogene, beside him, looks stunned. Opal reaches across Russell to pat Imogene's hand. The idea of love now, with a husband who no longer knows what season it is, must be a sad one. Imogene beams and clasps Opal's hand on top of her own for a moment. "Darlin'," she whispers.

It is a great relief when Travis says, "Didn't we come to *dance*?" and urges a reluctant Clancy to her feet. He's a good-looking boy; Clancy could act nicer.

Opal's not on the floor with Russell two minutes until her intestines are acting up. He holds his arm up high above her head, so that she has to reach for his hand, and then he gives her a twist, as if she's a lariat instead of a woman nearly sixty years old. "I *can't*," she pants, and walks right back to the table.

"Aw, Opal, honey," Russell pleads behind her. "Didn't we come here to dance, like Travis said?"

"Dance with your mother," she says. It's a good idea. Imogene looks bright and sassy as soon as Russell beckons her, and Opal, in relief, sinks onto her chair, one hand on her lower abdomen. She digs in her purse for an Equalactin tablet.

Travis is whispering in Clancy's ear while she stares at

her glass. She pulls away from him, and he leans back, shaking his head. In a moment he gets up and goes to the bar for another drink. He offers Opal a refill, too, but she's hardly touched her CC and water, which Russell got her because it's what he drinks. What she would like is a 7UP.

Joy's Otis is turning out to be a good dancer. He does a fast bit of stepping all his own. He's quite light on his feet. His elbows fly out from his body, like a bird's wings. Other dancers stop to watch and clap. He beckons Joy, who, not knowing the steps he is doing, stands in place and jiggles, like what you'd do to a rock 'n' roll song. When the music stops, he gives her a hug. They stand at the side against a railing, watching the far wall, where a dozen large screens show videos of the performers whose music is playing, and also of bucking bulls and cowboys, mountains and plains, pretty girls on corral fences. Watching them, Opal thinks Joy's chest is probably bigger than Otis's. He did bring them an anniversary present, though, the only one they got besides Imogene's old iron skillet she knew Opal admired. It was a carving, eight inches long, a man's and woman's faces whittled out of raw dried wood, the eyeholes surrounded by ridges, the man's mouth covered by a bark mustache. Opal didn't know what to say; you couldn't call it pretty. She said, "It must have taken a long time to do this."

Buddy and Leeanne arrive, dressed in matching red checked shirts, like pizza waiters. They head straight for the dancing, where Buddy waddles and twirls Leeanne with gusto, a display of talent Opal didn't know he had.

"Come on, Opal," Travis says. "Clancy's not in the mood; you better dance with me before I bust a gut." The music has changed to something a little slower, one of

those he-left-me-to-cry songs that allow a little hug dancing. Opal looks to Clancy, who arches an eyebrow, shrugs,
and waves her on.

"Why, sure," she says. He's a tall, sturdy man, with a
firm hand. He makes dancing an easier thing than with
Russell; Opal finds she enjoys it, now that her bowels have
settled down. "Clancy's not always in a bad mood," she
says, although the truth of that could be argued.

"She's sure in one tonight," Travis says. He pulls back,
to look better into Opal's face. "It's not anything I did, you
know."

She nods, but suspects that it is.

"I went to the races last weekend with some buddies.
She didn't want to go. She said, 'You go on,' like she meant
it. Do you think it made her mad?" he says.

"She didn't say a word about it," Opal says. "Maybe it's
something at work." Travis doesn't seem to distinguish
between *mad* and *sad,* fine points he may want to understand if he is going to keep on seeing Clancy.

"Yeah, I didn't think of that." Apparently mollified, he
pulls Opal closer. She can feel, but not hear, her stomach
growling. "She's real sour on getting married," he says, like
an afterthought.

Surprised, Opal says, "You asked her?"

"Not exactly. I mean, she told me all these times how it
doesn't work for her. She says she never keeps up. What do
you think she means? I'd get the place fixed up, you know.
Somebody could come in to clean."

Opal is dying to get home and talk to Clancy. She had no
idea Travis was a serious suitor. She thought he was unreliable, silly, from things Clancy has said. She thought he
had other girlfriends. You wonder about a man thirty-

something years old and still a bachelor, getting all he needs without marriage.

"Give her a little time, Travis," Opal advises. "And be real nice." There are a hundred things about Clancy she'd like to tell him, but she's made that mistake before and wished she hadn't. Clancy's husbands seemed to be challenged by her sad demeanor; they didn't realize it wasn't something she could toss off like a discarded blouse.

At the song's end, Travis gives Opal a little whirl, then catches her at the waist. "Put in a good word for me, why don't you?" he says.

When they get back to the table, Clancy is gone. Joy and Otis have come for a drink between songs, and Joy says she thinks Clancy went to the bathroom.

Russell says, "Come on, now, Opal, it's our party!" but she brushes by.

"In a minute," she says.

Clancy is in the bathroom, leaning against the wall by the sinks, her face on the cool tile. She's pale. When she sees Opal she looks up and says, "I want to go home, Mama." Opal leads her back outside.

Everyone except Travis is dancing. "I'll tell Russell I'm taking the car," she says, but Travis interrupts.

"I'll take her." He's rubbing Clancy's shoulder like she's come in from a cold day. He looks worried and perplexed, like you do when a pet is sick and can't tell you how it feels.

"Mama," Clancy whimpers. This is her little-girl word, a sign of shakiness.

"I'm coming," Opal says.

"I'm driving," Travis insists.

Russell and his mother are on the dance floor. From

behind, Opal taps him on the shoulder. "Why, sure!" he says, whirling around, ready to change partners.

He is astonished when Opal says she's going. "Leaving!" he bleats. "You can't do that!"

"Clancy's sick, Russell; I couldn't stay here now."

"We haven't been here an hour!"

"So stay and have a good time. Dance with Joy and Leeanne and your mother."

Russell grabs Opal's shoulders. "You going to Mineral Wells with me, Opal Duffy? I want to know right now."

The easiest way is to agree. "I'll go," she says. She figures, sooner or later, she will. She can drive there in a day. "But right now, I'm going home."

As soon as they are in the door, Clancy heads for the bathroom. Opal lingers in the hall, listening to her gag. It's the dry heaves; Clancy hasn't eaten all day. When Clancy's quiet and doesn't come out, Opal goes in. Clancy is sitting on the side of the tub. Opal wets two washcloths, one hot and one cold, and presses one then the other against Clancy's forehead. "Are you coming down with something?" she asks her. Clancy rolls her head and sways. Opal drops the cloth and grabs her. "What've you *got?*" she asks.

Clancy gets up and goes to her room without answering. Opal stands outside her closed door, trying to decide what to do. She decides that by the time she has a cup of tea or something, Clancy will have settled down, and she can take her temperature.

Travis is standing in the kitchen. "What is it?" he asks as soon as he sees Opal.

"I didn't know you were still here." Actually, she quite forgot about him.

"Should we take her somewhere?"

"I don't think she's that sick, Travis. Sit down, I'll make coffee."

Travis is too anxious to sit. "I'll go on home," he says, "but I'll call in the morning, hear?"

Right after, as she hears his truck drive off, Clancy comes out of the bedroom and wanders into the kitchen and sits at the table. "Sorry to be so much trouble," she says.

"Are you okay?" Opal asks.

"Mother, sit down."

Opal sits. She chews on one knuckle. She thinks maybe Clancy feels better, calling her "Mother" again.

"Why did you and Daddy divorce?"

"What in the world?" Opal slaps her hands palm down on the table.

"You've never talked to me about it. I just want to know. Did he do something?"

Opal sighs. "It's all so long ago. It all happened before I had time to realize what was happening."

"You didn't love each other? Did you ever?"

"Oh, yes, we loved each other. I think—no, I'm sure—we were happy at first. Partly, it was his job; he was always gone. When one of you girls was sick, he was never there to help. It seemed like he was always coming in in the middle of the night. I got used to not having him around, and then I minded when he was."

Clancy looks close to tears. Opal feels such a wave of nostalgia for Thatch and her babies. "It just happens," she says gently, patting Clancy's hand. She doesn't want so much from a husband anymore. She doesn't expect a daily miracle.

"He never told me he was sorry. I just came home, and he was gone," Clancy says.

"He was sorry, all right. We were both sorry. But you

don't know what to say to kids. You don't know what's happened yourself, and by the time you figure it out, it's done and you want to put it behind you. They didn't have books then, you know, to tell you what to say and how to act. You just got divorced."

"I don't think I loved Jeeter, but I liked him."

"He was a funny boy."

"I hate Travis's dogs."

"Maybe he'd give them away. He could put them on his parents' place."

"Why would he want big old mean dogs like that?" Clancy doesn't wait for an answer. She wanders back to her room. Opal fixes a bowl of Rice Krispies with a cut-up banana. While she's eating, Clancy goes out onto the porch, carrying the cat.

Russell calls. "Should I come on home?"

"We're fine."

"Mama's having a good time, and Joy and Otis, and Leeanne and Bones. It's not right with you gone, though."

"You stay, Russell. We can go another time. We can go next year." She is thinking about whether to tell Clancy what Travis said.

Outside, the cat is on Clancy's lap, its head tucked under her arm. Opal sits down beside Clancy and strokes the cat's back. "Look at that," she says. "She's out of her box."

Clancy sets the cat down on the step below her. The cat stands perfectly still for a moment, then leaps back onto Clancy's lap. "Miaow!" she scolds.

Clancy and Opal laugh.

"I don't want you to try to tell me what to do," Clancy says. "I want to make up my own mind."

"About what, sugar? About Travis?" She wants to blurt

out, *Go on and try again,* but how does she know it's a good thing? Has Clancy learned anything after two mistakes? Like, whose mistakes they were?

Clancy swallows, then speaks. "No, not about Travis. About this baby," she says. "It's for me to decide."

Opal waits until Russell is undressed and in bed to tell him about Clancy. He is fit to be tied when he hears the news. "A baby. Feature that!"

"What are *you* so excited about?" she asks petulantly. He doesn't act the least bit worried; does he think having babies is *easy*?

He's confused. "A baby'd be real nice. Travis is a nice boy."

"Oh, and Mick Jasonbee was a nice boy, and where is he?"

"Won't Travis want to get married?"

"I don't know, Russell! Travis can't have this baby for her. I know *that*."

"Neither can you." It's starting to dawn on Russell where this dialogue is going. "Hell's bells, Opal, let her have her baby, she don't need you for that. It's more Travis's business than yours, the way I see it."

"She's not big enough to carry a baby. She doesn't eat right. She had polio when she was four! She doesn't sleep right."

"So you're going to dog her every step? Spoon mush in her mouth? Forget about *your* being married?"

"I'm going to be here when she needs me," Opal says stubbornly. She really did expect Russell to understand. "I'm not the least bit sure Travis will be any help. I'm not sure Clancy wants his help."

"It's his baby, ain't it!"

"And she's mine."

Lines drawn, they glare at each other, then turn away and fall back on their pillows. Opal remembers she hasn't creamed her face, and starts out of bed. Russell grabs her by the elbow. "Opal, I want you with me."

"In Mineral Wells?" she says derisively.

"Wherever I'm living, working to support us both."

"I didn't tell you you had to go off on a pipeline!"

"It was time. You know it was. And now it's time for us to start being married by ourselves."

She jerks her arm away and rubs her elbow. "I can't," she says.

"Listen here. I know you've been hurt a bunch of times, sweetheart. I know that. Your first marriage, and your mama—I know it's been hard. But nobody's leaving you this time. What's happening is, you're running me off."

Opal climbs out of bed. "Oh, pooh," she says, and carries her cream back to bed. "I'll come see you every month," she says lightly.

Russell jumps up and grabs his pillow and blanket off the bed. He takes a couple steps toward the door, then turns around, trailing blanket. "I ain't talking about Mineral Wells, Opal. You don't want to live with me in my new trailer, I'm going a whole lot further'n Mineral Wells."

Opal slathers cream on her forehead. "You never been further'n New Mexico, Russell Duffy."

"Well, you just watch, and wave good-bye. I've had enough of not counting around here. You stay here and have Clancy's baby with her, girl. *I'm* going to Africa."

28

Joy was disappointed when she first saw where Otis lived. It helped to learn he owns it—the store downstairs (vacuum cleaners, small appliances), the apartment upstairs. There's a large studio with a kitchen, and only the bath is separate. He keeps the place tidy. He has built nice cupboards and cabinets and bookshelves, where he displays his carvings and a photograph of him with his wife, Linda, dead years ago of breast cancer. In one corner, by a window, he has set up his shop table and tools. He sits there every night, whittling. His brother sends him pine knots from Wyoming. He started carving after Linda died, to keep from going crazy. Now it's habit; he wouldn't know how to pass a day without picking up his knife.

Joy wouldn't want a photograph of someone dead, if it was someone you loved. The first time they had sex, she looked across the room and saw that picture. She imagined Linda watching Otis climb on top of her. She asked him, "How did you get over it? How do you forget?" He said it was like remembering when you were a child or a teenager, remembering when you lived in another house. It's over, but it's worth remembering. He was only thirty when Linda died. He said he loved her, but he is another man now. He has less hair and more patience; he expects different things out of life. She probably should have asked him what things, but she didn't want to know just yet, so she said,

"Well, if it doesn't bother you, it doesn't bother me." He doesn't seem to want to know about her husbands. She certainly doesn't have pictures of them sitting around anywhere.

"That smells good," she tells him, looking over his shoulder at Stroganoff cooking in a stainless-steel pot. He dips his spoon in, blows on it, and offers her a bite.

"Mmm," she says. She's glad he didn't use mushrooms. Generally speaking, she doesn't like fancy food.

Heather is across the room, sitting close to the TV. She has MTV on. Twice Joy has had to tell her to turn it down; now it's so low it can be heard only faintly from where Joy stands. If she told her to turn it down again, she bets Heather would sit with her nose against the screen, watching silent images out of spite. To Heather, it's boring here; almost everything is boring to Heather. Joy doesn't know why she brought her, except that it was Otis's idea. He said, "I'd like to get to know her." Now he's had his introduction. She barely managed to say hello, took a Coke without a thank you, and then turned MTV on as if they were all deaf.

"You can set plates out," Otis says. He's checking the rice. He points at the cabinet above the sink.

Joy takes out three stoneware plates, yellow, pink, and aqua, and finds forks in the drawer below. She calls Heather to eat.

Heather slumps in a chair as though she's just finished a long day's ironing. "Sit up," Joy says. Heather scoots her bottom back against the chair.

"Let's serve from the stove," Otis says. "Do you mind? The table's not so big."

Heather sighs. "I'll get yours," Joy says. "Don't get up."

When she sets a plate in front of her daughter, she has an instant when she imagines sliding it right off onto her lap. This sulkiness is deliberate sabotage. It would kill her to be nice.

"What is this?" Heather turns over a chunk of beef with the look of someone examining an insect.

"It's sliced steak," Joy says.

"Eye of round," Otis says.

"What's this *pink* stuff?" Heather moves the food around on her plate, her fork turned over.

"Tomato juice and sour cream," Otis says. He takes a big mouthful, and Joy self-consciously takes a small bite.

"I'll just watch TV," Heather says.

Otis puts his fork down. "I got a video for us. You could start it if you want."

Heather flops on the couch. "You don't have a thingie for the TV channels?"

Joy is avoiding Otis's eyes. He says, "It's an old TV."

"What movie?" Heather asks.

"*Coal Miner's Daughter.*" He gets up and shows her how to work the VCR.

"Are we going to stay long enough to watch a *whole movie?*" Heather asks.

Joy licks a grain of rice off her lip and throws her fork onto the table. "That's enough, Heather Lee!" she snaps.

Otis puts his hand on hers. She jerks it away. Slowly, deliberately, he takes another bite of food. Heather punches on the movie and it starts with a blast of Loretta Lynn's drawling voice.

"Turn it down," Joy says.

Heather ignores her.

Joy gets up and turns the TV off. "Maybe you'd like to wait for me in the car?"

"How long will it *take* you?" Heather says sarcastically. Anyone can tell what she means.

Joy turns around to look at Otis. Otis is sitting staring into his plate, his hands flat on the table.

"I like it better when they come to our house," Heather says slyly, and Joy slaps her.

Otis jumps up, but then just stands there.

Heather cries, "All I wanted to do was watch TV!"

Otis mumbles something and leaves the room. Joy hears him banging down the stairs.

"Why do you act like that?" Joy shouts.

Heather says, "He's *weird*."

"There is nothing weird about him, except that he's nice. Can't I like somebody nice for once?"

Heather flops back on the couch and crosses her arms across her chest. She stares at the blank TV.

Joy goes downstairs, but the store is locked up, and she doesn't see Otis on the street. His car is still parked in front, though, so he can't be too far. She returns upstairs and finds Heather has put *Coal Miner's Daughter* back on.

She sits down beside her daughter. "I like this movie," she says. "I like Tommy Lee Jones. They're always having fusses, but they still love each other." She loves it at the end, when Sissy calls Tommy Lee a "big ole b'ar."

They watch for a long time. Heather never does say anything. In a little while Joy forgets to be mad. They watch all the way up to the part where Loretta is so sick she has to stop touring.

Otis returns with a quart of ice cream. He closes the door behind himself gently, nods to Joy, and carries the ice cream to the counter. Joy joins him and without speaking they clear away the plates, and Otis takes out bowls. She thinks she smells beer on his breath. She should have gone out with him and left Heather alone to pout. She should have left Heather at home.

"There's ice cream," Otis says. He touches Joy's arm. "Sorry," he whispers.

For an instant she thinks: Well, you ought to be. Then she realizes he has nothing to be sorry for. "It's okay," she whispers back.

Heather comes to the table and looks into her bowl. She makes a face. She says, "You mean all they had was vanilla?"

Joy picks up Heather's bowl and carries it to the sink and dumps it. She goes back for the spoon, and throws it toward the counter, where it clatters to the floor. Otis says, "It's okay, Joy, never mind—"

"Don't tell me never mind!" she yells. "Don't look at me like you're looking right now. Like you know better!"

Otis throws his hands up in the air. "How'm I looking?"

"Anybody would know a kid wouldn't want tomato juice and sour cream!"

Otis backs away. He actually backs away. What does he think she's going to do?

Once Joy is in the car, Heather there beside her, she's shaking too hard to put the key in the ignition. "Will you please tell me," she says, "what happened up there? Will you tell me what the *hell* went on?"

"Otis doesn't like me," Heather says. "Nobody likes me."

"Think about that!" Joy says.

As soon as they're home, Heather goes straight out to the trailer. Joy hasn't been in the house two minutes until Otis calls. There isn't much she can say; she's about four feet from her mother, who's watching TV with Clancy. They're watching a special report on babies addicted to cocaine and alcohol. Maybe it makes Clancy feel smug to know there are some worries she doesn't have.

"She's so unhappy," Otis says.

"That's my fault?"

"I'm not criticizing. I'm saying something's wrong."

"Don't let it worry you."

"What are you down on me about?" he asks. "I called to see if you're okay. I called to say I'm not mad."

She can't think of anything to answer.

"We'll talk tomorrow," he says.

"Maybe," she says. "Maybe not."

"We will," he says back. "Unless the lines are down or something. Don't let her have her way on this, Joy."

"Oh, you read her mind?"

"Didn't have to. I could read the way she acted."

"I don't want to talk about it." She can see her mother is trying to listen. "I'm going to bed."

"Me too," Otis says sadly. "All alone. As soon as I clean the ice cream off the floor."

She hangs up without saying good-bye, but she's careful not to slam the phone.

29

In the trailer, Heather throws herself facedown on the wide bed and tries to cry, but she doesn't feel like crying anymore and it's too early to go to sleep. She gets back up and arranges herself on the blue plush couch in the main room, two fringed pillows behind her back, her legs stretched out. She is reading *Kisses for Georgina,* one of Clancy's paperback novels. Georgina is hired as an au pair for the summer at Cape Cod, and when the family decides to go to the South of France, they take her along. Right away she quarrels with the landlord's son, who is rude and terribly French and handsome. When the children stomp on some flowers, he says Americans are uncivilized. His mouth is always in a pout, like he's about to give someone a kiss.

It's for sure Georgina's about to fall in love.

Ohh, Heather sighs. Will she ever be kissed? Will she ever have a happy ending? She is fifteen now; is that old enough to think about endings? They always have to do with men. Women always get married in Clancy's books. Heather has never had a date. Other girls at school seem to have a secret they won't share; she watches them congregating with boys in the hall, giggling and posing and having fun. Sometimes she walks up to a small group of girls (certainly only a small one) and says "Hi!" as cheerfully as she can, and before she knows it, the group has disintegrated, is a group no more. Usually she's left standing by somebody's locker by herself. Nobody cares that it took her an hour to fix her hair, that she wears clothes just like the popular girls, bought from the same racks at the mall.

Lately she's been sitting with Jamaica at lunch. That is sure to lose her whatever friends she was on her way to making—the popular girls snicker about Jamaica, point her out, her outfits, her hair, her color—but it has turned out to be a reasonable trade. Friendship with those girls is at best a promise; lunch with Jamaica is company.

She isn't in the mood to read. The trailer is great, her own private kingdom while Russell is in Africa—when she asked him about it, he told her she could be his "caretaker"—but it has one drawback: no cable hookup, so she can't get MTV. She puts a tape of The Styph Dix in her player as loud as she dares and turns off the light and lies back down to listen.

She is so bored. The only thing worse than the thought of growing up—having to pay for everything yourself—is the thought of staying fifteen. At fifteen, you're nobody. If you don't have a house, a family, you don't really exist.

Her mother never does anything with her anymore. They work the snow cone concession on the weekends, and Joy drops Heather off and goes over to Otis's. Clancy is getting big as a bucket and *she* sure doesn't want to do anything. The last time Heather went to a movie was with Travis Murphy! He had come to take Clancy, who backed out. It felt so good, sitting in the theater next to a cute guy, imagining what it would be like if he were her boyfriend instead of Clancy's. For one thing it would mean she was older, because no way is some man over thirty years old going to go out with a high school sophomore, and that would mean she'd be out of school, maybe in college or working.

She would have her own apartment somewhere, maybe with roommates. Nobody would tell her what to do.

How do you get to that? she wonders, her eyes shut tight in the dark. If you can't stand school, how do you go to college, good grades or not? If you can't stand to have people tell you what to do, how do you get a job? If you don't have any money and nobody gives you any, how do you get to move out in the first place? She can't live with Opal forever! Opal has a heart that skips and sputters. Opal is old.

Jamaica says in another year or two she'll find a guy to live with and drop out. She says maybe she'll go out to California and live on the beach. Up until her mother brought her and her little brother to live with their grandmother, she's always lived in Queens. Queens, she says, is a lot better than Lubbock: There are more people, more noise, more things to do. You can hang out on your own front stoop. Heather isn't sure what a stoop is; she doesn't know what you do when you hang out.

She turns the light on and goes in the bedroom to look in the mirror and put on makeup. Jamaica says she goes to J.J.'s lots of evenings, and Heather ought to come. J.J.'s is a music store, video rental store, and arcade all in one, with a juice bar. The only time Heather's been in there has been with Joy, to rent movies, but there isn't a single reason she couldn't go there right now, except that it's too far to walk, and she doesn't think you can take a bus this late.

She can hitch a ride. Jamaica says that's how she gets around all the time. Heather has started taking the bus back and forth to school now, but she never has tried to get a ride on the street.

You have to start sometime, she thinks, as she draws a heavy black line on her eyelid. She is thinking she'll do something new with her hair, something not at all like how Lubbock girls look. She uses the tip of her little finger to smudge the eyeliner on her lid; she wants to look like the girl on MTV who has a British accent. She has the same eyebrows.

The first car that stops is really nice, an Oldsmobile. The passenger-side door is locked. This old woman rolls the window down part of the way and says, "Does your mother know you're out here, young lady?" Heather jumps back as if the old bag had taken a shot at her. She sticks her tongue out. The window zips back up, the woman drives away.

It's four or five minutes before she gets a ride. She has walked a couple blocks from the house, just in case anybody is coming or going from there, and she stands on the curb with her fist stuck out and her thumb stuck up. She's wearing jeans and a T-shirt, nothing spectacular, but she hardly looks dangerous. Why are people so stingy and hateful, to pass her by?

The guy who stops is driving a truck with high wheels and a noisy muffler. She's a little nervous climbing in, but what can happen on a city street at nine o'clock at night? There are cars everywhere. He has his radio on a country-western station.

"Where to, little lady?" this guy asks. He's wearing a black cowboy hat. The whole cab reeks of smoke, and empty beer cans roll around on the floor.

"Up to J.J.'s," she says, her voice not much more than a squeak.

"Where's that?"

"The video store, straight up, the other side." She points across the avenue. "Next to the supermarket."

He revs his engine and takes off with a lurch. He is too old to be showing off for her. She hugs the door and turns her knees away from him, but he's only interested in weaving in and out of traffic and cutting off slower drivers. He skids to a stop in front of J.J.'s and turns his radio down a little. "Want me to wait on you?" he says. "Want to get a movie and watch it with me? Uh, want me to pick it out?"

Now that they are in more light, she sees that he is older than Otis. She gets out of the truck as fast as she can. He leans out of the window on his side and yells, "Stuck-up pussy!" It's the first time she's ever heard that word, but she's sure she knows what it means. Like *bitch*. If you act like a bitch, more people want you. They think you know something special. All the popular girls are bitches.

She is going to have to learn the right thing to say to keep guys from getting the wrong idea—any idea—about her. She'll ask Jamaica.

Jamaica is playing pinball in the back of the store. She is wearing black leggings and a tight bright purple T-shirt. She has a straight-up-and-down figure, no breasts, but she stands with her hip cocked, and Heather thinks she looks cute. She walks back to her as fast as she can without actually running.

Jamaica says, "You're just in time."

"For what?" Heather leans on the pinball machine.

"Wait a minute." Jamaica has another try, then slaps the top of the machine and walks off. "Let's get a drink, okay? You by yourself?"

"Yeah." They get Dr Peppers and lean against the bar. There are half a dozen guys in the place, playing in the arcade, besides the ones looking at tapes and videos in the store. Most of them aren't any older than Heather, mouth-breathing boys with pimples.

Jamaica makes a face. "It's too early, nobody's out."

"Yeah," Heather says.

"We could go to a movie. You got some money?"

Neither of them knows what's playing.

Heather has an idea. "You want to go back to my house?"

"What's it like there? Can we play music?"

Heather smiles. "I've got my own trailer."

Somebody's father gives them a ride home. "You girls be careful," he says when he lets them out. "Everybody's not nice."

"We're real careful," Jamaica says. They start laughing as he pulls away. Old guys are such dorks.

Jamaica is impressed. An apartment in Manhattan, she says, would cost eight hundred dollars a month.

"Wow" is all Heather can think to say. She puts on a tape of Midnight Chains. She loves to watch their video, where the women are all lifting weights. It's so unbelievably disgusting; they have bumpy arms and legs. They breathe in and then go *hoo! hoo!* like Arnold Schwarzenegger. They get chained up, and they bust out, because they're so strong.

"You got any reggae?" Jamaica asks.

"No."

"That's what my dad plays, reggae. He and my mom are in Atlantic City this month. They go all over."

"Is that why you're here?"

Jamaica shrugs. "That's what she says."

Heather fills her in on her own household. "My mom

and me live with my grandmother Opal. Her husband is in Africa."

Startled, Jamaica asks, "He *black*?"

Heather giggles. "He'd have a heart attack to hear you ask that. He's working on a pipeline in Nigeria. He's Texas red up here"—she pats her cheeks, then draws her finger across her neck—"and white from here on down!"

"Africa," Jamaica says in a funny voice. Heather realizes it's something to do with being black, but she doesn't think of Jamaica as black or white; she thinks of her as from New York.

"I want to go to England," she says. "To see a castle."

"Listen, you want to do something?" Jamaica pulls a pouch out of her little paisley shoulder bag. It's full of ballpoint pens. "You want to give each other tattoos?"

"I don't know—"

Jamaica laughs. "Not real ones. Just ballpoint tattoos."

"Will they wash off?"

"Eventually. Take off your jeans." She's already pulling off her leggings. "We'll do flowers on our butts, want to?"

Jamaica has cigarettes, too. They take turns smoking and drawing. Heather asks, "Won't somebody wonder where you are?" The cigarettes have made her queasy. If Jamaica left, she would go inside and take a bath and drink a Coke.

"I think my grandmother forgets all about me," Jamaica says. "She hates my hair. She can't believe Mom married a black. And *his* mother hates *my* mother."

"I bet." Heather hopes it isn't the wrong thing to say. She wants to ask Jamaica how to wear her hair. She wants somebody else's opinion.

"She doesn't tell me what to do, and I don't get in trouble," Jamaica says. "She's pretty cool, for a grandma."

"Does she give you money?"

"There's money around," Jamaica says mysteriously. "And there's always baby-sitting." She opens her mouth and sticks her finger in. "Gag."

"I never have," Heather says.

Around midnight they slip into the house and get Cokes and a package of sliced ham and a bag of chocolate chip cookies. Nobody stirs. They go back outside and sleep in Opal and Russell's bed. They admire each other's tattoos, and tell about their parents. Jamaica's are really interesting: Her mother ran away at sixteen, ended up all the way in New York City, and now plays in Jamaica's father's reggae band. All Heather can say is her mother used to be a secretary and her father puts warheads on missiles. Jamaica is terribly sympathetic. They can't believe they've found each other.

Heather wakes up once and Jamaica is snuggled close against her hip. She touches Jamaica's arm lightly; it is skin, like her own skin, smooth and warm and tight over her bones. The next time she wakes up it's morning, and Jamaica is on the far side of the bed, her arms hanging off. Heather whispers, "You can sleep as long as you want." Jamaica doesn't stir.

In the house, Heather locks the bathroom door and uses a hand mirror to examine her buttocks. The tattoo is really just a big bouquet of posies. There's nothing shocking about it. If it was on her arm instead of her butt, she could show it to her mother, to anyone. She dresses in her ICE IS NICE outfit. Her mother will be amazed to get up and find her all ready for work.

She drew a snake on Jamaica. She assumed it was expected. She tried to make it look like one of those snakes that lift right up from their coiled body and weave and spit at you. It turned out to look a lot like a penis, if a penis coils, if a penis looks like she thinks it does. The only one she ever really saw was baby Andrew's; it looked like somebody's wrinkled thumb.

Dreams
of
Little
Birds

30

Clancy lies on the couch, oversized and lethargic, her parakeet, Pretty Bit, perched on the mound of her stomach. She has been watching Greta Garbo in an old movie about a queen who always dressed like a man and then fell in love, and it makes her cry even though she thinks it is a dumb story. Lots of things make her cry these days. It doesn't have to be something sad. Tears, like weeds, just spring up. If she isn't crying, she's bored, and she's terribly absentminded. Friday at work she spent fifteen minutes looking for a folder that was on her desk in front of her the whole time. Fortunately, nobody notices. Mr. Riddler has stuck her away down in the basement, to learn about foreclosures, he says. The real reason is she's pregnant, of course; he moved her when she started to show. She got a raise, though, fifteen dollars a week. If he disapproves (is there any doubt?), he isn't going to let her know, you have to give him that. And she isn't on display anymore, and foreclosures are a change, as long as you don't think about what it means for the people it's happening to, people who gave up and walked away, or dug in and hoped for the best when they couldn't make payments.

She would really, really like to have this baby and be done with it. "Cheer up!" she says to the bird. The bird says, "Cheer up," or something close to it. Clancy bought the bird the first time she went to shop for maternity clothes. She came home with three jersey dresses and a parakeet. She likes the company. She likes that a parakeet only says what you tell it to; it never asks a question. The baby—oh, the baby will listen too, and give back words learned from her. The baby will call her "Mama."

Her mother brings her a glass of orange juice. "Here, sit up," she tells her. "Take this." She hands Clancy a big red pill.

"I'm not supposed to take medicine, am I?" Her book says even aspirin can be bad.

"It's vitamin B. For your carpal tunnel syndrome."

Clancy swallows the pill. Her right wrist is swollen and numb; Opal has fashioned a makeshift splint for it for the weekend. She called her old boss, the orthopedist, to ask what to do. It's just one of many things, like the brown line from between her breasts down into her pubic hair, like heartburn and aching. Things are pressed and punished by the baby; things swell and hurt. At least when the baby's born, she can put it down sometimes. She can sleep on her stomach again.

It will all be over soon. She's due in a week. She's been doing her Kegel exercises to tone the vagina, just like it says to do in *What to Expect When You're Expecting*. It's hard to think how much her vagina will have to stretch, how much it will hurt, whether it will spring back. It's hard to think of everyone looking at her there, poking and grabbing, cutting and stitching. In her mind's eye, the vagina is a great wide mouth, and the baby pops out.

"What have you eaten today?" Opal asks.

Clancy puts her finger against the parakeet's breast and it steps on. "Pretty Bit," she says. "Pretty pretty pretty Bit."

"That baby must be gobbling you from the inside," Opal says. Clancy is large in the abdomen, and little every place else. It was a long time before she showed at all, and then it was like she was a balloon, *poof!* she was gigantic.

"I had a poached egg," Clancy says, revolted at the thought. She ate only the white part.

"Anybody home?"

Tanya and Rosa enter through the garage door. "Did Daddy call?" Tanya asks.

"He called Wednesday," Opal answers. "He's fine. Hot and dirty, tired and fine."

Rosa runs over to Clancy and jabbers at the bird, scaring it off Clancy's belly, onto the back of the couch.

"Don't be crazy," Clancy says. "He'll fly away." She can't remember how often she's supposed to clip its wings.

Rosa plants both her hands on Clancy's girth. "Baby," she says.

Clancy smiles. "Yes, it's my baby."

Rosa runs off down the hall.

"You stay in here," Opal calls.

Tanya follows her daughter, Opal follows her. Soon there is a discussion about Tanya's mother's sewing machine, which is stored in the hall closet. Tanya says she really needs it, and it's her mother's. Opal says it's Russell's, if it's in his house, and Tanya should wait and ask him for it.

Tanya sees that there are two sewing machines. "Look at that!" she says. "What do you want them both for?"

"Yoo hoo!" Imogene calls, now following the same path into the house, through the garage, past Clancy—"Hi, darlin'!"—and into the hall. Rosa runs past them back into the living room and climbs on the couch at Clancy's feet. She grins and flirts with Clancy, who doesn't have the energy to smile back. Clancy reaches down and takes her hand a moment and shakes it gently.

"I don't see one single reason I can't take whatever is my mother's," Tanya says.

"I don't see why you're even *here* when your daddy's *not*," Opal says.

Imogene says, "Lord, girl, your mama's been gone five years and now you want what she left behind?"

"Why not?" Tanya says. "I'm going to make some dresses for Rosa. I can't afford one of my own. It's my *mother's.*"

"Ohh!" Opal cries. Clancy hears her yanking things out of the closet, piling them into the hall. "Here's your *mother's* sewing machine. And her vacuum cleaner. And here's a box of your *mother's* dishes. Take them. Go on, take them all."

"I just want the sewing machine," Tanya says.

Imogene says, "Are you about ready, Opal?"

Opal says, "*All.*" She marches through the living room carrying a box and takes it out the garage door. Then she marches back for the vacuum cleaner. Tanya follows with the sewing machine, taking her time. She pauses and looks at Clancy sympathetically. "Don't you just want to have it *over*?"

"It's sure funny," Opal says when Tanya is gone, "that that girl comes around when Russell is in Nigeria, and not when he's here."

Clancy says, "Maybe she came when she needed to."

Imogene says, "I never see her. She never comes to my house. I see Buddy, but never Tanya. It's that Meskin husband of hers. He doesn't want her out of the house." She sits down in the chair near Clancy. "I haven't seen my Russell in six months."

"Well, who *has*?" Opal says. She sniffs. "I miss him."

Imogene sighs. "You always have company, Opal, honey. You don't know how lonesome it is, knocking around in a big old house by yourself. There's always something going on over here."

"I'll say," Clancy says. Her stomach suddenly protrudes. It hurts.

"Look at that!" Imogene says.

A big bump moves across the arc of Clancy's swollen belly. "I think it's a foot," she says, awed.

"I'm thinking I'll sell it," Imogene says.

Clancy laughs. It sounds like Imogene is talking about the baby's foot.

"Oh, I hope that baby isn't turning upside down," Opal says. "A breech birth would be the worst thing."

"Mother," Clancy says. "Stop it."

"I could get a trailer like Russell's," Imogene says.

"Hell, take this one!" Opal says.

Clancy says, "You'll have to take Heather with it."

"I heard there was a party!" Travis calls from the garage door. "And sure enough—" he says, standing in the living room. "Hi, there, Mrs. Duffy. Opal." He is holding a big sack.

"You might as well call me Imogene like everybody else," Imogene says. "Being part of the family."

Clancy clasps Pretty Bit in her hand and hauls herself to a sitting position. "Not *exactly*," she says.

Travis holds the sack up high, then sets it on the kitchen table. "Chicken, garlic bread, french fries, slaw. I figured somebody would be hungry."

Clancy puts the bird in its cage on the floor in the corner, between the couch and the lamp.

Opal says to Imogene, "Do we have time to eat before we go?"

"Where're you going?" Clancy asks. She's not eager to be alone with Travis.

"I told you, honey," Opal says. "We're going to the Church of Christ to hear a missionary who's home from Ethiopia."

"Since when do you go to the Church of Christ?" Clancy asks.

"It's because of Russell in Africa," Imogene says. "Don't you know we want to learn all we can?"

Clancy says, "I don't think Nigeria is anything like Ethiopia. I don't think they're starving in Nigeria."

"Oh, darlin', it's all *Africa*," Imogene says. "All those Negro people, and *dust*. Russell says it's an awful dirty place."

Opal plucks her shirt. "I can't go like this. Hold on, I'm going to change. We'll eat after, at Furr's."

Travis says, "You sure?" to Imogene, who says she's going to wait and have those enchiladas they make on Sunday night at the cafeteria. Travis says, "Heck, if it was me, I'd eat now *and* then. 'Course, you're just a little bit of a woman." Imogene is tickled. Travis makes a plate for himself and one for Clancy. "Come and get it," he says.

Imogene says, "It looks good, Clancy. You need to feed that baby."

Clancy lumbers over to the table. "How did you know I wouldn't already have eaten? How did you know I'd want chicken?"

"Clancy, honey, I was just driving by that fried chicken place, and I saw that big neon rooster, and my pickup came to a stop almost by itself. I was hungry, and I thought somebody else might be too. And don't I know enough about you to know you eat chicken?"

Clancy pushes on a chicken thigh with her splinted hand and tugs away a strip of meat with the other. She chews a bite slowly. Everything tastes pasty to her these days.

Opal nibbles on a chicken wing and a spoonful of slaw. "Don't you feel good?" she asks Clancy. "You don't look right."

"Mother, I'm pregnant. I just look *pregnant.*"

Clancy sees her mother and Travis exchange looks. They think they know so much.

"I thought there might be some reason you're so glum," her mother says.

Clancy scratches her belly. "Want a list?"

Opal says, "I heard a funny joke at the pharmacy yesterday. There's this guy in West Virginia, where they live in those hollers? One day he calls across the holler to his neighbor Luke. 'Luke,' he says, 'did you tell Rufus I was a son of a bitch?' Luke hollers back, 'Heck, no, I don't know how he found out.' "

Travis snorts.

Clancy takes a deep breath.

"You don't think that's funny?" Opal says. "I swear, Clancy, sometimes you act like you're deaf."

Imogene says, "We better go, Opal." It's a relief to Clancy when they do.

When the door's shut, Travis says mildly, "Dumb joke."

Clancy is annoyed that he wants to be on her side. She says, "I read this article in *Reader's Digest* the other day. There was this little girl they thought was autistic? She couldn't stand for people to talk to her. They put her in special schools and all? Well, it turned out, her mother found out from a specialist, years later, she had a hearing problem. When people talked to her, it was like they were shrieking at her. It was an awful sound. She wasn't deaf, it was worse. She heard too much. Her hearing was up way too high."

Travis turns his chair around so that his knees butt up against Clancy's thigh. He has such a sympathetic, sweet, earnest expression, it makes Clancy start to cry. "That's how I feel half the time," she says. "Like everything anybody says is just too loud."

"Have you been thinking about names?" Travis asks gently. "I'm awful partial to my grandma's name, Sarah, if it's a girl. If I have any say."

She sniffles. "Mother's mad because I won't tell her if it's a boy or a girl. They know, because of the sonogram. But I didn't look. I said I wanted to be surprised."

"Sure," Travis says.

"I don't care, boy or girl." And she isn't going to get in an argument about who gets to name *her* baby.

"Shoot, what good would it do if you cared?" Travis says. "You have a baby, you take what you get." He's trying hard to be cheerful. "Clancy, could we talk about the name? The last name, at least?"

"If you came over here to start in on me—" Clancy says.

Travis has taken her hands in his. "I'm through fussing at you, Clancy. Talking isn't going to make you marry me. But it is my baby, too, and you can't run me off."

Clancy nods her head miserably. "I wish you were having it, Travis Murphy. Then you wouldn't wonder why I don't laugh at jokes."

"Hey, I didn't think it was funny either! Listen, I came over for a reason." He digs in his pocket and takes out a stack of paint chips. "I'm having a lot of stuff done to the house. I thought you'd help me pick colors."

"Why?"

" 'Cause you're a woman and you'd know best."

She knows it's because he hopes she'll want to live in his fresh-painted house. For a moment she wants to topple forward into his arms, let him lead her out of her mother's house and back to his. But she got along without her daddy after he left; she got along without her husbands after they left. She and her baby can make it. They can count on each other. The two of them can be a family, for years and years. She just does not have the energy for Travis Murphy and his dogs.

"I don't care what colors you choose," she says.

He holds out the paint chips. She takes them. She's surprised; they are an array of soft, delicate shades, gray and green and lilac and rose. "They're pretty," she says. "They're all pretty."

Travis leans over and kisses her on top of the head. "I'm not going anywhere, Clancy. You'll always know where I am."

She leans over and puts her head down on his knees. He strokes her hair. It almost feels right.

31

Otis asks Joy, "Who are you so mad at?"

"My mother, for one." Joy doesn't even have to think. Then she realizes he'll want a reason: *And what does Opal do so wrong, except criticize?* "She killed my dog Daisy."

"When was that?"

"When Heather was three. I had surgery, and my mother came to stay with me. She kept feeding Daisy these jerky treats. She'd say, 'Treat! Treat!' and get the dog hysterical. Daisy would be running around and around in circles, barking for dog jerky. First it was one at night, after we had supper. Then she was giving them to her every time she walked in the kitchen."

"How'd she kill her?"

"That was how! The dog died of constipation. She just got all clogged up with dog treats." She bursts out laughing.

"Was that a joke?"

Joy makes herself stop. "I know it's not funny. I don't know why I'm laughing. Of course it's not a joke. I was crazy about that dog."

"And you're still mad?"

"She warned me not to marry every time. The first time—I was just out of high school—she said, 'You're both babies and you'll grow up first and where will you be?' She was right, and *that* made me mad—"

Otis raises his hands in that oh-stop-it pose he has. "I don't mean all that, Joy. You can't be mad about stuff that's a hundred years ago. I mean now. Where's all the anger coming from? Is it something I do? Is it something I don't do? Is it something I don't even know about?"

"I'm not mad." In fact, she's stretched out on his bed beside him, and she's been feeling happy. She could stay happy, if he'd quit quizzing her. "I'm not even mad at Wayne right now. This minute, I mean. I'm not mad at Mother, either. Don't be so serious. Who said anything about mad?"

"You're so quick to take offense. I can't be walking on eggshells all the time. I want to know what's what with you. I think: If I know what she doesn't like, I won't do it. I think: She needs somebody to be on her side. But then I wonder if I have any idea, if *you* have any idea: *what's the other side?* And I worry about Heather. She's got a father; I can't be that. I don't have any experience! Heck, Joy, I don't even have the space."

"Don't," she says.

"You're awful pretty, you know."

"I don't think so."

"Well, you are. You're a knockout in that shorts outfit of yours at the flea market. Both of you are—Heather, too, if she'd stop scowling for five minutes."

She turns over and props herself on her elbows so she can look at him. "When so many people have been mean to you, it's hard not to expect it."

"I'm not going to be mean, Joy."

"I never thought you were."

"Fact is, I'd like to be really, really nice right now."

She giggles. "Let me guess." She's relieved to get off the

serious streak. He gives her a kiss that isn't even warm yet.
She wriggles around to reposition herself.

"And then let's go bowling," he says. He always likes to
do things. He likes to have a good time. She kisses him
lightly. She wants him to kiss her harder.

"I was wondering one thing—" he says, though. "About
Heather. Does she get on with her daddy? Would he like it
if she stayed with him some time?"

"She goes up there once a month," Joy says. "I've got
custody." She thought they were going to do something,
here.

"Sure you do," Otis says, " 'cause you're her mama. I
was just wondering."

Joy sits up. "I don't really feel like bowling. Or talking."
Or anything, anymore, she could add.

Otis says, "We're going to have to talk about her, Joy."

"I don't see why."

"If we're going to talk about us."

"What's to talk about?"

"I thought you might want to live here," he says. "Later
on."

"Later on," Joy says, "we can talk about it. *Later on*
Heather'll be grown up and on her own."

"Not soon enough for us, Joy."

"Not soon enough for you, you mean," she says.

He doesn't contradict her.

Across town, Heather is playing Chinese checkers with
Travis while Opal grills cheese sandwiches for them all.
Clancy is lying down on the couch, the cat at her feet, its
head resting on her crossed ankles.

"Gotcha!" Heather laughs, jumping Travis's marble.

"I just let you win," he teases.

"Did not!" The parakeet hops from on top of Heather's head to the table and struts back and forth next to the checker set, like it's studying the game.

"Don't burn your mouth," Opal says, putting a plate of sandwiches on the table. "You eating, Clancy?" she asks, but Clancy is up and out the front door. Opal starts after her.

"She's okay," Travis says. "Sit down here with us, Opal."

Opal sits and idly chews on the corner of a sandwich. "She's been reading books, I know, but I wish she'd gone to childbirth classes," she says. "I said I'd go with her. Did she ask you? You wouldn't go?"

"She never asked."

"I guess she can get a spinal block," Opal says. "For anesthesia."

"Oh, gross," Heather says. "Like, in the *spine*?"

"Come on, Heather," Travis says. "One more game, rematch."

The bird hops onto Opal's shoulder. "Silly bird," she scolds. The bird says, "Cheer up!"

"My grandmother had birds," Opal says.

"What's that?" Travis is always polite.

"Canaries, at the farm. A whole room full of them. They sang all day, then at night she covered them with flour sacks."

"You start," Heather says to Travis, moving the marbles into position.

"Once my brother, Amos, let some of them out and I got in trouble. He said I did it, and my grandmother locked me in the cellar as punishment."

"Well, *gah*," Heather says. "Why didn't you just *say*?"

"He was such a little boy," Opal says. "I didn't want him to get a spanking."

Travis and Heather move their marbles.

"I don't think my grandmother meant to be so mean," Opal says wistfully. "I understand better now; those birds—that was all she had of her own. Everything else was work, work, work."

"That's farming for you," Travis says. "Weren't they farmers? Didn't you say?"

Opal gets up. "Sweet," she says absently, patting Travis's shoulder. She is out of breath and jittery. She looks at Heather and she wonders: Who's going to take care of *her* children?

She follows Clancy outside and finds her on the porch step.

"Hi, Mother." Clancy reaches up and Opal sits beside her, pulling her skirt down over her knees.

"That Travis is a nice boy, playing Chinese checkers with Heather. I don't know anybody else can make her laugh."

"Wait, Mom. Shh. Look." Clancy laughs as Chocolate streaks toward them out of the darkness beyond the yard. Chocolate climbs on Opal's lap and kneads her stomach with her front paws over and over, like bread dough.

"It's scary, having a baby, Mother," Clancy says.

The cat settles into a purring ball. "It comes to you," Opal says. "You'll see, you'll know what to do."

"And Travis, he's scary too."

"Pooh. Travis?"

"I can't do both. There's not enough of me."

"Oh, honey, don't you think it'd be easier with Travis? Don't you think your baby needs his daddy?"

"Maybe so. But I don't think I need him."

Opal doesn't know what to say. Her heart aches. If only

Clancy knew how hard it really is not to have your daddy.

She looks at Clancy in amazement. But of course she does know! Thatch left when she was twelve, just about the age Opal was when her daddy *died*. And they never talked about it. Not Opal and her mother, not Opal and Clancy. What were they all doing? Don't grown-ups know how much is going on inside their children's hearts? And Joy, too. How hard she tried to give Joy more; she even tried to let her know her real father, when she saw where her marriage to Thatch was headed. None of it was the right thing to do: not shutting Clancy out because she was a child, not sending Joy off and hurting her and Thatch both with it; maybe, even, not the divorce. It's hard to remember how hateful she and Thatch were to each other, how much the divorce seemed the only way. It's hard to remember what was so terrible. What can she tell Clancy about love and hope and patience? You can't know. That's all you can really say. You can't know. So you send your children out on leaky boats.

"Sweetie," she says, but doesn't know what else to say. She's suddenly so lonesome for Russell, his name rises in her throat. "Ahh," she sighs. She thinks sometimes the past crowds her heart and makes it jump.

The cat rises, stretches, steps off onto the walk in front of their feet. "Now watch this," Clancy says. "I've been coming out here with Chocolate at night. Watch what she does."

The cat stands a moment on three paws, her fourth curved in front, held high. Then, stalking some imagined prey, she disappears down the walk.

"Don't you see?" Clancy says. "She's getting up her courage. You wait. One of these nights she's going to stay out all night. She'll start dreaming of little birds, their tender necks. Ole Tiger Chocolate at last." She laughs. "Isn't it great?"

The cat comes back into view slowly and stops nine or ten feet away, her eyes strange and glittery. Opal feels herself pulled forward toward the eyes. Then Chocolate streaks away again. Clancy reaches over and takes her mother's hand in hers.

Opal would like to cheer the cat, who, she knows, will be back in the lapse of a minute, but she would sound foolish, and besides, the cat is too old for new courage, too set in its ways.

She squeezes Clancy's hand.

Clancy locks the door to the ladies' room at the bank and gets down on her hands and knees in the Dromedary Droop position. She raises her back, drops her head, and counts to five, then releases. She raises her back again.

It hurts too much. Whatever this is supposed to relieve is not relieved. The pain in her lower back has spread to her abdomen, and it is getting worse. It comes in a wave, then balls up inside her and holds on. Then, in a little while, it comes again.

She isn't ready for this. She isn't ready to climb up on a table and spread her legs wide and grunt and moan and push. She isn't ready for a baby that cries and needs things all the time.

She'll be ready later. If she can rest first, she'll feel up to it. Not now, though. Now is too soon.

She goes back to her desk to call her doctor, and Opal.

"I called Travis's mother and she's going out to the field to get him," Opal says when they're checking in the hospital.

"I don't care," Clancy says from between clenched teeth.

"Oh!" Opal cries. She waves at the nurse behind the desk. "It hasn't been five minutes!" she says. "She's in *labor.*"

"Yes, ma'am," the nurse says calmly. "We're going to take a look right now." She has a wheelchair for Clancy.

"Give us half an hour," she tells Opal. "You're the grand-mother?"

Of course Opal can't wait half an hour. Clancy has changed into a hospital gown and climbed up on the labor bed when Opal sticks her nose in. "What do they say?"

"Mama," Clancy says.

Behind Opal, Dr. Stone says, "Excuse, please," and pushes the door wide into the room.

"My mother," Clancy says. "Opal Duffy."

Dr. Stone shakes Opal's hand. "I'll just check her dila-tion, Mrs. Duffy." Gently he pushes Opal out and the door shut.

"You're in for some hard work, Clancy, but I don't foresee any complications," he says as he's taking off his glove.

"How long?" A cramp seizes her. She hopes he'll say, Let's go on in and get it over with right now.

"It's going to be hours. I'm going to send in a little Jell-O for you; you try to rest. Is your—is the father coming into the delivery room?"

They've never discussed it. "I don't think so," she says. The thought of Travis in a hospital gown and mask makes her giddy. She doesn't think he'd want it.

When someone brings in a tiny bowl of orange Jell-O, Opal takes the spoon and tries to feed Clancy. "Don't be stupid, Mother," Clancy says. "I'm not sick." She also is not hungry, but she puts a lump of Jell-O in her mouth and savors its tart coolness on her tongue. She takes another and lets it slide down her throat. She is grateful for the distraction.

"Not yet, you're not," her mother says. Then she settles herself in the armchair and opens a magazine. "*You* tell *me* when you want me to do something," she says in a hurt tone.

"Mama," Clancy says, "just be here, okay? Just wait."

She tries to breathe right when the pains come, the way she read in her books. Now she wishes she'd gone to one of those classes where they practice, but you go to them in pairs, and she didn't want to take a partner. She didn't want to think about labor till she had to. Now she has to.

She moans loudly and Opal throws the magazine on the floor. "Should I get somebody?" she says.

"Mother, you've had two babies, don't you know anything?" Clancy says when she can. "It just has to *happen*."

"When I had you, they didn't stick you in a room to yell it out," Opal says. "They gave you something to help. Now you have to ask. Well, I can do that, can't I? I can find a nurse and make her do something about your pain."

"It's not pain, Mother," Clancy says with great effort. "It's—labor." And, oh, it hurts.

Before Opal can say anything more, Travis enters the room. "I couldn't get here sooner," he says. "I had to clean up."

"Nothing's happened yet," Clancy says, just before another pain. Travis looks stricken, as if she's been in an accident. "It's going to be hours." Suddenly she's so aggravated with them both, she says peevishly, "It takes *time* to have a baby."

"Maybe I'll go get some supper," Travis says. "Or should I stay?"

Clancy leans back on her elbows. "I think you should go, and take Mother with you, and let me rest, like Dr. Stone says. What can you do?"

"Leave you by *yourself*?" Opal says.

"Mama, I'm in the *hospital*," she says, but it sounds more like a moan. "And I'm really, really busy."

While they're gone an aide comes in with a razor. "What's that for?" Clancy demands. The woman says she's going to "prep" her. Clancy says, "Dr. Stone says I don't have to be shaved."

"Oh, dear, everyone is shaved," the nurse says. She pulls Clancy's gown up.

Clancy jerks it right back down. "I don't want to!" she says. "Dr. Stone says he can find his way through my hair!" she yells, and the aide laughs. "Stubborn, aren't you?" she says, but she goes away.

Clancy lies back, exhausted and pleased. She remembers something one of the women at work told her. "Just remember, everyone expects you to make noise. Make a lot of it and they'll pay attention."

She smiles and rubs her belly. Maybe she can do this after all.

By the time Opal and Travis return, labor is steady and hard and takes all her attention. She has learned the pattern of the pains, though; she knows she can ride them out; she gets through the hard part because she knows she's going to slide down, down again, to rest. She's annoyed at her mother and Travis, standing around looking helpless; she wants to get on with this baby business, and something about their helplessness and their fussy looks makes her think they're holding things up. But somehow she never finds the energy to scold them, and when the pains are harder, after the nurse checks and says, "Good girl, you're two more centimeters dilated," she's glad for them, one on each side, squeezing her hand. They talk to each other over her body; she hears their voices but can't quite tell what they're saying. She hears the buzzing in her head she knows so well, only louder than it's ever been, and she hears the grunting sounds that seem to be coming from somewhere *over there,* although she knows they are sounds she's making, sounds she's never made before.

"Oh, oh," she cries in the late afternoon, "I can't stand it! I don't want to!"

"I'll get somebody," Travis says.

"It'd be better another time," she says most reasonably. "After I have a nap. Tomorrow. Tell them—oh, oh!"

The nurse brings her fresh ice chips and says it won't be much longer.

Clancy can't stand the pain in her back. She pulls herself up by Travis's arm, squeezing it with both hands. "I want to—turn over—" she manages to say.

Opal says, "You need some Demerol! Why haven't they given you anything?"

"I didn't want it—" she says. She doesn't want to feel fuzzy and crazy and lost.

Opal goes out and comes back with a nurse who has a needle.

"A pinch in the thigh—" the nurse says.

Clancy slaps her hand away.

"Clancy!" Opal says.

The nurse says, "She has to say."

Travis says, "Squeeze harder," taking her hand.

She has climbed up to a kind of squat. The nurse pulls guardrails up on the sides of the bed. She says, "They get in every sort of position these days." She's probably talking to Opal. Nurse to nurse.

Clancy brays. Travis wipes her forehead. In a moment

she lies down again. "My feet are cold," she says. She's wearing cotton crew socks with her hospital gown. Travis begins rubbing her feet.

"C-cold," she chatters.

Travis falls back into a chair and pulls his shoes and socks off. He puts his socks over Clancy's.

"Travis!" Opal says. "She can't wear those."

"They're clean," he says. He wipes Clancy's face again.

"You need a shot," Opal says.

"I hate Demerol," Clancy says. She had it when she broke her ankle, years ago. She remembers still the panic she felt, even as she floated above it.

"Phenergan. I'll find the doctor. He can give you Phenergan."

Clancy, holding on to Travis, pulls herself up again. "Go away," she says to her mother. "Go wait somewhere while I—uh-uh—" She waits out the hardest pain yet, a long slope of it. Then she looks at her mother. "You think I can't do this, don't you? *You think you have to do it for me!*"

"Clancy!" Opal says.

"Go away. This is my *baby."*

Travis turns away too. "Not you," Clancy says. "Not yet."

Opal, with a startled whimper, goes out of the room. Travis says, "What can I do, honey? What can I do?"

"My back," she moans. "Press—there—"

The pains are so bad, and fast. The nurse is in to check. It's time; she's going to have this baby.

Clancy leans into Travis. "My back," she moans again. And suddenly, he has climbed up onto the bed with her, behind her, and he straddles her, pressing her back and holding her arms, his long strong thighs warm against her legs. "You're going to have a baby," he says softly into her hair. "You're going to have my baby." He kisses her neck. "I love you, Clancy. Get used to it."

It's her baby, though, all hers, and when they wheel her into the delivery room, she leaves Travis behind. The doctor says, "Let it go, Clancy. Yell if you want, and *push!*" They jab a needle into her down there, but she doesn't feel it. *"Come on!"* she shrieks. "It *hurts!*" The nurse says *not now*, then *now, push, push;* *"Fuck!"* Clancy yells. *"Whoo!"* she brays. *"Unhh! Fuck!"*

"Here it comes," the doctor says. "Look, Clancy, don't miss this!"

In the mirror, she sees the head crown. Her creamy baby slithers out. The doctor holds the baby up. Her eyes blur and she lays her head back. Someone puts the baby on her for a moment.

"It's a boy," someone says.

She touches his tiny hand. "I did it," she tells him. She means to be serious—*she has done something wonderful all by herself*—but she's laughing. The baby, solemn, waves his free fist. Clancy waves hers, too.

Then it's morning. She lies bathed and rested on her bed, and they bring the baby wrapped in a blanket. At the sight of him, her breasts pulse, and her womb. *This is her child.* Opal and Travis tiptoe in and stand, one on each side of the bed.

"It's a boy," Opal says reverently.

"He's got hair," Travis says.

"What'll we name him?" Opal asks. "After his daddy?"

Clancy looks at her mother, then at Travis, and then at the baby. She realizes that the buzzing in her head has gone away.

"His daddy, and mine," Clancy says. "Murphy Thatcher."

"This beats everything," Travis says. "This is the best yet."

Clancy doesn't say, but she agrees.

Shy Dogs

33

Russell is in bed, zonked on codeine, and whimpering, but at least he's home. When he stepped off the plane and Opal saw him, tan and lean and grinning from ear to ear, she forgave him everything: all the months of running the household alone, with nobody to talk to when she was blue; all the bills to manage and the car to fix and his mother to entertain. All the lonesome nights. She forgave him for liking Africa, for feeling cocky about seven months out of the country. He proved his point; he went far enough away for long enough for her to know she needs him around. She wants to be with him. They haven't talked about where that will be. They haven't talked about why he went to Africa, or why he can't look for a job in Lubbock. He's bound to see Clancy needs her here. He's already crazy about Murphy. And what can he say: That little fellow needs to get out on his own? Hardly!

They had just walked in the house from the airport when she saw the funny blue-brown color edging the mole by his lower lip. She had turned her face up to kiss him, and she thought: Oh, no, squamous cells. She didn't ask him; she went and called the dermatologist herself, and before Russell could wink, had him in for an exam. "Boy, you don't give a guy a minute to enjoy hisself," he teased, but he found it less funny when the doctor said he had five spots that had to go, and came at him with a needle and a scalpel. Now he has little bandages stuck on his cheeks and nose, and on that spot under his lip, and he feels mightily sorry for himself, but he can be glad she paid attention, she knew what to watch for, she was right.

She sits on the bed a few minutes and watches him sleep. His mouth is open and he is snoring. He is curled up like a big cartoon version of the baby in his crib. Opal puts her hand on his hip. "I'm glad you're home," she whispers.

Clancy is on the couch, nursing Murphy. Her eyes are closed. The baby is sucking greedily. Opal sits down beside them and watches him working hard to get his mother's milk. She doesn't think Clancy's milk is rich enough; she thinks he needs cereal. She tried to warn Clancy what breast-feeding would be like. "He'll be at you every three hours," she said. Clancy is like a broom straw with breasts. Milk leaks through her bra and T-shirt day and night. "What are you going to do when you go back to work?" Opal asked. Clancy said she'll keep on nursing at night and wean him onto a bottle for the day. She would have done better to start out on a bottle right away, so that anyone could feed him. The first week she cried for lack of sleep. Then she started taking the baby to bed with her. That worries Opal, too. She lies in her own bed and pictures Murphy tucked in the crook of Clancy's arm; she wonders if his little head is clear of the covers, if Clancy has turned over across his body.

The nipple slips out of the baby's mouth and his head droops. If Clancy doesn't burp him, he'll be crying with gas pains in half an hour. She reaches for him.

"Mama, don't," Clancy says. She blinks, sits straighter; she *was* asleep.

"Why don't you lie down? I'll change him in a minute and rock him a little while."

Clancy yawns and yields her son.

"I don't see how you're going to go back to work," Opal says. She's already told Clancy she doesn't see the point. Travis has the baby on his medical insurance, and she's sure they've worked out some child support. His parents have been over—his mother every other day—and brought boxes and boxes of diapers, sleepers, toys he won't know what to do with for half a year. They bought the crib and bedding, too. And can Clancy doubt that Russell and Opal's home is hers? Where does she think she's been for nearly two years, in Albania?

"Want to go see Granny?" Clancy asks sleepily. "Could you drive?"

"Why, of course I'll drive," Opal says. She relishes the thought of a few days away with her two babies. She always feels like seeing Elizabeth. "Whenever you say." Maybe, driving, Clancy will talk to her. Travis moved his dogs to his parents' place; doesn't that mean something? The baby's still feeding frequently; shouldn't he be getting a supplement? If they put the crib in the front alcove, away from Clancy's room, wouldn't they both sleep better?

"When Russell feels better," Clancy says.

"Of course," Opal agrees. She had forgotten her husband and his carved-up face for the moment.

"He could go, I guess," Clancy says.

"I'm sure he'll have things to do here," Opal replies. She'll make him a list, in case he can't see on his own. He can start by cleaning the garage. He can work on the yard, if he wears a hat.

She is rocking Murphy, singing a lullaby she hasn't thought of in thirty years: *Summer night, sweet and bright, lay your head on my shoulder—*

Heather comes in from the backyard, giggling and talking, followed by her odd, skinny friend, Jamaica. Heather's
head is wrapped in a towel. She stops when she sees Opal.
"Shh," she says, turning to Jamaica. "Come see our baby."
As she bends over and touches Murphy's cheek, Opal sees
there are black stains around the towel where it meets her
hairline.

"What are you doing to your hair?" she asks.

Jamaica says, "Heather is going to look so cool."

Heather says, "Can I go in your shower?"

"No," Opal says. "Russell's asleep. He feels awful."

Heather groans. "How am I supposed to get this guck
off?"

Jamaica says, "You can lean over the tub, I'll help." She
looks at the baby more closely. "He's cute."

Heather says, "That's why I get Pretty Bit. Clancy
doesn't pay him any attention anymore. Go get him out of
my room, Jamaica. He can come in the bathroom with us."

"What's your mother going to think of your hair?" Opal
calls after them as they go around the corner into the hall.
Heather leans back around to answer.

"Like, do you think she'll notice?" she says. "Like, does
she care?"

"You clean that tub!" Opal yells. "You don't leave it for
me to do!"

Opal changes the baby and takes him into the bedroom.
Russell has turned onto his back, his arms flung out. She
lays the baby carefully on the bed and arranges herself
beside him. She has no intention of sleeping; she wants to
think. A lot of things have not been discussed in this household since the baby came, since Russell arrived. Clancy is
wrapped up in a cocoon of secretiveness. Languidly, she

ignores Travis's attentions and Opal's advice. She says, to any question, "I don't know yet." She lies stretched out with the baby on her belly and the cat at her feet, and she smiles to herself. As soon as she sees someone looking, she stops.

She hopes Russell will understand how much the baby—and Clancy—need her. The baby gives them a reason to get up in the morning. Uncomplicated, he bears no grudges. His history is all ahead of him. When he cries, he has a reason, and most of the time Opal can figure out what it is. You can make babies happy with so little. When does that stop? When do they start wanting more than you have to give? When do they get angry that life has bumps in the road? Why do they blame their mothers?

34

Elizabeth looks frail. Maybe it is the contrast: she so old, with the baby on her lap. She doesn't say anything, or fuss or coo over the child, but she rocks her knees gently back and forth while the baby stares up at her, mesmerized.

"He looks just like Thatch did," she says. "I'm surprised I remember, but I do. It's the hair, and the nose."

"He's got his daddy's chin," Opal says.

"Oh, Mother," Clancy says. "He just looks like a *baby.*"

"Travis is thrilled," Opal says to Elizabeth. "He's been over every day."

Elizabeth glances at Clancy, then back to the child.

"Will you take him to your daddy's this trip?" she asks.

Clancy says, "I'll go up later by myself for a real visit, when I can stay a while. Mother needs to get back. Russell's sick."

"Oh?" Elizabeth says, concerned.

"All that sun," Opal says. "Skin cancer. They got it all. He's okay." She pats her own nose.

"What a worry," Elizabeth says. She always sees to the heart of things. The baby fusses.

"I guess he's hungry," Clancy says, taking him from her grandmother's lap. She settles into a chair and pulls up her shirt. Opal wishes Clancy would use a blanket to shield her nursing just a little. Elizabeth must think her very casual.

"He's always hungry," she says, without thinking, and then, sensing Clancy's defensiveness, adds, "That's all babies are, eating machines."

"Not quite *all,*" Elizabeth says, laughing. "The machine puts out what it takes in." Her little joke surprises Opal. She has never heard Elizabeth say a coarse word. Maybe she doesn't think of baby poop that way.

She leaves Clancy and Elizabeth talking and invents an excuse—a trip to the drugstore for some antacids—so that she can go over to Grant Street and see her mother's house. She leaves Elizabeth's street and has to pull over, her breath is coming so hard. She puts a hand to her chest. She has learned that these attacks are not what they seem: the sense that her heart is skipping and may stop, that her lungs are starved for air. It's a false alarm, her heart playing tricks on her. As long as she takes her medicine, takes it easy— nobody has given her a definition of that!—she will be all right. Until something leaks or clogs, bursts or stops. Until some part of her says *enough.* None of them believe she's sick. When she has a moment—she's worried, maybe scared, and it shows on her face, in her hand on her chest—they turn away. They get busy all of a sudden. They have no patience for her pain and fear. Even Russell, who acted so scared for her after that first attack, said to her last night, "You don't know how bad this hurt, Opal." He thinks his little bandages are marks of valor. He asks her to bring him things: Kleenex, juice, one of his old Louis L'Amour books. He says, when she gives him her list of things to do, "I don't know when I'll be up to it, honey."

She leans against the seat back. She hears her mother's voice in her head: *There's someone on the line.* Why should

she remember that? Why not a pleasant moment, a ten-
derness, a joke they shared?

It is something she has done to herself, resisting the
boxes from her mother's house. She hasn't opened either of
them. They are in the corner of the front room, stacked up
near Joy's computer, as if they contained files or paper. She
forgets them most of the time. Even when she sits tinkering
with Joy's machine, trying to learn to run the editing program, she ignores them. *Later,* she thought when she put
them there. Later she will be able to think about her mother
without choking on her grief. Later she will be able to look
at pictures and not weep, read letters curiously, as the
artifacts they are. Much, much later.

She sits up and rubs her eyes. Has she dozed? Her heart
beats regularly, her chest doesn't hurt. She should go to the
drugstore after all, then back to Elizabeth's, but she knows
she won't. She must see her mother's house again; she is
resolved that this will be the last time. She doesn't know
who is living there. She hopes they haven't killed the roses.
She hopes they aren't trashy people who don't pick up the
cups and papers people throw out of their cars onto the
yard. She hopes they are not unhappy people, a family that
says terrible things, or doesn't speak.

The house belongs to someone else now, a landlord,
probably, who lets it out to people who cannot afford
something better. Neither the owner nor the renters will
feel anything of the stubborn pride her mother felt for her
house. It would have been better to give the house away to
someone who would be grateful, a family of Mexicans, or
those Asians you see moving in all over Texas. Someone
who has known what it's like to have no place at all.

She turns the ignition and pulls back onto the street.

*   *   *

There is no house on her mother's lot. Opal parks across the street and walks over to the edge of the yard. The old house has been cleared and a new foundation laid. The frame of a new house has already been built, something larger than the old one, but not grand, not in this part of town, not on this street. Something sturdy, and new.

Carefully she picks her way across the yard and around the lot. With her back to the new foundation, she looks out across the large backyard to the apricot trees. Rotting fruit lies on the ground. The lot is a tangle of weeds up to the area where the ground has been turned and disturbed by the construction. She walks to the edge of the framed house, leans her arm against a post, and peers in where a room will be.

She drives to a filling station and calls Russell.

"They tore my mother's house down," she says.

"Opal?"

"They're building a new one."

She wonders if he's going to say anything, and then he does. "There won't be anything of her left there now."

"No." It surprises her, but she isn't crying.

"So you might as well get Clancy and come on home."

"There are things—" She doesn't know if she can say it.

"What things, honey?"

"Things I needed to say to her and didn't."

"It's been over two years."

"She was my mother for fifty-seven years."

"Come home, sweetheart," Russell says. "I'm lots better."

"In the morning. I still want to get out to the cemetery."

"They called me about another job."

"Where?" Is he going to lean on her about this so soon? Does she have to explain to him what's happened while he was gone?

"Colombia," he says.

It takes a moment to sink in. "South America?"

"Yup."

"That's where those drug lords are!"

"Wouldn't be to fight drug wars, Opal, it'd be to put in a crude-oil line."

"Are you teasing, Russell?"

"More like testing the water."

"I don't want you to go to South America."

"Can't go yet," he says. "I'm too ugly with these holes in my face. I'm feeling better, though. You come home. You can shut your eyes."

"Nobody picked Mother's apricots this year," she says.

"I miss you. Get back here."

She drives by her mother's lot one more time, but she doesn't stop. She looks in the rearview mirror once, but she doesn't turn around. She goes to visit her mother's grave alone, and doesn't stay very long. Everybody's doing the best they can, she tells her mother. Just like you did. Russell hasn't turned out to be the sorry man you thought.

Her heart aches, but she knows whatever's hurting has to be fixed with the living and not the dead.

When she gets back to Elizabeth's, she sees from the way she and Clancy look at her that they know where she's been. "The grass was green and damp," she tells them. "Somebody's watering like they should."

In Benjamin, on the way home, they buy hamburgers and then find a place to park on the street near an elementary school closed for the summer. A couple of little boys are kicking a soccer ball around on the playground. Clancy nurses Murphy, and Opal closes her eyes and rests.

"I asked Granny if she'd still like me to come stay with her in Wichita Falls," Clancy says. "She's got lots of room."

"You've got a room where you live now," Opal points out.

"I need to do something. I don't want to go back to the bank right now. I want to be with Murphy."

"And not Travis." Opal holds her eyes shut tight.

"Not right now."

"And not me?" That's what hurts. She has to look.

"It's not that," Clancy says. "I'm not leaving anything. I'm trying to go *to* something. Murphy changes everything, don't you see? What I do really matters. I can't sleep my life away. I don't think I can explain. I need to think about it. Maybe I'll see a counselor. You've wanted me to do that for years. Now maybe I will."

Opal sighs. "I was hoping you'd go on and be a nurse, like you were thinking. There's that good program at Tech."

"I was never thinking that far," Clancy says irritably. "It wasn't *my* idea."

"That's just one more thing I need to think about," Clancy says. "School. What I want to do. Something more than now."

"Now you're a mother."

"That's not everything," Clancy says. "I was thinking like it was, but when I talked to Granny I realized there's a lot ahead of me, a lot of my own life."

"You could go to school in Lubbock, I could take care of Murphy. Why wouldn't that be perfect?"

"Have you asked Russell about that?"

"I don't have to ask him anything."

Clancy lays the baby down across her thighs and pats his back gently. "It might be a good idea, Mama."

Opal says, "Who's going to watch Murphy if you want to go to school in Wichita Falls? Elizabeth's too old."

"I'm not thinking about school. I'll watch Murphy myself. Mama, every time a person does something, it isn't forever."

"A lot of the time you think it is. A lot of the time, it keeps coming back to you. Some things, you do them once, and then they worry you ever after. Other people don't let you forget."

"Do you want me to drive?"

Opal's throat flushes with pleasure at the thought of the baby in her arms. "And I can hold him," she says tenderly.

Clancy opens her door. "You know you can't, Mother. He goes in the carrier, in the back, where it's safe."

"Never mind," Opal says. "I'll drive, you nap." She starts the car. If Clancy thinks an infant seat makes her baby safe, let her. She'll find out soon enough how many dangers there are. She'll find out what it's like to have your heart in your throat half the time, worrying about your children.

She wonders what Elizabeth came up with to make this happen. She feels betrayed. It's wicked of Elizabeth to lure Clancy away because she's lonesome. She should know how Opal would feel about Clancy's baby. She should let things be.

"It's not right away," Clancy says in a little while, as if that helps. "It's just an idea."

35

Heather wears her black, black hair slicked back in a tiny blunt ponytail, to show off her new earholes and earrings. She has pierced each lobe in the conventional place, and then made a parade of other holes up the lobe, three on one side, two on the other. She has spent over sixty dollars of her snow cone money for gold studs, loops, and one dangling silver bird. Only one of the holes still oozes a little; she used hydrogen peroxide three or four times a day, just like Jamaica said she should, until they were healed, and she found some Neosporin in Opal's bathroom, for the one that needs it. It doesn't hurt. Jamaica says some people believe that when you pierce your ears, you free up energy in your body, kind of open new lines. She can believe it; she loves her ears, her hair, her new look.

Her mother says she might as well wear a sign on her back: CHEAP. *She* doesn't do anything to *her* hair except pull it back in a ratty ponytail. But when Opal says, "What do you think you look like, Heather, walking around like that?" Joy snaps at her mother, "She looks like she *wants* to look!" Privately, she asks Heather, "What next? Am I going to come home and find you crying because you're pregnant? Am I going to get a call to pick you up at the station stoned? What are you working up to?" She really wants to be mad at Heather.

"It's just my *hair*," Heather says.

She's afraid they'll start in on Jamaica, so the two of them lay low. Jamaica stays with her in the trailer; they hang out at J.J.'s or the mall. A couple times Russell takes them for tacos; he never gets in on Opal and Joy's little fits. "Whaddaya call that hairdo?" he asks Jamaica, and she tells him, seriously, as if it were an important question. Heather had no idea grown-ups were so hung up on hair. You wouldn't think so, to look at them.

Sometimes in the afternoons the girls go to the park where the prairie dog city is, and watch the holes for signs of life. Heather tells Jamaica what she remembers hearing about the prairie dogs—how, when the pioneers first came, the dogs had huge underground cities, linked for miles. You always hear about how white men came and took over from the Indians, but when you see the prairie dogs limited to this stupid park, you realize men came along and messed up animals, too. Jamaica says, "And for what? Why'd they want to live here anyway?" It makes them sad, thinking about it.

Once a couple of Mexican guys tried to flirt with them. They were cute, in their own way, in black T-shirts and tight jeans, with long pretty hair, and bandanas tied around their foreheads. They were lots older, maybe nineteen, twenty. They asked the girls if they wanted a beer out of their cooler. Heather couldn't help it, she giggled; Jamaica sighed with boredom. "I wish we were in the Village, in New York," she told Heather. "Or the park. I wish we were in SoHo. Or even Queens."

"I wish we were, too," Heather said. "I wish something would happen."

*   *   *

Heather was surprised when Joy asked Kay Lynn about having Jamaica work, too. That way Kay Lynn won't have to fill in on the weekends Heather goes to Amarillo. Heather didn't think Jamaica would want to, but she did, probably for the money. She even agreed to wear an ICE IS NICE tee. "What about *her* hair?" Heather asked, although she felt disloyal. Joy said Jamaica looked foreign, so the hair fit. Nobody expects Jamaica to look normal.

Heather thinks the fuss is finally over about her hair, especially since Joy is gone a lot. When Joy is home, she's hunched over that stupid computer, clicking away and cursing, printing out piles of paper and calling people up to come and get them. She doesn't pay any attention when Heather is home, and usually doesn't notice when she isn't. Then one afternoon in the middle of the week, halfway into August, she says Kay Lynn is driving to Amarillo to see a friend, and Heather can ride along.

"Why would I do that?" Heather asks. "Why would I go up there when it's not my weekend?"

"I talked to Wayne," Joy says. "I said I thought you ought to spend some time up there; I don't know what you're getting into here."

"Getting into! I go and watch prairie dogs run from one hole to the other! My only friend is Jamaica, and you know she's nice; you even let her work with you. You talked to Daddy? You never talk to him. What'd I do?"

"Look at you," Joy said.

"Look at you," her father says sarcastically.

"It's just my *hair*."

"It isn't just your hair," he says coldly. "It's your ears. It's your shorts. It's your attitude."

There's nothing wrong with Heather's shorts. They're short, that's all. It's not like she's fat.

"Wayne, leave her alone," Joanne says. "You're making a fuss about nothing."

He gives Joanne a look that could kill cows, but he doesn't say anything. Later, when he has to go to a meeting, Joanne makes them iced tea with slices of orange.

"I never had tea like this," Heather says, grateful and surprised and apprehensive.

"The orange is nice; you don't need sugar," Joanne says. "Of course, you're young and thin, you can have sugar in your tea if you want. Here—" and she scoots the sugar bowl toward her.

Heather takes a long drink of the tea. It is so cold she can't really taste it. "It's great just like this," she says.

Baby Andrew, up from his nap, starts squalling. Joanne says, "Excuse me."

Excuse me?

"Sure," Heather says. It would be pretty funny to say to her stepmother, *You're excused.*

Joanne comes back with the baby. He's over a year old. Compared with Murphy, he's a giant and a genius. His legs and arms are chubby, and his face is more like a person's now. A little more. He wants to be down all the time, getting around. Joanne has gates on the kitchen doors so he can't get in when she's not looking.

She gives him a cracker and some juice while Heather looks on. He's cute. He slobbers cracker and grins at Heather. When he's eaten the cracker, he puts his hands over his eyes.

"He's playing with you," Joanne says fondly.

Heather puts her hands over her eyes and takes them away. "Peekaboo," she says. Andy laughs and laughs.

"Let's go in the other room," Joanne says. Heather finds this all funny; you'd think she was a visiting neighbor instead of the brat stepdaughter.

Andy has a pile of toys in his playpen under a window in the living room. He tugs at a teddy bear through the slats, where of course it gets stuck. Heather reaches in and gives it to him, and takes out a toy train, too, an engine and a caboose. It's green and yellow, with circus animals painted on the side. Before she even thinks, she's down on the floor, pushing it toward Andy. *"Woo, woo!"* she calls. He laughs and runs to his mother.

She feels silly crouched on the floor over Andy's toys. She moves to a chair and sprawls in it, her legs stuck out.

"We've joined a swim club," Joanne says. "We can go tomorrow, if you want. Did you bring a suit? Or we can get one."

Heather shrugs, suddenly embarrassed at this cozy intimacy with Joanne. She wonders where it's headed, what she's done, what they're up to.

"Are you guys moving?" she asks.

"Where'd you get that idea?"

"I thought maybe Daddy got a new job. So you might be moving." It'd be just like them to be nice before they moved.

"I love my house," Joanne says. "I'm not going anywhere." The baby shrieks and runs around, stumbles, howls, and crawls to a ball by the TV. Heather can't take her eyes off him. He's like a toy with a long-lasting battery, like on that TV commercial where they pretend it's an ad for something else.

"It's a nice house," Heather says.

"You have to look upstairs. We've carpeted the third bedroom. Blue. Do you like blue?"

"Where's Daddy's train?"

"I moved it into the dining room. We always eat in the breakfast nook anyway. I wanted to fix the bedroom up."

"For guests," Heather suggests.

Joanne smiles. "Why don't you go look?"

There is a sleek white metal double bed in the room now, and a nightstand with a lamp and a clock. The bed isn't made up, but there are sheets and a cotton blanket folded in the middle of the mattress. There's nothing on the walls, no other furniture. At the door, Joanne says, "It needs a lot of stuff. I thought you might want to help me pick it all out."

"I don't know," Heather says. She is near tears. She doesn't want to misunderstand.

"You're the most likely tenant," Joanne says.

"Tenant?"

"We wanted to make you your own room."

"Yeah," Heather says. "Like I have at *home*." She would like to crawl under the sheets and go to sleep. She absolutely does not want to have a heart-to-heart with her stepmother.

"Excuse me," she says, brushing past Joanne. "I have to pee." Her daddy likes for her to say "go to the ladies' room." He'd have something to say, if he heard that.

He has something to say about Joy. "I guess your mother's launched a new romance."

Heather isn't going to add to that.

"I guess that's why she doesn't have enough time to watch what you're doing."

"I'm fifteen," Heather says. "Nobody watches somebody fifteen."

"They should. Look at you."

Joanne is right there. "We were just talking," she says to Wayne. "Heather could use a trim, and then her new hair will look chic. I thought I'd take her in to Vicky's tomorrow. You wait, you'll be surprised!" She's so cheerful, Heather and her father actually give each other a look: Believe *her?*

Suddenly she's inspired. "Short," she says. She laughs, almost happy. "But not as short as Sinéad O'Connor's." Both Wayne and Joanne have blank looks. "Like, she's bald," she tells them. Joanne thinks it's funny. Her daddy looks like he's eating lemons.

That night she sits propped up in the new bed, looking at some of Joanne's magazines. She takes *Ms.* and *New Woman.* Heather bets her daddy doesn't read them. None of the articles interest her, but turning pages passes time. The women in pictures in *Ms.* are kind of ugly. They're probably real people.

Sleepy, she pulls open the nightstand to put the magazines in there, and sees a book. She takes it out. It's the journal Joanne tried to give her ages ago. She opens it. There are her notes: *"four phones,* king-sized bed, eight skirts—"

Her face is so hot she thinks she'd faint if she wasn't already in bed. She tears the page out and crumples it into a ball. She wonders if Joanne read it. Of course she read it! For a *year* she's known Heather is a sneak.

There isn't a trash basket in the room. Heather holds the crumpled paper and looks around for a place to put it. Finally she stuffs it in her overnight bag, under her shirts and underwear. Then she turns off the light and gets back in bed.

She hopes Joanne's hairdresser isn't some old lady. Joanne's hair is okay, and Heather can say what she wants. Of course, she doesn't know what she wants. It was Joanne's idea.

Joanne saved the day.

36

"**M**an, are you *down* or *what*?" Jamaica exclaims when she sees Heather's new hairdo the next Friday. She has come to spend the night. Joy and Otis are at a crafts fair in Santa Fe, selling his unbelievably dumb carved heads, so the girls are going to run the snow cone concession together on Saturday.

In the trailer they can listen to music really loud, but Opal says they should sleep inside so she doesn't have to go out in the yard to wake them. Like the trailer was in China.

They share Heather's bed. The bird squawks. "Uh oh, forgot to cover Pretty Bit," Heather says. She throws a dirty shirt over the bird's cage, then snuggles down under the covers. Opal has the air conditioner on Siberia because it's been so hot.

"We never had an air conditioner in New York," Jamaica says. "In the summer you lie on your bed naked and sweaty. In a way it's awful; I mean, who wants to be that hot? But in another way, it's like, *summer*. People are all out on the streets. Kids play in the water from fire hydrants. You see kids dancing, jiving, arguing, making out. There's just so much going on all over. I miss it. I miss New York. I'm going to go back as soon as I can. Texas is awful. I hate it."

"I thought you were going to L.A."

"They have planes. You can go both ways."

They lie quietly for a while, then Heather says, "Do you

think it'll be any better this year in school? Do you think it won't be so bad?"

Jamaica rolls over onto her tummy and props herself up on her elbows. "School sucks," she says, "but it's got to be better, being friends. We'll get the same classes and all. We can be together all day."

"For sure," Heather says. If she's not worrying about the other kids, she realizes, she can worry about her subjects. She'd like to take French and art. She'd like to take a harder math.

She reaches for Jamaica's hand. "Friends," she whispers.

"If you're not a pair," Kay Lynn says when she sees the girls in the morning, but she's not mad. She stands back with her hands on her hips and gives a whistle. "They'll buy snow cones just to see the two of you."

The girls have taken scissors to their T-shirts. They've cut the necks out and chopped off the hems to the hips, then slit them up the middle and tied them above the navel. Heather was nervous about Kay Lynn, but Kay Lynn doesn't care. She just cares about making money. She gives them the till and goes off, promising to come back to give them a lunch break.

Jamaica is tired of dreadlocks. She's chopped them off a couple of inches and is letting her hair grow as well as it can. She is thinking of cutting it right to the scalp if she needs to.

Heather's hair is cropped close all around, with a little length in the bangs, and a long purple streak of hair she can flip with a movement of her head. It was Vicky's idea. "If you're going to do this, do it big," she said. Joanne had left Heather and then come back to pick her up. Heather thought she would yell at her and Vicky both, but she didn't. She just said, "Your father is going to have to get used to a few things, isn't he?" Andrew had a baby-sitter so Joanne could take Heather swimming. Heather didn't go in the pool, though, not with her hair just fixed. She lay on a towel and dipped her arm in the water. She played eyes with a couple of teenage boys, but they never came over. They grinned and stared, and once one of them waved, but they never got up their nerve. She might have, if she'd cared, but she wasn't going to act anxious over a couple of *boys.*

"Look what just happened in," Jamaica says. She points to a pack of guys in leather pants. "Bikers."

"There's a dealer with parts and stuff over by the fence," Heather says. "Those guys are always in here." She's never been interested.

"You see Kay Lynn? I'm going to take a little break." Kay Lynn isn't in sight, and in a minute, Jamaica is at the same end of the lot as the bikers. Heather is too busy to watch her every move, but she can see she's talking to a couple of them. She looks back at Heather and waves.

"Oh, *cool,*" she says when she comes running back. "They're coming this way, aren't they?" She nods her head back, so Heather will look.

" 'Ice is nice,' " the first one says when he arrives at the stand. "That's not all."

"This is Heather," Jamaica says.

The guys are really old. One has long hair, pulled back in a ponytail, and one has a ducktail, like he's Elvis or somebody. They are cute, in a really ugly way.

"We've added coffee syrup," Heather says. She points to the jar. "And we have regular flavors."

One guy says, pointing back at Heather, "She's got regular flavors."

"That's nice," the other says, "but I think I'll go for a beer instead. You girls want a beer?"

Heather and Jamaica exchange looks. Of course it's a stupid question.

Jamaica is almost whispering. "Not now we don't," she says, "but I bet you'd be nice and get us some after a while, wouldn't you?"

Heather kicks Jamaica on the calf.

Kay Lynn is headed their way.

"Tell us where to bring it," the guy with the ponytail says.

"Hi, there," Kay Lynn says to them.

"Two cherry," one says. "To go."

They do come back, around four o'clock. Jamaica talks to them away from the stand, then runs back to Heather and says they're going to bring them beer at nine o'clock.

"Bring it where?"

"To your house."

"*Gah*, Jamaica, they can't do that. Opal would never let them in."

"Not in the house," Jamaica says. "You think I'm retarded? I told them about the trailer, and how to come in the alley. You want some beer, don't you?"

Heather never really thought about it. Russell always has a couple in the refrigerator, but sometimes they sit there for a week untouched. Joy drinks at Otis's but not at Opal's.

"Did you ever get drunk?" Heather asks Jamaica.

"Not *drunk*," Jamaica says. "Just high." She whispers. "They might bring some pot, too."

"They're old," Heather says.

"I know," Jamaica says. "And they've got Harleys."

*   *   *

She and Jamaica are in the house until eight-thirty. They eat microwave pizza, then change into jeans and tank tops and play Chinese checkers at the kitchen table. Every few minutes they look at each other and giggle. Opal and Russell are watching a tape of *Far Pavilions*. About the time Heather and Jamaica need to go out to the trailer to meet the bikers, there is this big dust storm in the movie, and a soldier and an Indian woman are hiding out in a cave together and you can see they're going to do it.

Heather goes in her room and gets Pretty Bit in his cage and carries it back into the living room. "We want to listen to music out in the trailer, okay, Russell?" she says casually. Russell sort of waves them on. Opal says, "It's a waste of electricity being out there," and Russell says, "Fifty cents' worth for peace and quiet," and waves them on again. He and Opal are sitting close together on the couch. Clancy and the baby are at Travis's parents' house. If Heather and Jamaica go outside, Russell can move in on Opal right there in the living room. Heather can't believe old people do it.

They're not going to be out checking the trailer.

"Thanks, Russell," Jamaica says. "We'll be real careful with everything."

Russell says, "That durn trailer'd set empty if Heather hadn't watched it for me all year."

"We'll go on and sleep out there," Heather says casually.

"Wash your faces," Opal says.

Russell says, "Watch the bedbugs."

"You girls want to take a ride?" the guys ask. Heather is so nervous she feels like throwing up. She hears their names and then can't remember them. They're standing out in the alley by their motorcycles. She thought sure when she heard them roar up that Opal and Russell would be out to see what it was, but they weren't. Russell is probably feeling around on Opal, the two of them alone in the house for a change.

Ponytail lights a cigarette, then passes it around. Jamaica shows Heather how to take a drag. It's not a cigarette, she says, it's pot. Heather is a little scared, but she doesn't see how a couple of puffs in her own alley is going to kill anyone. The stuff burns her lungs and makes her cough, but the third time around she does okay, and the other three cheer.

"Shhh!" she says, and giggles.

"Did you bring beer?" Jamaica asks.

They produce two six-packs, one from each bike. "Think this'll do it?" Ponytail asks.

Ducktail says, "That a new trailer?"

"Practically," Heather says.

"It's nice inside," Jamaica says. She's giggly, too.

Ponytail puts a hand right on Jamaica's chest. "How old are you?"

Jamaica says, "Seventeen."

"In a rat's ass," Ducktail says. He's standing right next to Heather, and she is scared to death he's going to put *his* hand on *her* boob the same way. Instead, he leans over and gives her a fast, wet kiss. She's too surprised to do a thing. "Twelve is more like it," he says, pulling his head back.

Heather says haughtily, "We're seniors in high school."

"I'm from New York," Jamaica says. Ponytail's hand has slipped down to her midriff, under her tank top. "My daddy has a reggae band."

"My daddy has hard time in Huntsville," Ponytail says, rubbing his hand around on Jamaica's front. He licks her earlobe and says, "They do this in Africa?" Jamaica has earring holes all the way up to the top of her ears. "You are part African, ain't you?"

Ducktail leans down. "Try again?" he says to Heather. Heather thinks he might be making fun of her, but she nods. The only way to get better at anything is practice. She turns her face up to him. She's so nervous she's almost chattering.

"Loose up your lips," he says.

She tries to make her whole face loose. Her mouth sags.

"That's better." He sticks his tongue in her mouth. He tastes like cigarette and pot and beer. He puts his hand between her legs.

She jumps half a foot straight up in the air. "Don't!" she says loudly. She sees that Jamaica has crawled up on the seat of Ponytail's Harley and wrapped her legs around his hips.

"Seventeen," Ducktail says.

"Sixteen," Heather amends.

Ducktail laughs and opens a beer. He takes a long drink, then hands it to Heather. "Here, this'll make you older," he says. She can manage only little sips, but she keeps working at it while he opens another beer for himself. "You guys want a beer?" he asks the others. Behind Jamaica's back, Ponytail waves Ducktail away.

"Let's go in your trailer," Ducktail says. "And find out how old you are."

Heather says, "I don't want to."

Ducktail hoots with laughter. " 'Course you don't, baby girl. Did you think I did? I don't diddle baby girls."

Jamaica turns and looks over her shoulder. "Heather?" she says.

Heather is in tears. "I'm going in the house," she says.

Jamaica squirms out of Ponytail's embrace. "We'll go in the trailer," she says.

"Not them," Heather says quietly and carefully. She can't tell how loudly she is speaking. She is suddenly aware there is a full moon, and a sky full of stars, and any neighbor could look out to the alley and see what's going on. It's not even ten o'clock yet. Someone could be taking her trash out.

"Let's get the fuck out of here," Ducktail says. He mounts his bike.

"I'd kinda like to stay," Ponytail says.

"Can we have the beer?" Jamaica asks. She tugs her tank top back in place. "Please?"

"For free?" Ponytail says. "You do nothing, and take the beer?"

"Aw, give it to them," Ducktail says. "They're just teenyboppers. Let's go find us some grown-up women." He throws what's left of his beer on the ground. Ponytail hands his six-pack to Jamaica and says, "Bye, now. See you at the flea market." Both guys start laughing loudly. "Ice is *nice,*" one of them says.

The bikes make a terrific racket, and then they're gone. Heather stoops down and picks up the beer. She's afraid Jamaica is going to be mad. They're friends, aren't they? She can tell a friend she was scared and didn't want to.

Jamaica says, "Hey, let's go drink it," cheerful as can be. "Didn't they think they were hot, though?" She laughs all the way into the trailer. "They'd get run over in Queens."

Ponytail had given Jamaica another joint, too, so she and Heather drink two beers apiece and then smoke. Jamaica tries to teach Pretty Bit to say, "Want a hit?" The bird squawks and flaps frantically. Heather says, "It's way past his bedtime," and they almost yell, it's so funny. They put a small towel over the top of the birdcage and set it by the door. Then they describe the guys to each other, and quote what they can remember them saying, and laugh hysterically. "You part African, ain't you?" Jamaica says.

It takes a long time to drink another beer. Heather's head is heavy, and she's sleepy and numb. She doesn't want to go to sleep, though. She's never had more than two swallows of beer before, never smoked pot. Nothing's going to happen sitting in Russell's trailer with her best friend, Jamaica. She might as well enjoy it.

Jamaica crawls up on her knees and runs her finger along Heather's ear. "It wasn't so bad, was it?"

"They were creeps," Heather says. "Except for giving us the beer."

"I didn't mean them. I meant piercing your ears." She did it, stuck the needle through Heather's ears all those times, cleaned the holes with hydrogen peroxide.

"It only hurt a little," Heather lies.

"I've got an idea, if you're not scared."

Heather belches loudly. They laugh so hard they fall down onto the floor, flat. Heather farts and they shriek.

"Let's pierce our noses," Jamaica finally says.

They sit back up. It takes a long time to get situated for this consideration. "I don't have any more earrings," Heather says.

"We'll use a post out of our ears. One hole, right here—" She touches Heather's nose.

Heather says, "I will if you will."

They still have a needle and peroxide in the trailer. Jamaica says they should wash their faces first.

Now Heather is the one with an idea. "I've got to go in the house," she says. "You wait."

"For what? You gotta be quiet!"

"I'll be right back."

She tries to be quiet going inside, but Opal hears her. "Is that you, Clancy?" she says.

She steps to their bedroom door. "It's Heather, I'm just coming in to get something in the bathroom."

"Close my door tight," Opal says grumpily.

Heather rummages in all the stuff in the bathroom drawers, looking for something for tooth pain. Then she thinks of Mrs. Murphy's packets she brought for the baby, boxes and plastic pouches of powders and thermometers and creams and—sure enough, teething gel.

She sits right there on the bathroom floor and laughs. That baby isn't going to have teeth for forever! And that old lady brings teething gel—just when Heather needs it.

She takes it back out to Jamaica, along with a bag of doughnuts Russell has bought for breakfast.

"Oh, God, food!" Jamaica says when she sees the sack.

"And something for the pain," Heather says, showing the tube to Jamaica.

While they eat doughnuts, they rub the gel on their noses over and over.

"Does your nose feel numb?" Heather asks.

"My whole face feels numb!" Jamaica says.

This is the funniest thing yet. Heather's face is numb too. "You first," she tells Jamaica.

They wipe the needle with peroxide. "Where are those matches?" Jamaica says. "Let's sterilize it in a flame, too."

"*Gah,*" Heather says when the needle is ready. "I don't see how you can do it."

Jamaica hands the needle out toward Heather. "You do me and I'll do you."

"No way!" Heather cries. "You do both."

They crowd in front of the little mirror in the bed alcove, and on the second try Jamaica gives up trying to stab a needle through her nose. She takes a post out of her ear and punches it right through the soft cartilage of her nose. "Oh, fuck!" she yells, and then hugs Heather.

"It's so cool!" Heather says. She takes out her post, and, not stopping to be afraid, punches her own nose. Blood gushes to her head as the pain stabs her, and then, almost before she can groan, it subsides. Her face really is numb; she can hardly feel it. Her heart is beating way up in her ears.

They sit side by side on the bed, eating the rest of the doughnuts. They dab at their noses with bits of toilet paper. "My daddy is going to die," Heather says happily.

"I've been wanting to do that a long time," Jamaica says. She gets that *look* again. "Listen, Heather. Let's drink the last beers. Stay here, I'll get them." When she's back, and they're drinking, she says, "I know girls who pierce something even better. I mean, something your daddy won't know about."

"I'll do whatever you'll do," Heather says. A wave of nausea passes over her, though, and makes her feel shaky. She sets the beer can down on the floor. "What is it?"

"Get that tooth stuff," Jamaica says. "We might need it."

So it is that Joy and Otis, back from Santa Fe, look out the living room window and see lights at eleven o'clock, and Joy, who has been talking with Otis about moving in, while Otis has been hinting about but not really saying the word *marriage,* says sadly, not at all seriously, "Maybe we could borrow the trailer and park it in your alley for her," and Otis says, "Heck, Joy, I'm sorry I'm not a rich man with a mansion and five cars, you know I am," and Joy feels suddenly so torn, so divided, and so guilty, she wants to see her baby, kiss her good night, tell her she's not mad about the hair anymore, tell her she loves her lots, even if she loves Otis, too.

And so she flips on the patio light and walks out to the trailer while Otis watches from the patio door, and, in her tender and motherly mood, walks in just in time to see her daughter on her back on Russell's trailer bed, her legs spread wide, while that little half-black Yankee girl pulls a needle through the lip outside her vagina.

Opal, who was finally sound asleep beside Russell, hears Joy's screams and thinks: My God, someone's dead. She hears Otis shout, too, and she grabs her robe and runs to the yard, followed by Russell and, a few steps later, Clancy, carrying the baby in her arms. There is so much yelling going on, it takes a minute to realize that nobody is dead, nobody is even attacked or injured, there is no reason for this ruckus, but then Opal sees the beer cans on the floor of Russell's trailer, and sees Joy slapping Heather over and over.

Otis pulls Joy off her daughter, and Russell says, "It's nothing, Joy; Jesus, a little beer!" The girls have pulled the cover off the bed and across their bare bottoms and legs. *What* were they doing?

Heather screams, "It's none of your business!" and Joy is screaming, "You stupid little bitch! You stupid bitch!" while everyone is saying, Joy, Joy, Joy.

"Oh, you've done it now," Joy screams. "And I know just what to do with you! You're going to your daddy's! I don't have to worry about it anymore! You did it to your-self, drunk and dyed and poked and—and—" and at the top of her lungs, Joy yells: *"Homosexual!"* at which point

Heather, with a shudder and a cry, bends forward and throws up on Russell's trailer's bed's quilted cover.

Then Opal hears Pretty Bit squawk, and sees the cage knocked on its side, and the bird flapping about the trailer. Behind her, Clancy stands with the door held open, and the bird flies out.

"Pretty Bit!" Opal cries. "Oh, no, the bird is out!" She rushes out the door and sees the bird flapping along the edge of the roof of the trailer. "Reach him!" she screams. "Somebody come and get the bird!"

Russell, soon beside her, says, "Oh, to hell with the damned bird, Opal, your daughter is killing Heather," but for all the crying and noise in the trailer, Opal can't take her eyes off the parakeet above her head. The bird lands, finally, a foot, foot and a half, back of the ledge of the roof, shivering and fluttering.

"He's scared to death," Opal says. "Russell, get the ladder."

He tries to shimmy up the side of the trailer, using the door for toeholds, but he can't manage. The bird, just out of reach, seems to watch bemused, its flapping wings now quiet. "The ladder!" Opal shouts.

Clancy has gone inside. Otis and Joy come out. They look up to see what Opal is looking at. "Oh, Mother, for God's sake," Joy says. "Who cares about a *bird*?"

"I do," Opal says. Russell brings the ladder and props it up against the side of the trailer.

"I'm going to get my shoes," he says.

Opal doesn't wait. She grabs the towel from by the cage, and she climbs the ladder to the bird.

"Mother!" Joy says.

Opal turns and frantically waves her hand. "Shhh!" she says. She moves slowly, the towel in her hand, toward the bird. He stares at her, then flaps and moves a few inches to one side. He is teasing her.

"Shh, Pretty Bit," Opal croons. She can just reach over the ladder. "Pretty pretty Bit," she says, and tosses the towel over the bird, then reaches forward and clamps her hand over that. "I've got it!" she cries, and pulls the bird toward her. Then, with her other hand, she clasps the ladder tightly and cries, "Russell!"

Russell says gently, "I'm right here behind you, honey." She feels his arm around her. Slowly he talks her down. Her heart is pounding fiercely, but it doesn't hurt. She feels the bird's heart in her palm.

She takes the bird inside the trailer. Jamaica and Heather, now in their jeans, sit side by side on the couch, their faces smeared with tears.

Jamaica says, "We're not lesbians, Opal, we're just friends."

Opal holds her hand up, the towel still draped over it. "I got your bird, sweetheart," she says to Heather. She kneels down and puts the bird in her lap. She takes the towel off, and the bird says, "Cheer up!"

37

While Opal lies sleepless
through the night and worries that decisions have been
made too quickly, Russell beside her sleeps deeply and
well, his dreams seamless and undisturbing. So much in
Russell is at once comforting and provocative: his stubborn optimism, his simple solutions, his forgiving nature,
his unguarded affection. His pains are so surface, so evi-
dent: excisions in his face, lonesomeness away from home,
indignance at a driver who cuts into his lane. Yet he is a
man whose first wife came home one day, packed her bags,
and left a note saying, "The rest of my life would be far too
long here." He is a father whose children have never, in the
years since Opal met him, given him a gift, although they
appear on Christmas and Father's Day for a meal and a
video, and now and then in between, if they need something. He is a man who wanted to be an engineer and
couldn't get past calculus, a man who believes that it's
easier to give things away than protect them. What does it
mean, that he thinks he loves her? He has thrown his hat
into her ring. He knows that in the construction of your
life's plot, you narrow the options with age and error, and
he wants to make the best of what he's got. Maybe he's
right. Maybe what you've got is out of your control; all
you can affect is who you are.

It's always been more important to be a mother than a
wife; when Greta was alive, it was more important to be a

daughter. Now her mother is dead, and her children, like little blind rats, are stumbling out of the nest. Who does that make her, if not Russell's companion? What does it give her, if she won't take what he offers? Is it so bad?

Sometime before dawn she makes coffee and sits at the table leafing through *Pipeline Digest*. Russell has circled "Jobs to Let." He has circled announcements for work in California, Delaware, Pennsylvania, Alberta, India, and Brazil, but he has taken a job to lay fifty-four miles of twenty-inch pipeline from Pampa to Wheeler, Texas. Does he mean to keep her close to her children? Was Africa, once done, enough for one man's life afield? Whatever his reasons, she accepts them and desires no explanation; she can live with him in his trailer anywhere. She can be his wife.

She reads that Saudi Arabia has discovered a vast deposit of superlight oil, so like gasoline in color and consistency, "you could probably put it straight into your car and run it." She imagines cars lined up at a hole in the ground, their drivers' heads swathed in white turbans—or is that India and not Arabia? She knows she will never see another country, and she is sorry.

Morning comes, and she begins it early with cooking. Mad or glad, everyone has to eat. She makes biscuits and waffle batter, a platter of bacon and fried potatoes. She sets out margarine and jellies, dishes and silver. She dresses, and sits down to wait.

The first person up is Otis, arriving at her door with a vacuum cleaner in tow. Such a bargain, he says. It is a repossessed model, one of the best, and he wants Opal to have it. It's too good to sell, he says; he wants to keep it in the family. He looks around and sees only Opal; behind him Joy enters and, without speaking, goes to her room and shuts the door. "I'd show you," he says, "but it does make noise." At this moment Russell appears, zipping his trousers.

Murphy is fussing to get up in Clancy's room. "Oh, go ahead," Opal tells Otis. "You can run it in our room." She pours coffee for Russell. "See what he's brought," she says.

Otis calls them into their bedroom. He has pulled the sheets back off the bed, and a long attachment sucks up and down the mattress in rows. "Now watch," he says, "you aren't going to believe it." He pulls out the bag from the vacuum cleaner, and dumps its contents back onto the mattress. There is a pile of dust. "There was nothing in it when I came," he said. He taps the bag: "New bag this morning." He points to the debris. "This is on your mattress, can you imagine? Dust and mites and scales of skin."

Russell says, "I'll be dipped."

Opal says, "Can you get it back up?" In a single long suck, he can. She says, "Maybe you could do the carpet in here, and then leave the rest for later?"

Otis, humming, attaches the proper extension and tackles the carpet. Opal goes into Clancy's room to see if she's up with the baby. The sight of their boxes and suitcases piled at one side of the room shocks her. Clancy is changing Murphy on the bed. "Hand me his blue sleeper, Mother," she says. As she does this, Opal starts to cry.

"That isn't going to do any good," Clancy says.

"I can't be sad that you're taking that baby—?"

"Wiggle-butt," Clancy says to Murphy, as if her mother were invisible. Opal bends over, kisses Murphy's tummy, and leaves.

Otis and Russell have dished up big plates of breakfast.

"Sit down, honey, you have to hear this," Russell says. "I meant to tell you this when I first got home, but I got distracted with that surgery and forgot."

Opal butters a biscuit and pulls up a chair.

"This fella from Grants Pass, Oregon? His name was Emory. He was head mechanic on the heavy equipment in Nigeria. I was telling him about my stepdaughters living here—" He smiles sheepishly. "I wasn't complaining, Opal, I was just talking. And he says, oh, hell, he can top that— your girls moving in, he meant. He had two kids of his own he couldn't get rid of! Lived with his wife and these boys in this little-bitty house in Oregon; those boys grew up to be big devils, football players and rowdies, banging off the walls, driving Emory and his wife plumb nuts. So Emory —he don't have a bunch of money to spare—decides they need a basement for the boys. And durned if he doesn't dig the damned thing himself, I mean with a *shovel*—"

"You don't mean it!" Otis exclaims.

"Yup. Took him a lot of one year, but he digs it, and he finishes it, and he tells his boys, 'It's yours, just don't come up here and bother us.' "

"Isn't it nice you had a big house, instead?" Opal says archly. She can see Russell blundering right into insult here. But with Otis sitting by, she doesn't want to say anything. A man doesn't want to be chided in front of another man.

"So—here's the good part—these boys, they settle in. They get out of high school, and they just stay there. They get a job here, a job there, they spend months at a time on their butts watching TV—"

"Russell, does this story have a point?" Opal takes Russell's plate and stacks her little one on top in front of her.

Russell laughs loudly. "So one day he says, 'What you boys need is a change of scenery,' and he gives them money

—wouldn't you think they'd suspect something?—he gives them money to take a little trip. They go to Reno, I think he said. And while they're gone, *he fills the basement back in*."

"Oh, shit!" Otis says, and guffaws. The two men hit each other on the shoulders, laughing.

Opal says, "I don't believe one word of it."

Joy, in the hall, says loudly, "I mean it, Heather Lee!" and marches over to her mother. "She's still in bed."

"Her daddy won't be here for an hour or so," Opal says. "We worked on packing her last night, Joy; let her be."

Joy narrows her eyes at her mother. "I will tell her what to do right up to the minute she's in Wayne Ronnander's car, Mother, and you can stay out of it. And I want you to know I don't appreciate going in there and finding that Jamaica person, either."

"They're best friends," Opal says. "They're really sad."

Joy rolls her eyes. "Is that what they call it?"

"Joy, you are imagining—" Opal begins, but Russell slaps her shoulder.

"Don't, honey," he says. Joy gets a Coke and sits down glumly.

Just in time to lighten the mood, Travis appears. He is carrying a cardboard pet carrier and a box of diapers. He sees there's food and helps himself. The fellows exchange pleasantries and Russell starts in on his same story again, but Opal cuts him short.

"Travis doesn't have any reason to think that's funny," she says. "His parents moved out and gave him the house he's in."

Russell stares a moment, until the truth of what she says registers, then he laughs. "By golly, that's so," he says.

Travis, confused, says, "My ma wanted everything new and electric. She's even got this machine, makes bread. You put the stuff in this kinda box, and after a while, what do you know? Bread. She doesn't even have to get her hands floury."

Clancy appears with Murphy and hands him to Travis. She pours herself coffee and sits at the table. Murphy is gurgling and bobbing on Travis's lap; Clancy smiles, watching.

"You got everything ready?" he asks her.

"It's all piled up in my room."

"I'll load up whenever you say."

"Might as well," Clancy says.

"Everybody eat," Opal pleads. "I plugged in the waffle iron."

"Shoot, I'd never turn down a waffle," Travis says.

"I could eat a piece of one," Clancy says.

"And the girls," Opal says, more or less to herself. She's made a lot of batter.

"I can eat one more," Otis says. He could stand to, no bigger than he is.

Heather is the first to go. Wayne drives up and honks. It's Clancy who looks out and sees who it is, while Travis is packing her car. Otis, too, is carrying stuff out of the house from Joy's room and putting it in the back of his pickup. Opal feels like she's at a clearance sale. She stands in the hall and calls to Heather, "Your daddy's here."

Heather and Jamaica come out of the bedroom, red-eyed and silent, and move slowly through the house and into the yard. Wayne has gotten out long enough to open the trunk of the car, then climbed back in. It's Joanne who gets out and greets Opal and the others. "Nice day for all this," she says to Clancy. "Not so hot today."

Clancy says, "I've got an air conditioner."

Heather turns around, runs back into the house, and returns with Pretty Bit and his cage. From where Opal is standing, by the garage, she can't hear the conversation with Joanne, but there has to be some sort of consultation with Wayne, much talking by Joanne, and then the birdcage is placed on the backseat. Opal sees Wayne gesturing; he wants to get out of there. It's not only rude of him, it's out of character. Usually he likes to swagger a little and let them know he's glad he escaped the family. Opal looks around for Joy, who's not in sight, then back at Heather, who is embracing Jamaica and crying. Joanne moves up to the girls and speaks in a low voice. The girls nod, she talks more, and then she moves closer and puts her arms around them, pulling them in close to her body.

Joy strides across the yard to Heather, and Opal follows. Clancy and Russell, too, gather. Joy touches her daughter lightly, says, "I'll be up in a couple of weeks to see you, see how school's going." Heather's face is sullen, withholding. Opal goes to her and gives her a hug. "You come down and see Jamaica and me," she says, knowing she's making some sort of promise she'll have to pay off. It would be cruel not to mean what she says. She reaches her hand out for Jamaica. "You come anytime," she tells her. Jamaica and Heather hug again, and Opal says, "Jamaica, honey, go in there and eat something, there's so much food," and Jamaica, sensible enough to see that Opal is closing the scene, runs inside.

"Bye, darling," Opal says, waving and waving as Wayne pulls away. He's hardly moved when he slams on the brakes, backs up, and Heather jumps out. She runs to her mother and gives her a hug, then runs back to the car.

"Oh, my," Opal says. Otis and Travis go by, each carrying a box.

"I think that's it," Travis says, "except for the cat." In a moment he's back with Chocolate in the carrier. He puts her in the front seat of his truck.

"I didn't know you were taking the cat!" Opal says.

"Oh, no, ma'am, I'm not. I'm just driving it. Don't you know? I'm going behind Clancy, make sure she gets there safely. Her daddy's coming down, too, and I'll meet him. Then I'll have to get back to my cotton." He smiles. "I gotta know where they are, don't I?"

Clancy, carrying Murphy, stands on the walk with a lost look. "Oh, Mama," she says, then turns to put the baby in his carrier in the backseat. Opal finds she cannot move her legs. She cannot think of a single word to say. It's Travis who kisses her on the cheek. "We'll drive real careful," he says.

"We'll be back in town next Monday," Otis says. Joy walks past him and gives her sister a good-bye embrace. "We're going to do a little camping, over by Chaco Canyon."

"Oh oh," Opal manages to say. Before she has found any words, Joy and Clancy are settled, each in her car. Joy gives the horn a short honk. Clancy calls out, "Bye, everybody, bye, bye."

Opal stands in the driveway, looking right, then left, as Clancy pulls away, followed by Travis, and, the other way, Otis drives off too. She stands with her arms up, one in each direction, and she waves, and waves, and waves.

"Aw, honey, they're not gone so far or long," Russell says. Already both cars have turned off the street, out of sight. From the avenue, with a squeal of wheels, Imogene drives to a sudden halt in front of the house, jumps out, opens her back door, and pulls out a suitcase.

"Oh, shoot, I missed them, didn't I?" she says.

"They're gone," Opal says.

Imogene says, "I'll look after the house while you're gone. I'll be here if anyone needs anything." Russell picks up her suitcase, and she says, "I'll be here when you get home."

"Sure, Mama," Russell says. He winks at Opal. He sets the suitcase back down, steps between the women, puts an arm around each waist, and ushers them inside. "What good's a house with nobody in it?"

About the Author

SANDRA SCOFIELD's novel *Beyond Deserving* was a 1991 finalist for the National Book Award and received an American Book Award. She has also been awarded a Creative Writing Fellowship from the National Endowment for the Arts. She is a member of PEN and the Authors' Guild. A native Texan, she now lives in southern Oregon.